A GATE OF NIGHT

A Shade Of Vampire, Book 6

Bella Forrest

Also By Bella Forrest:

A Shade Of Vampire (Book 1)

A Shade Of Blood (Book 2)

A Castle Of Sand (Book 3)

A Shadow Of Light (Book 4)

A Blaze Of Sun (Book 5)

Beautiful Monster

For an updated list of Bella's books,
please visit: www.bellaforrest.net

Contents

PROLOGUE: Natalie

As a rogue, I had been to more vampire covens than any other vampire out there. I was the ultimate diplomat. I had the trust of every coven and that was something I'd valued for the past five hundred years. I'd never had any reason to fear entering a coven. I would be treated with the respect that was due a rogue.

This time, however, I was terrified. I would have been a fool to think that I still had diplomatic immunity. Not with all the rumors running amok. Apparently, Derek and Sofia Novak, joint rulers of The Shade, had actually done it—they had found a cure to vampirism. I couldn't wrap my mind around it, but if it was true, Derek and Sofia had just opened a Pandora's Box of disaster. I doubted they were aware of the magnitude of trouble they'd caused.

I took a deep breath as I made my way toward the staircase leading down to the basement floor of an old building in Amsterdam. Of all the vampire covens, The Underground was my least favorite. The coven inhabited a series of bunkers beneath the city, connected by old sewers and tunnels.

The Underground was a testament to how unsafe the world had become for vampires. The hunters were always on our trail and it was becoming more and more difficult to hide from them. The Shade had long been heralded as a haven for vampires, but now there were rumors that hunters had overtaken the island. That rumor, however, I had trouble believing. *I know Derek Novak. He would never compromise his own people by working with the hunters.* I would soon visit The Shade again. *Times are calling for it, but right now, I have to deal with The Underground.*

When I arrived at the basement, I immediately made my way toward the wall that concealed the secret passage leading to the main hall.

"Well, if it isn't Natalie Borgia."

I winced. "Kiev." I turned around to find the tall, broad-shouldered man with dark hair and blood-red eyes standing right beside me. A smirk was on his handsome face as he looked me over from head to foot.

"It's been a while since I last saw you, Natalie. How's my gorgeous Italian rogue?"

My entire body shuddered at the recollection of my last encounter with him. It was one of my darkest memories. Kiev was a man who knew what he wanted and took it whether one was willing or not. He was the son of the Elder, the very first vampire.

I fought to regain composure. Men like Kiev gained power from fear. I refused to give him that, not again… so, ignoring my quickening heartbeat, I stood to my full height, kept a poker face and tried to look him straight in the eye.

"Why are you here?"

Before he could open his mouth to respond, a chilling wind passed by me, and his sister, Clara, appeared. "Hello, Natalie. I think the question is why are *you* here? The Underground is no place for a diplomat like you."

She began brushing her fingers over my hair, her mouth so close to my ear I could hear her every breath.

"I was asked to deliver a message," I explained. "That's my job as a rogue, lest you forget."

Kiev gave me an accusing glare. "How come you never come to give *me* messages, Natalie?"

"I don't know where you live."

Clara chuckled. "We're going to fix that soon."

They were the Elder's children and the home of the Elder—*if* he even truly existed—was a huge secret. I was about to ask her to clarify, but Kiev stepped forward and towered over me. I shuddered at their closeness as I was sandwiched between the siblings, Clara behind me and Kiev in front of me.

"Get out of here, Natalie," Kiev hissed, before pushing his lips against mine. I trembled at the memories his kiss brought about. "Remain as you are. Neutral. Just like Switzerland." He snapped his fingers and I knew then that I wasn't going to be able to meet with The Underground's leader. One thing was clear: blood was going to be shed that night.

As the Elder's vampire warriors stormed through the secret passage down to the bunkers, I ran after them, shouting, "Why?"

Kiev shrugged and I thought I saw a flicker of remorse in his expression. I wondered if there was any trace left in him of the man he used to be before the Elder possessed him; of the man I'd once fallen in love with. But I was fooling myself. If there was anything about the Elder that I knew, it was that he was pure evil. And so were his children.

When Kiev looked at me, his red eyes gleamed with pleasure. "They chose the wrong side," he grinned. "Now, I'm going to enjoy seeing them suffer. Just like you suffered the last time you made the mistake of choosing Derek Novak's side. But with them, I won't be as merciful."

Chills ran down my spine. My last encounter with him had been the farthest thing from merciful and he knew it.

"Make sure everyone finds out about what happened here tonight, Natalie," Clara whispered.

They both chuckled before rushing through the entrance of the main hall.

Like father, like children. Their very presence left me feeling dark and dirty. I wanted to leave the place, but for reasons I couldn't fathom, I didn't. I stood rooted to that spot for what felt like hours. My heightened sense of hearing made it impossible for me to not hear the screams of all the vampires they murdered that night. That was the price that had to be paid, because Kiev had already made it crystal clear.

Choose Derek Novak's side and you will suffer the same fate as the vampires of The Underground.

Those screams were going to haunt me in my dreams. I wanted to do something—*anything*—but I couldn't. I'd become the rogue because I was a coward. I never chose sides, and the one time that I had chosen, I'd paid a heavy price for it. I had a better chance of survival if I did what I always did best. Stay neutral. This time, however, staying neutral felt like I was siding with the Elder, and that was selling my soul.

Are you willing to pay that price, Natalie?

Chapter 1: Derek

The image of Sofia emerging from the ocean, that red swimsuit highlighting her curves, would forever be etched in my mind. My wife was a stunning sight to behold and spending my entire lifetime with her was more than I could've ever dreamed of.

I was sitting on the sand, finishing a sandcastle that she had started but abandoned in order to take a dip in the ocean. When she reached me, she slapped my shoulder.

"What was that for?"

She sat beside the sandcastle and pouted as she looked me over from head to foot. "It's annoying. I don't get it."

"Don't get what?"

"I've been living under the sun for most of my life and I'm still as creamy white as the day I was born, but you..." She groaned. "You've been under the sun for a week after hiding out in darkness for five hundred years, and you already have a tan!"

I doubled over with laughter at her outburst.

"It doesn't make sense." She lifted her arms and stared at them. "The Prince of Darkness himself can get a tan, but no matter what I do, I never can."

My laughter subsided. She was right. We'd been on our honeymoon for over a week now and a good chunk of our time had been spent outdoors. My skin had already bronzed nicely, but Sofia's skin was still as pale as the day I'd first met her.

"That *is* odd." I frowned, narrowing my eyes at her. "Are you sure you're not a vampire, Sofia?"

She sighed and stretched out on her towel. "Ben used to tease me about it. He always got a beautiful tan during the summer while I just ended up red and sunburned."

I kept my eyes on her, amused. Sofia was an old soul and she had accomplished so much at The Shade already. Moments like these, however, reminded me that she was an eighteen-year-old, young and with her whole life ahead of her, a life she'd decided to live with me.

I found it humbling. *She's mine. She willingly gave her life and love to me.*

The expression in her green eyes changed to something more pensive. I didn't need to ask.

"You miss him, don't you?" I asked, referring to Ben Hudson. She'd grown up with the young man. He had been her best friend and the fact that he'd died not so long ago—at the hands of my older brother—wasn't lost on me. It was a reminder of how resilient and strong Sofia was. She'd been through hell and back the past year.

She nodded. "Of course I do. And I feel guilty I haven't spoken to Ben's family since the funeral. It's been difficult to contact them. I couldn't bear the thought of facing them, you know? Besides, with what's been happening with us and The Shade and... I haven't even really thought about them until now. That's awful, isn't it?"

"Don't be so hard on yourself, Sofia. There was no way you could've communicated with them." I paused and gave it some thought. "But we're out here... we can do whatever we want. Maybe we should pay them a visit."

"We're in Tahiti, Derek. Are you seriously proposing that we fly to California?"

"They deserved to be at our wedding, but since bringing them to The Shade wasn't an option, I don't see why we can't visit them now."

A smile broke into her lovely face as she gave me an affectionate look. "I love you, Derek Novak."

I flashed her a wide grin and shrugged a shoulder. "I know." I threw a plastic shovel toward her. "Now, get to work, lazy. You started this sandcastle. Come help me finish it."

Sofia jumped up from her towel and she was in my arms, her slim form comfortably settling on top of me as she kissed me. Her kiss was gentle and sweet, and to my delight, lingering. Even with my eyes closed, I could sense the smile on her face—that beautiful smile that always had a way of melting my heart—that same smile that I got to see once our lips parted.

"I adore you, Derek. You know that, don't you?" She grinned.

I squinted my eyes at her. "All right," I drawled. "What do you want in exchange for that?"

"You." She bit her lip. "Just you."

She wrapped her legs around me and pulled me on top of her. Being with her was like a piece of heaven—one that I wished would last forever. But I knew that our honeymoon was borrowed time. It would soon be over, so I intended to enjoy every single moment.

I was needed back home. The Shade was crippled without us

there—especially with the hunters looming over us and the discovery of the cure that had created all sorts of enemies and all kinds of threats—but this was my one shot at normalcy. This one-month honeymoon was the only time I could just be a young man in love with his wife.

I let all the responsibilities I had as ruler of The Shade roll off my shoulders. I had one month to have Sofia all to myself and I wasn't going to trade that for the world.

Chapter 2: Vivienne

"We need your brother back here." The blonde vampire slammed her palm down on my dining table, glaring daggers at me.

I sat still, maintaining a cool and collected front—a façade that was completely opposite to the chaos going on inside of me.

"Claudia, calm down," my best friend, Liana Hendry, reprimanded our co-council, who was known for her mood swings and temper.

Yuri Lazaroff glared at Claudia, which was enough to reel her in and make her settle down in her seat beside him.

The surviving leaders of the twelve clans that composed The Shade's Elite were all gathered around Aiden and me at my dining room table. When Derek and Sofia had left for their honeymoon, they'd left her father, Aiden, and me in charge of The Shade. We'd been tasked to "cooperate with the hunters" who'd been sent to "guard" the island. Little had we known what the hunters had in mind.

"The hunters are taking over The Shade. We can't keep living this way. They're calling all the shots. Did they even consult you and Aiden when they shut down the Port?"

The Port was the main entry point to the island. Recently, the hunters had placed it on full lockdown. No one was allowed to enter and no one was allowed to leave without their express permission. We were prisoners in our own home and the only explanation was a cryptic, "Orders."

"We can take these hunters down, Vivienne," Claudia hissed.

"That may be true, but at what cost? We can take down those who are present here at the island, but we stand no chance against a full-on attack from the hunters. We all know that."

"Vivienne's right." Aiden nodded. He was the only human among us vampires, but if anybody knew how the hunters worked, it was him. "Under no circumstances can we afford to retaliate against them."

"The problem is that they know that." Cameron spoke up. "They're using that knowledge against us."

"They're provoking you," Aiden explained. "They *want* you to retaliate. They *want* you to lose your cool so that they have a reason to destroy you. These are hunters with decades of vendetta against vampires. Make no mistake about it—most of these hunters hate you with every fiber of their being."

"Well, that's comforting." Claudia grimaced. "They can do whatever they want with us and there's nothing we can do to make them stop."

"Not if you want to maintain peace with the hunters, and that's exactly what Derek wants us to do," Aiden reiterated.

"It's just one month," I added. "We already have a week down.

We're immortals. What's three weeks to us? Derek and Sofia will be back from their honeymoon and he can iron things out with the hunters." That silenced everyone.

I felt ill at ease with the position Derek had placed me in. After having been captured by the hunters, imprisoned, tortured and brainwashed at their headquarters, I'd lost a huge part of who I was and everyone could tell. I wasn't in the best condition to be running a kingdom waiting to implode or explode—depending on who was going to light the fuse.

I'd spent the greater part of five hundred years living in The Shade. Our coven had been founded and ruled by my family—the Novaks. After the deaths of my father, Gregor, and my older brother, Lucas, the weight of ruling The Shade had fallen entirely on Derek's shoulders.

I was the Seer of The Shade and I'd always known that Derek was destined to rule. He was prophesied to bring our kind to true sanctuary. With the help of Sofia, he'd found a cure, a way to turn vampires back into humans.

This cure, we believed, was our true sanctuary. Derek longed for it. He'd never wanted to be a vampire, so he'd turned his back on immortality and become human again the first chance he got—right after he'd married Sofia. They deserved their happy ending, but happily ever after wasn't easily achieved. Not in real life.

When Derek had left for his honeymoon, some saw the move as selfish. I saw it as a well-deserved break, but of course their reprieve came at a price for those of us who were left behind. Now, while Derek and Sofia enjoyed their honeymoon, the island was overrun by hunters.

None of us trusted the hunters. Aiden's experience alone was a testament that we could not put our faith in them. Because of his love for Sofia, he'd sided with his daughter and for that, even after he'd given his whole life to the cause of the hunters, they'd turned their back on him.

After discussing other matters, the council left the penthouse and, feeling suffocated by the loneliness of my home, I decided to take a breath of fresh air. I strolled past the giant redwood trees which supported the Residences.

The Residences used to be one of the most beautiful areas of The Shade, but after the Elder had attacked the island, many of the homes had been destroyed, along with half of the Crimson Fortress and the entirety of the Vale.

I looked up at the homes at the Residences still intact, now being shared by several vampire clans. At the thought of everything that we'd been able to establish at The Shade—everything that was now threatened—a wave of melancholy came over me. Everything I loved about The Shade was about to disappear. I swallowed back the tears.

"Well, if it isn't Vivienne Novak," a voice from behind me cooed.

I didn't need to turn around to recognize the voice. Memories returned to me. Of all the hunters who'd come to my cell to torment me, he was the worst. Chills ran along my spine, settling at the nape of my neck, as he began to circle me.

"What do you want?" I snapped.

He stopped circling and stood in front of me—too close—crossing his arms over his chest. "I heard you were in charge of this island while your brother is out frolicking around the world with his new wife. Kind of selfish of him, don't you think?"

"My brother is a lot of things. Selfish isn't one of them." Avoiding eye contact, I gazed at the tattoo of a small blue star on his temple.

He chuckled. "Well, I don't care. It just means that we get to deal with you instead of your brother."

I swallowed hard, knowing that even though I remained a vampire and Derek was human, I was still nowhere near as intimidating as Derek. "What do you want?"

"We appreciate the quarters you provided us at the Crimson Fortress, but I have to say that the Residences seem to be far more comfortable."

"If you want comfortable, you can leave anytime."

It was Aiden who'd suggested that the hunters be assigned to the military bunks at the Crimson Fortress—the large hundred-foot wall surrounding the entire island. A good chunk of the wall and its towers had been torn apart when other vampire covens had attacked The Shade under the command of the Elder. Still, the hunters' quarters were quite comfortable, especially with a full staff to cater to their needs. As far as I was concerned, they were being treated like royalty, certainly better than the other humans.

He chuckled. "You always were a feisty one, Vivienne. I have to admit it's interesting to see you in your element." He gestured with his arms as he looked around. "I never thought The Shade would be like this. I mean, apart from the fact that the sun never rises here, the place is rather breathtaking."

I didn't know how to react to him. *Has he forgotten what he did to me?* "How long are you going to be here?"

"For as long as they tell us to be." He shrugged. "Look, Vivienne, I know we started off on the wrong foot, but you have to understand that back at headquarters, I was just doing what I was supposed to do."

"You were doing what you were *supposed* to do?" My voice was deceptively composed, but I was fighting the urge to strangle him. "You did what you did to me out of hatred. You enjoyed it."

His jaw tightened and an infuriating smirk formed on his face.

I wanted to hurt him. I could sink my teeth into his neck, claw through his flesh or even rip his heart out, but I wouldn't. There was more in the balance than just my revenge.

"Now"—I sidestepped him—"as much as I'm enjoying this talk, I have better things to do."

He grabbed my arm. "Wait a minute. You can't just walk away from me."

I gritted my teeth. "In case you haven't realized, you are at The Shade. I am princess of this place. Touch me again and you will regret it."

"Okay then, *princess*, we want better quarters. Do something about it."

The nerve of this man. My fists clenched and it was all I could do not to inflict some serious pain upon him.

"You are truly a magnificent sight to behold, Vivienne Novak." He leaned toward my ear, so close that I could feel every breath. "It grates at you, doesn't it? Everything you fought for all these years is crumbling before your very eyes. I must say that I am honored that I'm here to see it happen."

I was losing control. I was about to attack him, but to my relief, a familiar voice came to my rescue.

"Vivienne? Is everything all right?" I'd known Xavier for as long as I could remember. He was one of the constants of my life and, among the Elite, he was also one of the most loyal to our family.

The hunter took a step backward, letting go of my hand. Xavier stood beside me. His hand protectively settled on the small of my back.

"Is this guy bothering you, Vivienne?"

"The princess and I were just talking about our living arrangements."

Xavier cocked his head to the side. "Why? What's wrong with your living arrangements exactly?"

"I'm sorry." The hunter returned Xavier's glare. "Who are you?"

Xavier was attempting to reel in his temper. "I could ask the same thing about you, boy. You have no business talking to our princess. The next time you wish to address her, you go through me."

The hunter began laughing. "And what do you think you're going to do if I talk to her, vampire? Do you honestly believe that Princess Vampire here is still in control of this island?"

I went from wanting to attack him to trying to prevent Xavier from breaking his neck.

"Let me maim him," Xavier whispered beneath his breath.

"He's not worth it." I shook my head. "Let's just walk away."

"That's right. Walk away, Vivienne. I hope you realize that you are just as weak and vulnerable here as you were at headquarters." He then curtsied. "I'll leave you two alone... for now." He walked past us and was already several feet away when he screamed. "By the way, princess, I'm not sure I ever told you my name. It's Craig. Don't you ever forget!"

Xavier eyed me after Craig was gone. "You know that guy?"

I couldn't break down. I shook my head as I clung to his arm for support, hoping that my knees wouldn't buckle beneath me. "I don't want to talk about it."

I wish Derek and Sofia were here, because I can't handle this. I knew that chaos was up ahead. My dreams and visions told me as much. I also knew that I was completely incapable of handling it on my own.

I shut my eyes for a moment. *Derek, wherever you are, I hope that you're having the time of your life, but I also hope that you remember how desperately we need you back here.*

Chapter 3: Sofia

The moment Derek and I arrived at California, we took a cab to the neighborhood I'd lived in for nine years, since Aiden had left me under the care of Lyle and Amelia Hudson. As we passed the local elementary school and the familiar suburban homes—all of them attached to specific memories from my childhood—I was beginning to choke up with tears. I reached for Derek, who was sitting in the passenger's seat beside me, and he put his arm around me.

"So this is where you grew up," he eventually said, gazing out of the window.

I tried to wipe away the tears that were brimming in my eyes and threatening to fall down my cheeks, but not soon enough.

Derek placed his hand over mine, squeezing hard. "It's going to be all right, Sofia."

"I know." I smiled. "It's just that this place brings back so many memories."

It didn't take long before we pulled over in front of the Hudsons' house—one that contained so many of the memories I held dear, memories of my best friend, Ben, whom I'd been in love with for most of my teenage years. Ben was the only one who'd ever posed a threat to my love for Derek. He was that important to me. *And now he's gone.*

As Derek paid the driver, I swallowed hard when my eyes settled on an estate agency sign in front of the yard that said, "For Sale."

I sat frozen for a couple of minutes before the sign registered. "They're no longer here." The Hudsons might not have been the kind of family I'd always dreamed of having, but they'd been good to me. "I want to see the house one last time, if that's okay with you."

"Of course." Derek looked at me sympathetically.

We got out of the car and walked toward the house. I was expecting it to be locked, but when I twisted the knob, the door opened. A middle-aged woman with brown hair, glasses and a beige suit skipped down the stairs toward us.

I swallowed hard at the familiar scent and homey atmosphere that came with standing in the Hudsons' hallway before focusing my attention on the woman.

"You must be the Millers! Oh my goodness, you are such a lovely couple!" she exclaimed before shaking our hands. "I didn't think you'd be so young! Are you ready to tour the house?"

I was momentarily speechless. The woman looked from me to Derek, awaiting our response.

"Oh, I'm so sorry. I'm Monica Andrews. I'm the real estate agent. We talked over the phone. We had an appointment for you to check out the house? You're actually an hour late."

Derek and I exchanged glances. It seemed the Millers had ditched her.

"So?" Monica asked. "Shall we start?"

Derek shrugged a shoulder, his blue eyes still on me. "Sure. Why not?"

So, for the next half-hour, Monica gave us a tour around a house that I knew far better than she did. I was still doing pretty well around the living room and dining room, but when our tour reached the second floor I knew that I wasn't going to be able to keep myself together.

The moment I stepped inside my old bedroom—now empty—vivid memories of times spent with Ben came flooding back. Every cherished memory I had with him: charming and funny, endearing and sometimes lonely. I could practically imagine their faces inside—his and his younger sister, Abby's. We'd had so much fun in that room, but all the feelings of loss that I'd struggled with since Ben's death returned to me at full blast.

"He used to call me Rose Red," I whispered to Derek, memories of Ben's kisses making my lips tingle. I was clinging to Derek's arm so tightly, my knuckles were growing white.

Derek nodded and whispered back, "I know. Sofia, if this is too hard for you, we don't have to go through this…"

Monica was talking about how marvelous the rooms were. She was showing us the cabinets and the wide windows and all I could think of was that I'd spent hours with Ben in that room.

Derek kept one hand on the small of my back. "Still up for this, Sofia?"

Monica spun around and froze when she saw me close to tears. "Oh. What's the matter? Is something wrong?"

Derek forced a smile. "The room just reminded her of someone important to her. That's all."

Monica gave me a sympathetic glance but she obviously had no idea how to handle the situation.

"We're just going to get a breath of fresh air," Derek said, before gently tugging me to follow him before I could break down in tears.

We were in the front yard when the waterworks began. I buried my face into Derek's chest, my arms wrapping around his waist. Guilt was taking hold of me. After the funeral, I'd kept telling myself to give the Hudsons a call, but there had been just too much going on. I owed Ben and his family more than I could ever give them.

Derek seemed to be reading my thoughts. "Sofia, we both know everything that happened after Ben's funeral. I'm sure they will understand that you weren't able to communicate with them. I'm sure *Ben* would've understood."

"I know, I know…" I tried to get a hold of myself as I pulled away from Derek.

He began gently wiping my tears away. "What do you want to do now?" He cupped my face with his hands. "We *are* still on our honeymoon."

I gave it some thought. Monica had just stepped out of the house, locking the front door behind her. She had probably realized that there was no way we were going to buy the house. She shifted her weight from one foot to the other and looked at Derek. "I'm not sure if I'm being insensitive here, but would you maybe want to check out another house?"

Derek looked at me. I shrugged. "Why not?"

The smile on Derek's face said that he loved the idea of exploring homes with me. He turned toward Monica and said, "Do you have any beachfront homes available?"

Monica's shoulders perked up. "Yes, actually… however, I have to warn you that most of those homes are outside the budget range you gave me in our initial conversation…"

That charming grin I loved so much appeared on Derek's face. "Let's just say our finances have improved."

Monica looked as if she'd just hit the jackpot.

Chapter 4: Derek

The six-bedroom oceanfront villa was situated on the edge of a cliff and had one of the most breathtaking views I'd ever seen. The home was already fully furnished and I could see myself building a life and starting a family here.

"You like it, don't you?" Sofia asked as she took a step into the master bedroom's terrace with me.

It was the third home that Monica had brought us to, not counting the Hudsons' house, and so far, this was my favorite. I nodded enthusiastically. "Don't you?"

Sofia gave me a smile as she breathed a deep sigh and nodded. "I do. I love it actually. It's bigger than what I'm used to, especially for just the two of us, but…"

I smiled at her suggestively. "Well, it's not going to be just the two of us forever, is it, Sofia? I can see our kids running all over this place."

"Oh really?" She blushed.

I gave her a nod as I placed my hands over her waist and pulled her slim form against me before claiming her lips with mine. After all this time, I still wasn't used to how fragile she felt in my arms, like I could snap her in two if I wanted to. Even without being of a vampire, I was still a lot stronger than she was. Yet, in so many other ways, she was stronger than I was.

When she pulled away from me, her milky skin was flushed red and her lips were swollen. *I can see why Ben called her Rose Red.*

"Derek," Sofia muttered, motioning to our guide.

Monica cleared her throat. I suspected she was starting to think that she was wasting her time with us. After all, Sofia and I looked like two teenagers way in over our heads when we'd decided to get married at such a young age.

So, without thinking it through, I decided to ease her doubts. "We're going to buy the house, Monica."

Her face lit up with delight. When she told us the price of the property, Sofia's jaw dropped. "Derek, what are you doing? How on earth are we going to afford this?"

I couldn't help but smile at Sofia's naïveté. "Sofia, do you really think we could run a place like The Shade if we didn't have money? Besides, your father told me to look at houses if the chance presented itself. In case you have forgotten, your father is a multi-millionaire."

Sofia's face was priceless. Queen of The Shade or not, she was one wealthy young woman.

"When shall we discuss payment, Mr. Miller?" Monica asked.

"It's Novak. The name is Derek Novak, and this is my wife, Sofia. We have no idea who the Millers are. For all we know, they showed up at the house wondering why their agent didn't show up."

Monica looked taken aback, but then said, "Oh, it doesn't matter.

I'm just honestly relieved to make a sale today!"

"Uhm… Could we give you a call tomorrow?" Sofia stepped forward. "I'd like to talk it over with my husband first."

"I thought you said you liked the house, Sofia."

"I do, but *Derek*…" She gave me a sharp look before muttering beneath her breath. "I don't understand why we're buying the home. What for? Our home is The Shade, isn't it?"

The truth was that I wanted this. I wanted to forget The Shade and live a life with her. I wanted to be the father of her children and to see them grow up to have normal lives, away from hunters and vampires. I was exhausted. I'd been bearing the weight of being the ruler and savior of The Shade for centuries. Now we had found the cure, wasn't my role done? I had brought my kind to true sanctuary.

Wasn't it time to find a sanctuary of my own?

Chapter 5: Sofia

Back in our hotel room, I snuggled against Derek on the king-sized bed. His fingers brushed over my bare shoulders.

"Don't you want that, Sofia? A home, a family, a safe place for our kids to grow up in? Away from all the wars and…"

"Derek, do you honestly believe that we can get away from all that? My father tried to give me a shot at normalcy, and look where I ended up. And we can't abandon The Shade. This time away has been wonderful, but people we care about are back at that island, and as much as I've tried not to worry, I'm anxious over what's going on back there. Aren't you wondering?"

"Of course I am, but…" Derek heaved a sigh. "Sofia, we've done it. We brought the vampires to true sanctuary. We found the cure. Maybe it's time someone else took over the burden of ruling The Shade."

"And who would do that, Derek? Would you abandon Vivienne?

She's still trying to pull herself together after what the hunters put her through. She needs a life of her own too." Sitting on his lap, I looked him straight in the eye. "I know you, Derek. You care about The Shade. You care about everyone there. Don't even deny it. No matter how much we both want to start a family together, we can't just turn our backs on The Shade."

It was so unlike him to even think of running from the responsibility of ruling The Shade. I adored him for wanting to build a family with me, and I wanted to dream right along with him, but I also knew that running away from everything... it wasn't him. It wasn't us.

"You dream, you know. Every night since we left The Shade. You begin mumbling stuff about the island. What's going on, Derek? This isn't you."

His face softened as his eyes glistened. "I guess I'm just tired, Sofia. I feel like we're going to return to complete chaos, and... I'm human now. Ruling The Shade as a powerful vampire was difficult enough. Stepping up to that responsibility as a human... it feels like I'm just putting myself, you and our future children in danger."

I swallowed hard. I'd never thought about it that way. In my eyes, Derek was just as powerful as a human as he had been as a vampire.

He sat up, leaning back against the headboard. He ran his hands over my thighs and let them settle over my hips. "I don't know if this is a risk I want to take."

It didn't take a genius to know that we had trouble ahead. I wouldn't be surprised if trouble was already happening back home at The Shade as we were gallivanting around the globe on our honeymoon. The one month we'd asked for was already selfish. Still, I never would've imagined that Derek could entertain the idea of abandoning the island entirely.

"Tell me about the dreams you've been having, Derek. What do you think is up ahead?"

He pried his eyes away from me and let them settle on my kneecap while his hand slid down from my thigh to my knees. A mischievous grin appeared on his face and he began tickling me.

He was trying to distract me and it was working. I screeched and tried to get away from him. Of course, that was futile, considering his strong grip. By the time he was done, I was lying on my back on the bed, unable to control my laughter. He was kneeling on the bed, looming over me.

"Hey!" I squealed. "You can't just do that to avoid a conversation, Derek."

He responded by slipping his hand beneath my shirt and tickling my ribs.

"No!" I screamed. "Enough! Please… Derek, enough! Have mercy!" I was practically in tears.

He chuckled. "You're my wife. I can do whatever I want."

"No, you can't!"

He narrowed his eyes at me. "You're objecting?" His fingers once again threatened to knock the breath right out of me.

"No! I'm not," I conceded. "You win, you win."

A self-satisfied smile appeared on his face. "No one ever said this marriage was going to be fair, Sofia."

He might have known my weakness, but I sure knew *his*. I gave him a naughty grin. "That is so true." All I had to do was unbutton the first three buttons of my shirt and he was putty in my hands. When I was sure that he was pining for me, I slapped his hands away just as he was about to pull at my underwear. It was my turn to smile. I fluttered my eyelashes. "Only if you promise that you will tell me about these dreams you've been having. If not today, tomorrow."

His eyes went from roaming my body to giving me a glare. "Sofia, that's not fair."

I grinned. "No one said this marriage was going to be fair."

"You win." He rolled his eyes.

"Perfect." I reached out and planted a kiss on his lips.

Derek was the first and only man I'd ever made love to. When he'd still been a vampire, he'd spent a lot of energy just trying to maintain control whenever we slept together.

The first time we'd made love after he turned human was the best I could remember. It was perhaps because of his abandon. He wasn't busy trying to restrain his cravings and appetites. He was enjoying every moment of it.

"I'm hungry," Derek confessed after we both rolled over on our backs, breathless. "Why am I always hungry?"

I chuckled and rubbed his stomach. "Weren't you the same when you were a vampire?"

"True," he admitted. "Let's go get something to eat."

One of the things I enjoyed most about our honeymoon was introducing him to new delicacies. In fact, the first time he'd begun to crave food, he'd asked if people were still making salted pork and ale. It had been a pleasure watching the delight in his eyes whenever he tasted something new.

So my eyes lit up and I sat up on the bed. "I think this would be a great time to introduce you to ice cream. I can't believe I totally forgot about ice cream. Let's go." I tried to think back to the last time I'd had it. My stomach turned. *Ben.* He was the only person who knew what my favorite ice cream flavor was.

"Uh, Sofia… What's wrong?"

"What? Oh, it's nothing." I shook my head. "Let's go get you your first taste of ice cream."

The reaction on Derek's face was priceless as he tasted his third flavor of ice cream. "This is delicious. Aren't you going to have more?"

"I already had a second serving," I told him. "That might go straight to my hips. We're going to get some exercise now."

"Exercise?" He wrinkled his nose.

"As a vampire, you never needed it." I smiled. "Now, you do."

He took a huge bite from his ice cream cone. "Well, let me just finish this first."

I enjoyed watching him. He had a childlike delight at everything we saw during our honeymoon. He found pleasure in the things I took for granted—vending machines, phones, bells, food… Derek loved every second of being human, of being alive. He embraced every new experience he encountered.

Or at least it seemed that way to me. I remembered what he'd told me about his apprehensions, and I had to face the fact that as strong and as virile as he still was, he was no longer the most powerful vampire there was. As Derek Novak the human, he was vulnerable and so was I.

I'd never thought that he could have misgivings about being human again, but when the reality of the situation began to sink in, I found myself battling with fear.

Derek was prophesied to bring his kind true sanctuary. I was prophesied to help him do just that. Both of us were convinced that true sanctuary was the cure to vampirism, but by discovering that cure, we'd created enemies. Our lives were in danger and I knew it. Derek knew it.

As I stared at him, trying to make light of each moment we spent on our honeymoon, trying to just enjoy the temporary reprieve we'd been given, I caught myself wondering… *How could this possibly be true sanctuary?*

CHAPTER 6: DEREK

"Woman, why would you do this to me?" I groaned at Sofia, who gave me a grin as she wiped the sweat off her brow and grabbed a towel to wipe away mine.

We'd been "exercising" for the past hour and a half and every muscle and bone in my body was screaming in agony.

"I've trained at the Crimson Fortress' battle grounds for hours every day for weeks. I never ached like this."

"Welcome to being mortal, Derek. You're flesh and blood just like the rest of us. You need to get used to experiencing pain in order to get what you want."

"And what exactly do *I* want? Remind me again why I'm doing this."

She smiled at me as she slipped her hands under my shirt and over my lower torso. "We want to keep those abs of yours, Derek. That's what we want."

"No." I shook my head. "That's what *you* want."

"Maybe so, but as my husband, you're supposed to make sure that I get what I want."

"Oh, is that so? I never thought you could be so selfish…"

"And yet you're still madly in love with me." She stepped forward and gave me a peck on the cheek.

"The things I let you get away with…" I heaved the duffel bag containing our belongings over my shoulder. "Could we get something to eat? I'm famished."

"Again?" She wrinkled her nose.

She managed to convince me to settle for a salad—something she was easily able to do with a few suggestive quips and gestures. I wolfed down my dinner. I couldn't wait to get Sofia back to our hotel room. I already had her on the bed and was about to undress her when I heard quick footsteps and a voice I was sure I'd already heard somewhere before saying, "Find them."

I swallowed hard and looked around the room.

"Derek? What's wrong?" Sofia asked from beneath me.

"We have to get out of here."

"What? Why?"

A shadow moved from the terrace. *Vampires.* I motioned for Sofia to look towards the veranda. "That's why," I whispered.

Her eyes widened. "Who could possibly…"

"I don't know, but we don't want to stay to find out." I got off her and quickly replaced my clothes, my eyes set on the terrace. Now there were two figures. "Sofia, hurry."

She was already moving as quickly as she could, but the glass doors that led to the terrace slid open. My heart dropped when I saw who our intruders were. *Kiev and Clara. The Elder's children.*

My stomach turned. Never before had I ever felt as incapable of defending Sofia as I did at that moment. When Kiev's red eyes settled on Sofia—her hair a mess and her clothes still disheveled—I wanted to rip his throat out. I pulled her closer to me, stepping forward to block her from his view.

Kiev only scoffed as he eyed me from head to foot. We both knew how powerless I was against him.

I was so focused on Kiev I barely noticed Clara until she was standing right beside me, tracing a claw over my arm.

"I love the tan, Novak," she drawled before pushing the point of her claw into my skin. I winced when blood trickled down my arm. She smirked when the wound didn't heal. "I wonder what Emilia would think if you hadn't killed her. She became a vampire because you were a vampire. Now, you're nothing but an ordinary man."

"Yes, which is why I'm wondering what you could possibly want from me."

"Who says anything about wanting you?"

Kiev's stare fixed on Sofia. "We're here for *her*. We're here for the immune herself."

Sofia shivered and her grip tightened over my biceps.

"You're not touching her." I shook my head. "You'd have to kill me first."

Kiev and Clara exchanged glances before chuckling.

This time, Kiev pried his eyes away from Sofia and stared straight at me. "Oh, trust us, Novak," he said in a slurred accent, amusement glimmering in his red eyes, "after what you did to our sister"—his claws came out with a glimmer against the moonlight from outside our hotel room—"killing you would be both our honor and our pleasure."

CHAPTER 7: AIDEN

A full orchestra played a Bach classic through my earphones as I hit the punching bag in front of me over and over and over again. I wanted to see it in pieces. I wanted to tear that bag apart.

I want it ruined… just like my marriage.

I'd loved Camilla with all my heart and I couldn't understand why she would choose to be a creature of the dark—how she could choose it over our daughter, over me.

I refused to break down. From the moment I'd found out what she'd really done to me and our daughter, I'd determined that this wasn't going to destroy me.

Camilla was just another thing that the vampires had taken away from me and they were going to pay. The vampires were going to pay dearly for ruining my life… mine and my daughter's.

Burning midnight oil at hunter headquarters, I spent all my energy and anger at the atrium, where the hunters held combat training. Every ounce of my strength was being expended to muscle out the rage I felt inside. I had an endless supply of it and all I had to do was think of my little Sofia. Every time, the rage would shoot up to an all-new high and I would begin hitting that bag with all the might I could muster as I contemplated questions I had no idea how to answer.

How am I going to tell Sofia about this? How am I going to tell her that her mother left us in order to become a vampire? How am I even going to raise her? How on earth could I ever be the father that she deserves? How could Camilla do this to us? Does she not realize how much we need her? How could Camilla stand losing her own daughter?

Memories of how sick Sofia had been came back to haunt me. I'd thought I was going to lose her. Ever since Camilla had left, Sofia's life had been placed on the edge by some sort of disease that doctors could not even diagnose. She'd been in and out of a high fever for days. I'd been in way over my head, going crazy over how to take care of her. I was supposed to protect her and keep her safe and in the span of those days, I realized that I had absolutely no control of her fate. If anything ever happened to Sofia, I wouldn't be able to forgive myself, but there would be times when all I could do was stand and watch and hope that she would make it.

I hated that. I wanted to always be in control and yet it was so clear to me that my life—much more the lives of those I loved—was never meant to be manageable.

I jabbed at the punching bag before letting out a frustrated scream. Tears and sweat made a mess out of my face, but I held the sobs in. Camilla never could've known how much she'd hurt me by leaving. I doubted she even cared.

What am I going to do with Sofia now? How on earth am I going to be a father to her when all I know in life is to play the part of Aiden Claremont, the millionaire, and Reuben the Head Hunter?

"Reuben," a deep familiar voice called me by my hunter name. "What

are you still doing here?"

I spun around and found Arron studying me. Arron was a senior of the Order of the Hawk, which controlled all hunter activities. He was one of the most influential figures among the hunters and one to avoid crossing.

I nodded toward him. "Arron. I had no idea you were here. I was just..."

"Blowing off some steam?"

I nodded, trying to maintain composure. Of all the seniors I'd met, Arron intimidated me the most, and I couldn't even figure out why. There wasn't anything striking about him. He was known for being ruthless against vampires, but among the hunters, who wasn't? I raised my eyes to his, wanting to place what it was about him that silenced even the most fearless of hunters.

"I heard what happened to your wife and your daughter."

My fists clenched, the leather of the boxing gloves squeaking. I swallowed hard, refusing to break down in front of one of our strongest leaders.

Arron began circling me, his hands tucked behind his back. "Tell me, Reuben, how do you plan to raise a nine-year-old child? You kept your family life so well hidden all these years. How you sheltered your wife and your daughter amazes me, but now that the vampire world is aware of Sofia, do you really believe you can keep this up?"

I was in no mood to discuss Camilla or Sofia. "What are you saying? Kindly get to the point."

"Just like your father. No time for nonsense, ruthless in battle, loyal to the cause of the hawk. You impress me time and time again, Reuben, but I digress. What I'm saying is that you have a decision to make. This is the forked road. You are either going to introduce little Sofia to our world or you are going to push her away from your life in order to spare her all this."

"Push her away?"

"Do you honestly believe that she could live a normal life? If so, then you are a fool."

"It can happen. She will only know Aiden Claremont. She will never have to know Reuben."

"She is a walking target as long as she's connected to you."

"She just lost her mother. I can't cut her out of my life. I just…"

"Then make a hunter out of her. I've known you since you were a child. Your father was a good friend of mine. You were meant to be a hunter, Reuben, but you know what the life of a hunter is like. Look ahead of you and you will find nothing but bloodshed and violence. Thus was the life of your father and thus will your life be also. Should you decide to keep Sofia close to you, then you had better prepare her for this life."

"And if I don't want her to be a hunter?"

"Then stay as far away from her as possible."

"Just like that? How can a father do that to his own child? How can I live with myself knowing that I abandoned my own daughter?"

"How can you live with yourself knowing that you put her life in danger?"

With that, Arron left me to muse over his words. No words of comfort, no hint of empathy—just an expressionless face the entire time.

Right then, I understood what was so chilling about Arron's presence. He was a man without a family who saw nothing but the bottom line. He looked at people and saw them for what use they could be to our cause. If one was no longer of use, then he was no longer of worth. That was what made him so terrifying. Unlike the rest of us, Arron acted like a man with nothing to lose and everything to gain.

The hunters' occupation of The Shade was a dream come true for anyone with a deep-seated hatred for vampires and I was keenly aware of it. I could practically feel the hatred oozing out past their veneer of calm confidence. It was a matter of time before things turned out for the worst. I would be a fool to think that they wouldn't capitalize on the power they had over the vampires of The Shade.

Soon after our first council meeting at Vivienne's penthouse, the hunters had taken over the Residences. They wanted the vampires to retaliate. They wanted a valid reason to harm the vampires of The Shade. They were just waiting, prodding, allowing the tension to increase.

I walked past a group of hunters as I made my way along the cobblestone pathways of what was left of the Vale.

"So this is The Shade." Zinnia, a young hunter whom I'd mentored, began walking in stride with me. "This is what you left our cause for."

"You know why I left our cause, Zinnia. I did it for Sofia and Sofia alone."

"So you admit it." She tucked a loose strand of her blue-streaked, shoulder-length hair behind her ear. "You *have* left our cause."

I chuckled as I waved at one of the humans from the Catacombs manning one of the stalls at the Vale's main market, or at least what was left of it. They were making a valiant, but rather shoddy, attempt to rebuild what we'd lost at The Shade after the Elder's devastating attack. "A cure has been found, Zinnia. You and I know that changes everything. Perhaps you should be asking yourself what exactly your cause is."

"Revenge. Hasn't that always been a hunter's cause? We can talk about the big picture all we want, but the only reason any of us ever became hunters was because vampires took something—someone— from us. And we want them to pay."

"So what are you proposing now? What do you intend to do?

Spend your whole life chasing after vampires—none of whom are personally responsible for your loss? And what happens when these vampires turn back to humans? What then?"

Zinnia shifted her weight. I was getting to her and I knew it. I couldn't blame her. After years of devoting oneself to a cause, it was difficult to have what you were fighting for seem meaningless.

"What happened to you? You were the infamous Reuben. Ruthless... merciless... devoted to our cause."

"Again with this cause. Revenge is not a cause, Zinnia. It's a controlling obsession. It accomplishes nothing."

"That's not what you taught me."

"It's the truth nonetheless. Most of what I taught you was born out of hatred. I found a better way, a higher cause."

"Go ahead. Preach it." Teeth gritted, Zinnia glared at one of the vampires nearby. "How can you stand them?"

"Sometimes I can't, but I remember that my daughter risked her life too many times to make a home out of this island, so I convince myself not to compromise everything she worked for."

Zinnia was about to say something, but was silenced by the sight of Vivienne and Xavier making their way to us. Worry was traced in the countenance of the beautiful vampire.

I took a step forward, ignoring the way Zinnia was seething over the idea that they'd found the largest, most influential vampire coven in history, and there was nothing she could do to ruin it.

"Vivienne?"

"Natalie just arrived at the Port. She's badly wounded." Vivienne's gaze lingered on me before she shuffled her feet nervously, glancing at Zinnia.

"I thought the hunters shut down the Port."

"For a catch like Natalie Borgia, do you really think they wouldn't re-open it?" Vivienne narrowed her eyes at Zinnia.

"They've taken her to Corrine's," Xavier added. He paid little heed to the spunky hunter beside me.

Zinnia raised a brow, never one to enjoy being ignored. "Take us to the witch's temple then. Hurry, vampire. We wouldn't want to miss what your messenger has to say, would we?"

Xavier's steely eyes shifted from Vivienne to Zinnia. His fists clenched tightly.

Though Vivienne didn't quite have Derek's authoritative temperament, she still had fire in her. She was still princess of The Shade and in her eyes, Zinnia was a brat threatening her home and everyone she loved. Her face hardened.

I could tell that Xavier was just waiting for one word from the princess. Should it come to that, I had no idea whose side I was going to take. Despite our current differences, Zinnia and I had history. She was like a daughter to me.

Xavier took a step toward Zinnia.

I wasn't a huge fan of the teenager at that moment, but I didn't want to see her mangled either. She was one of our most well-trained but she stood no chance against vampires as powerful as Xavier or Vivienne. The hunters' strength was always in the element of surprise, strategy and cunning. She had none of those at the moment. I gave her a quick glance and saw nothing but defiance. *Did I train you to be this way? A complete fool?*

To my relief, however, Vivienne's shoulders sagged and she heaved out a long sigh—probably to reel her temper in. "Take her to the Sanctuary, Xavier. Aiden and I will soon follow."

Xavier's jaw twitched. He was clearly not happy, but he had no choice but to obey.

Once left alone, I studied Vivienne. "What's going on, Vivienne?"

"Something's wrong, Aiden. I've had a bad feeling all day and then Natalie shows up and…" Stark panic was in her eyes.

"Vivienne, get a hold of yourself."

"I can't. I can't take Derek and Sofia's place here at the island. I don't have it in me to lead. Not when all this is happening." She wasn't listening to me. Her eyes were blank, staring into the space between us.

I grabbed her by the shoulders and shook her. It did little good. Instead, she just began to sob.

"If anything happens to them…"

I found it strange seeing a powerful vampire have a nervous breakdown right in front of me, but more than the awkward situation, I felt guilt. *We did this to her.*

Vivienne had been attempting to convince Sofia to return to The Shade after she'd left with her best friend, Ben, when we'd caught her. Before being taken to hunters' headquarters, she was strong and enigmatic, with a lot of confidence and fight in her. By the time we were done with her, however, she'd become a broken, whimpering and frightened woman.

As she stood before me, shaking like a leaf, afraid of everything and nothing, I did the one thing I knew how to do at the moment.

I slapped her square in the face.

"Snap out of it, Vivienne," I hissed. "Remember who you are. You ruled The Shade for four hundred years. I know you'd like to think that it was your father or your brother, Lucas, but while Derek was asleep, it was you. You kept this place together and you're going to do it again as soon as you get a hold of yourself."

Vivienne stared at me, shock in her bright violet eyes. For a couple of seconds, we stood frozen. Finally, she broke the silence through a gasp. She shrugged my grip off her shoulders as she stood to her full height, her chin tilting up.

Gratefulness flashed on her face when she finally looked me in the eye. No words came out, but Vivienne Novak and I had an understanding that day. I don't know what it was that made me so sure, or how I understood her mere gaze, but I knew three things to be true:

One, we were about to see a very different Vivienne Novak—or at least the one The Shade had always known before we broke her.

Two, I had her forgiveness for what I'd put her through back at the hunters' headquarters.

Three, I was never, *ever* allowed to hit her again.

CHAPTER 8: SOFIA

I was close to throwing up.

It felt like a flurry of little creatures were doing cartwheels inside me. The cold air seeped through my skin and penetrated my bones. I shivered as I tried to get a grip on our dark surroundings. Flashbacks of my first night at The Shade returned to me in full force. The darkness, the musty atmosphere, the feeling of being inside a dungeon… I half-expected to be thrown over the wall on my back.

Then I remembered everything I'd gone through over the past two years. No. I wasn't back at The Shade, but there was a great chance that I was indeed inside a dungeon.

I tried to recall what had happened before I'd lost consciousness. Two vampires—one red-eyed and one brunette—had been in our hotel room. From the look in Derek's eyes, he knew who they were. For the first time in my life, I'd seen terror in Derek's face.

I'd known without a doubt that the two intruders wouldn't

hesitate to end my husband's life. Derek had been poised to fend off an attack from Kiev when something sharp had stuck me on the neck. I'd lost consciousness after that—but not before Kiev hit Derek over the neck with his sharp claws.

Now that I'd jolted fully awake, terror filled me. *Where's Derek?* The thought of what they could've done to him began eating at me. I tried to recall who they were and remembered how the brunette had spoken about Emilia. *Could they be...* My breath hitched. If they were who I thought they were... the Elder's children...

I fought back all negative thoughts. I refused to sink into that kind of darkness. I needed to believe that Derek was okay. He was a survivor, the strongest man I had ever known. I wasn't going to lose him—not even in my thoughts. Not ever.

Please be all right, Derek. I love you. You know I love you.

I was whispering the words out loud when a movement nearby jolted me to attention. I blinked several times, trying to adjust to the dimness. To my relief, the trace of moonlight streaming through a high window allowed me to make out a small figure nearby.

I creased my brows. "Hello?"

I was answered by shuffling and a quiet whimper.

A lump formed in my throat. *Is she a child? What monsters hold us captive?* I tried to keep my voice as soft and gentle as I could. "It's all right, honey. I'm not going to hurt you."

I barely heard her voice, hoarse and frightened. "I'm afraid."

I nodded, though I doubted she could even see me. "I know, dear. I'm frightened too, but we need to be brave right now. We have to be brave if we want to make it out of here."

"There's no way out of here. The last one who tried to escape..." She choked on her own words.

I couldn't imagine what kind of terrors the young girl had already gone through. I tried to steer the conversation away from the painful memories. "What's your name?"

She said the words in a soft, hesitant tone, but the effect it had on me was so thunderous, it knocked the breath right out of me.

"I'm Abby. Abigail Hudson."

I was so stunned, I wasn't able to respond. I was overjoyed that she was alive. Ben's little sister was practically a sister to me too, and the thought of seeing her after all these years in a place like this was tearing me apart.

"Abby?" I managed to squeak out. "It's me. Sofia."

A gasp and a sob cut through the tension and within seconds, soft arms wrapped around my neck, tears wetting the nook she buried her small face in. She held me so tight I could barely catch my breath. The way she clung to me said a lot about her relief, about what kind of things she'd been put through.

We stayed that way for a couple of moments before I pried her away from me. The questions running through my mind begged to be answered and I doubted we had a lot of time. I knelt on the ground and stood her in front of me. I reminded myself that Abby was barely seven years old and that she had probably been more traumatized than any child her age should have to be.

"Abby, I need you to answer a few questions for me, okay? I'm here now and I'm going to look out for you, but I need to know if…"

"They killed Daddy and Mommy. The red-eyed man and the scary woman with brown hair… they did it." Abby was sobbing, but the words were clear enough, each one cutting me to the core.

I tried to search for words to comfort her, but all I could do was hold her in my arms, guilty over what part I might have played in the deaths of Lyle and Amelia Hudson, the couple who had raised me for nine years. On the other hand, I was also consumed by the hope that the love of my life had escaped a horrifying demise.

I held the little girl in my arms for what felt like an eternity before the wooden door swung open and a flood of light streamed through the room.

We really were in a dungeon—rusty shackles at the end of chains hooked on the stone walls, with hay on the ground. I blinked to adjust to the change of lighting. I gasped when a figure was pushed to the ground, causing a loud thud to echo across the room.

Abby shrieked at the sight. A man beaten, bruised and bloody lay on his stomach on the hard stone floor. One could barely decipher what was skin and what was flesh.

"Derek…" I managed to squeak out, reaching for him.

"Impressive. You recognized him."

The red-eyed man leaned against the doorpost, his arms folded over his chest. Abby cowered behind me. I wasn't going to give him the same satisfaction. Ignoring him, I set my focus on Derek, gently brushing my fingers over his damp hair. "Derek, baby, can you hear me? I love you… I love you. Please say something."

"Sweet," the vampire said. "It's fascinating to see firsthand the kind of undying love you two are known for."

My eyes shot up at him, forcing myself to look into those eyes. I tried to see a trace of compassion, of regret, and saw none. He seemed to be enjoying seeing us suffer. I held my gaze, channeling all my attention on him. "What made you like this?"

He smirked, but the expression in his eyes changed. Still, he said words meant to prove himself unswervingly cruel. "Pleasure, Sofia. I became a monster because I enjoy it, and believe me that I feel no regret in mangling your beloved. Not even a single ounce of it. Seeing the expression on your face when you lay eyes on him—how tortured you are—it's fulfilling."

I pried my eyes away from him. I was hoping Derek would heal. He always did, but I had to remind myself that he was no longer a vampire. He was as human as I was. Vulnerable. Mortal. So easily broken.

All because I wanted to be with him, build a life with him, *cure* him.

Sitting there, jolting in surprise when our captor slammed the cell door shut, I tried to remember why I'd ever thought finding a cure was a good thing.

How could we have fooled ourselves into believing that draining Derek of his power was the vampires' true sanctuary?

CHAPTER 9: DEREK

Every bone in my body screamed out in pain. Those red eyes were ingrained in my memory as a symbol for excruciating agony. I wanted to heal. I wanted to somehow recover the ability I'd taken for granted all those years. I was surprised to even be alive. I couldn't understand how a mortal human being could survive what Kiev had just put me through.

The things we survive, I mused, thinking of the many things Sofia had had to endure. *Was it this painful for her too?* A wave of guilt swept over me at the recollection of all the pain she'd gone through ever since she got entangled in my life. I struggled to meet her gaze, moaning at how even the slightest motion caused currents of agony to flow from the nape of my neck to the tips of my toes.

I drew a breath at the look on Sofia's face. "I'm so sorry, Derek," she whispered, obviously afraid to even touch me. "I'm so sorry."

I couldn't understand why she was apologizing. She wasn't the one who'd done this to me. "No. Don't."

"If I hadn't pushed for a cure... If I'd just... I'm so sorry."

I hated the Elder and his children more than I ever had before. "I love you, Sofia, but you really need to stop this nonsense you're sputtering out." I tried to chuckle but the attempt only caused spasms of pain to go through my throat.

"You're not supposed to be kidding around, Derek." She choked back her tears. "What have they done to you? Who are these monsters? What do they want with us?"

I pressed my palms on the ground and pushed my upper body up, groaning. "Help me up."

She helped me sit up, leaning my bleeding back against the wall. Now that I was sitting upright, my head began to whirl.

"You should lie down." Sofia's gentle hands ran over my matted hair before she pulled me to rest my head over her lap.

I tried not to groan too much, noticing how she winced. She was trying to be as gentle as possible with me—as if she were afraid that if she touched me, I would break.

Is this how she used to feel around me? So vulnerable?

"It's all right, Sofia. We'll be all right," was my feeble attempt to assure her. Soft lips touched my forehead then my cheek then my lips. The contact caused my bruised face agony and yet my soul came alive just to have her shower those kisses on me.

I dared not groan, steeling myself against the pain. I had an inkling that the memory of those kisses would be the only thing I could hold on to in the coming months.

"Rest," she whispered as she brushed slender fingers over my hair. I shifted my head on her lap to find the least painful position I could manage.

Only then did I notice the little girl backed up into one corner of the cell. She had her arms wrapped around her knees, her big eyes set on me. I felt like I was being assessed. I tried to recall where I'd seen the little blonde before. She looked awfully familiar.

"That little girl," I moaned, my voice hoarse from all the screaming I'd done in Kiev's hands. "Is that Ben's sister?"

Sofia frowned. "You see her?"

"Why wouldn't I see her? She's right there."

"It's pitch black in that corner."

I blinked as I scanned the room. The light left something to be desired, but I could still see everything clearly.

The little girl spoke up.

"Sofia?" she squeaked out.

"Abby, do you see me?"

"Not so much. Who are you with?"

"He's my husband, Derek. He was there during Ben's funeral. Don't you remember?"

"Is he safe? He won't hurt me, will he?"

"Honey, he's not going to hurt you. Derek, you remember Abby, right?"

"I'm too hurt to even move, Abby. So yes. You're safe with me."

We were met with silence. The little girl was just staring straight right in front of her.

"Come here where I can see you, sweetie," Sofia coaxed.

Abby crawled toward us, following the sound of Sofia's voice, feeling the space in front of her.

Questions were running through my mind—ones I wasn't sure I wanted answered. Why was she here? What had happened to the Hudsons? What would the Elder want with a little girl like her?

Abby finally arrived by Sofia's side, snuggling against her. Small hands began to brush through my hair. "They hurt you really bad,

Mr. Derek."

"They did, didn't they?" I groaned, her statement reminding me of the dull ache I felt all over my body. I was desperately trying to make light of the situation, perhaps draw a laugh from my wife. I was afraid that we only had a few moments left with each other, and I would've rather seen her smile rather than her tears.

"I thought Sofia was going to marry Ben. I saw them kissing a lot."

I could already see the blush on Sofia's face without having to look at her. I grinned, remembering how jealous I'd been of Sofia's best friend. At that time, I'd lost all hope that I could ever be with her. How was I going to compete with all those years of history? Now she was my wife. *A wife you're about to lose.*

I swallowed hard. I would've shaken my head, but it would be too painful so I just shut my eyes and bit my lip, trying to regain hope that both Sofia and I were going to get out of this mess in one piece.

"Sofia." I spoke up. "I need you to listen to me. We're being held captive by the Elder and his children. The vampires who took us at the hotel—they're his children. The red-eyed one is Kiev. The brunette is his sister, Clara. I think they want to kill me."

"Derek, don't…"

"Listen to me." I cut her off. "There's little chance we can get away from this, Sofia. I'll be honest with you. Even as a vampire, I was already vulnerable against them. Right now…" I tried to choose my words carefully, to assure her that I wasn't blaming her for what I was now, that I adored her for finding the cure and making me feel like normalcy was a possibility. "Sofia, whatever they ask you to do, don't give in."

"Of course. I would never—"

"Even if they threaten to kill me."

Her breath hitched. I could almost see the wheels turning furiously in her mind. I knew then that no matter what she said, even if she promised me that she wouldn't risk her life or everything we worked for to save me, she wouldn't be able to help herself.

I wondered then if the prophecy that we were strongest together and weakest apart was true, because I had become Sofia's greatest weakness and she had become mine.

I would do anything to keep from losing Sofia and from the looks of it, the same was true of her.

CHAPTER 10: VIVIENNE

Aiden Claremont had knocked me to my senses. Our confrontation had shaken me and the full reality of what was happening sank in.

Derek and Sofia aren't going to return soon enough to spare you. Get it together.

The moment Aiden and I arrived at the Sanctuary, I resolved to just suck all my fears and weaknesses in and channel as much Derek Novak as I could. My twin brother had a way of silencing people with the full force of his presence. I wondered if I could do the same thing with the calmness of mine.

We arrived at the Sanctuary to find Zinnia and Xavier standing face to face, fists clenched, both warriors geared up for a fight. Aiden took a step forward, about to say something. I raised my hand to silence him.

I walked forward, stopping between my old-time friend and the petite hunter. I glanced Xavier's way, flicked my head to the side. He knew the gesture all too well already. He'd seen it many times over the centuries that we'd been working side-by-side. He followed me as I continued to walk forward, ignoring Zinnia. She didn't like that.

"Hey. I have a score to settle with your man."

I spun around and glared at her. "I suggest you be silent, little girl. I don't care how many wooden stakes you have or how many UV-ray guns you wield, trust me when I say that I can take you. Say another word that irks me and you will have a score to settle, but not with *my man,* as you so aptly put it. The score you're going to settle will be with *me.*"

The fool actually smirked. "Like you've ever been a threat to someone like me."

Within seconds, my hand was coiled around her neck, her petite body raised two feet above the ground, her back against a marble pillar. She retrieved a wooden stake with one hand. I used my free hand to knock the weapon out of hers. I let go of her neck and quickly pinned her wrists above her head, using my own legs to keep her from kicking at me.

"I know your moves. I spent enough time at your headquarters to observe your training. Don't mess with me."

"We broke you," she mocked.

"Oh, yes, you did. All the more reason for me to break you now. Revenge, that's what you want, right? We both know how defenseless you are against me right now. Perhaps I should do it. Take revenge. That's what you would do, right?" My fangs appeared. The act was painful in itself, considering that my fangs were removed at hunters' headquarters, but back at The Shade, without the suppressing chemicals that the hunters had injected me with, the fangs had been growing back. I hadn't used them yet, but at that moment, I couldn't think of a better way to use them.

It seemed like poetic justice. Truth be told, I wanted to do it. Teach her a lesson. Sink my teeth into her neck and show her that we weren't to be messed with. But I knew that all I could do was threaten her. It was a bluff, and I couldn't help but wonder if she knew it.

"Go ahead," she challenged. "Do it. Go against what your king told you. Let's not play around. We all know you're just your brother's pawn."

"Maybe so, *if* he was here, but he isn't, is he?" I pressed my teeth into her neck and she gasped. *I don't think she's ever actually had a vampire suck her blood before.*

"Vivienne..." Aiden spoke up. "Don't. We have other things to take care of."

I guess the bluff is working. I stepped back and stared Zinnia down. Rage flashed in her eyes and for a moment, I could have sworn that she would be foolish enough to try and fight back.

"Don't be a fool, Zinnia." Aiden spoke up.

"Listen to your boss, baby hunter."

Her eyes darted across the room. Save for Aiden, who was more on our side now than hers, she was the only hunter present. She had to choose her words and actions carefully if she wanted to survive.

Her shoulders sagged. Even though she was clearly attempting to reel back her temper, her fists clenched so tightly her knuckles had already grown white.

I smirked at her before glancing over at Aiden. He had a serious expression on his face, although I thought I saw a hint of amusement—perhaps even pride—behind his gaze. He nodded my way. I found myself missing my own father. It was probably wishful thinking on my part but I could swear that there was a trace of Gregor Novak in him. I turned toward Xavier.

The look Xavier was giving me knocked my breath away. His eyes bore into me with an intensity I'd never quite seen from him before. It was as if he saw me for the first time that day, his eyes moist with tears.

I gave him a curt nod even though I wanted to do so much more. I made a mental note to have a long, meaningful talk with him. He deserved that.

"Let's go meet Natalie." I broke the silence, trying to put my focus on work. I walked past Xavier, my arm brushing against his. The contact sent shivers down my spine. *Dear heavens, Vivienne, what is happening to you? Get a grip.*

As I walked on, ignoring the fact that I was keenly aware of his presence right behind me, I tried to push away the same truth I'd been denying for the past five centuries.

Xavier Vaughn had always had that effect on me.

We arrived at the room where Corrine was keeping Natalie. The rogue vampire was still unconscious. The Shade's witch was sitting on a couch, cross-legged, sipping a warm drink. She made it look like everything in the world was just as it should be, which was the farthest thing from the truth.

"Corrine," I acknowledged her.

"Princess," she responded, eyeing me from head to foot before gazing at Xavier who was standing right behind me.

I could practically feel his eyes settled behind my neck.

Corrine smirked. "Tense, your highness?" She always had a way of making the title seem like an insult.

I kept my cool and perused her the same way she had me. "Hello to you too, Corrine. It's nice to see someone here at The Shade can afford to remain relaxed." I looked toward Natalie. "When will she wake?"

"Something's different about you." Corrine cocked her head to the side. "Your old fire... it's back."

I didn't know how to respond so I just made my way toward Natalie, standing by her bedside. "Come on, Natalie," I whispered. "Wake up."

As if on cue, Natalie stirred on the bed. I drew in my breath when she slowly opened her eyes, blinking several times to get a clear look at me. "Viv..."

"What happened to you? Do you know if Derek and Sofia are doing well?"

For the first time since I'd met Natalie, I saw terror in her eyes.

"They're opening the gates, Vivienne. The Elder is opening the gates."

I had no idea what she was talking about, but anything that involved the Elder couldn't possibly be good.

Corrine stood, her knuckles growing white as she gripped the cup between her hands so hard it seemed she intended to break it.

"That's impossible." The witch shook her head, her brown locks wildly swaying behind her.

"What's going on? What is she talking about?" I directed my eyes toward Natalie. "What does all this have to do with my brother?"

"I don't know." Natalie shook her head. "But I was there when Kiev and Clara wiped out an entire vampire coven because they chose to side with Derek. The Elder seems to have quite a vendetta against your brother, the cure being a threat and all."

My knees weakened, and I leaned against Xavier, who had already taken my side for support.

"What coven are you referring to?" he asked.

"The Underground," Natalie managed to rasp out before breaking into coughs.

"Kiev and Clara." Corrine said the words with utter spite. "The Elder's children."

I asked the question I was dreading the answer to. "Do they have my brother, Natalie?"

She nodded. "I tried to stop it, but Kiev and Clara… they're powerful. I didn't stand a chance. They have both Derek and Sofia."

My stomach turned. My brother was mortal. How on earth was he going to protect himself? "What would they want with…"

"They're after Sofia," Corrine announced. "They're after the immunes."

Aiden's hands balled into tight fists, a muscle on his jaw twitching. Behind him, Zinnia stood, arms crossed over her chest, leaning against the wall, seemingly enjoying everything that was happening.

I tried to ignore how irritated I was by the little brat. "And my brother?" I was afraid for his life. They only wanted Sofia. That meant Derek, especially now that he was a human, was dispensable.

"They told me to tell you that they would return Derek alive in exchange for one thing. They want The Shade's side of the portal activated. The Shade's gate."

"No. Never." Corrine shook her head violently.

"What?" I blurted out. "What is going on, Corrine? What portal? What gate?"

"We can't have that, Vivienne. Trust me. We can't allow something like that to happen. The stakes are too high."

Collect yourself, Vivienne. I breathed a deep sigh. "Something like what, Corrine?" I said through gritted teeth. "Make it clear to me what's so important about this portal that you are willing to exchange my brother's life for it."

"Surely they wouldn't kill Derek," Corrine muttered.

"Why wouldn't they?" Natalie said. "Derek has been a pain in their ass since he woke up. Now is the best time to get rid of him. As a human, he's the weakest he's ever been in centuries."

"If they wanted him dead, they would've killed him when he was in their territory—when Emilia was madly in love with him."

"There's no Emilia now to protect him, is there?" I added. "Corrine, what is this gate?"

"I can't tell you." Corrine shook her head. "But it's the only reason I ever agreed to come here, Vivienne. I need to protect that gate. It can never be opened."

"I'm getting my brother back, witch. I will strike a deal with the Elder himself if I have to."

"You know that I'm powerful enough to stop you."

"Then do it. You'll have to kill me, because that's what it will take."

Seeing the witch so alarmed daunted me. Corrine was so much better at keeping a calm and collected exterior than I was. We'd never been friends, but we'd always had an understanding—we were on the same side. Until now. Staring at her, I wondered if Corrine would go as far as killing me to prevent that gate from getting opened.

She eyed me, her inner conflict evident in the heave of her chest and the firmness of her expression. "There are three gates that will open a portal to Cruor, the realm of the original vampires, the Elders. And yes, there is more than one Elder. One gate is in The Blood Keep, one is here at The Shade, one is at The Underground. From what Natalie said, they already have control of The Underground. The only one left is The Shade."

"What does that mean? Why should it matter to me that the portal be opened?"

"You have no idea what the original vampires are like. *Elders.*

They are nothing like you. Your kind are their creation, a mere mutation of the original. Should they come to earth, then those of the other supernatural realms will come too. That means war, Vivienne. A war of supernaturals. Do we really want to be a catalyst of that?"

"Why now? Why do all these Elders want to come now after all these years?"

Corrine shrugged. "Your brother found the cure. That cure has been the greatest threat to their presence here on earth. If that cure has the potential to eradicate all vampires…"

I stared at Corrine, unable to breathe. I couldn't help but feel like her very existence had been a lie. I'd thought that she had become an ally to us, but I should've known that it was a mistake to ever trust a witch.

Derek trusted Cora and he paid dearly for it.

"Do you really think for one moment, Corrine, that the Elder isn't going to find another way to activate that portal—with or without Derek as a bargaining chip? If this war is—"

My sentence was cut off because a vision flashed right in front of me—a vision so vivid I dropped to the ground. I was known as the Seer of The Shade for a reason but never before had I seen a vision so disturbing.

The sky was a deep crimson red. Deafening thunder rolled overhead. Torrents of hot rain poured from the clouds, soaking the blood-stained ground. Giant winged creatures and immortal vampires were in full-on war. The earth was their battleground, humans their casualties.

By the time the vision was over, I was trembling uncontrollably. When I came to, Xavier's arm was around me and Corrine was kneeling right in front of me.

"What did you see?" she asked.

"War. Violent… bloody… too many deaths…"

"*That's* what's going to happen if the portal is opened."

"The portal *will* be opened, Corrine. The real question here is whether or not my brother will be alive when it does. I don't know about you, but I'd rather go through that war with an ally like him."

Something sparked in Corrine's eyes. "Vivienne… I don't know…"

I opened my mouth but Aiden cleared his throat, interrupting us. "I understand the discussion on whether or not to save Derek, but you forget his number one weakness. My daughter. In the rush of your discussion, you ignore one key thing. What are they going to do with the immunes? What are they going to do with Sofia?"

Chapter 11: Sofia

Derek was trying to keep a brave face, but he was in agony. I was barely able to sleep because he kept stirring on my lap, moaning. I wasn't sure if it was because of the pain or because of the nightmare he seemed to be having. Abby remained snuggled beside me and my body was beginning to feel the strain caused by their weight leaning against me, my back aching, the hard concrete wall behind me not helping.

The Elder's children had us and I had no idea what they wanted from us. I didn't have the heart to pry information out of my Derek. He'd already been through enough. I could only imagine the trauma he was going through now that he'd been tortured as a human being and not a powerful vampire.

I wanted to help him, but what was there to do? I actually missed the days when all it had taken was a cut on my wrist and a few uncomfortable moments feeling him drink my blood. Neither of us were fans of the whole thing, but at least it had healed him. *Now, I'm helpless to do anything. I've ruined him. I've ruined Derek Novak.*

The door swung open. Abby took a short intake of breath before burying her face against my arm. I looked up, squinting at the light that streamed inside the cell.

"We're starving. Are you ever going to feed us?" I hadn't even been conscious of how hungry I was until I said the words out loud. My stomach grumbled in agreement.

Kiev stepped inside the cell, his red eyes first falling on my face. He smirked at the sight of me. He then looked at Derek and his face fell. His brows met. "How is it possible…"

I looked down at my husband and was washed with complete relief. I had no idea how it had happened, but his face—which I'd barely recognised right after he was brought into the cell—was almost healed save for a few scrapes and scratches.

"What did you do?" Kiev glared at me.

I smiled before shrugging. I caressed my husband's cheek with my fingers, hoping that he looked less disturbed and more at peace. "It's not easy to break a man like Derek Novak."

To my dismay, however, Kiev had already recovered from the shock. His chuckle grated at my nerves. "Maybe you're right, but I always did love a challenge. I see surprise in your eyes, Mrs. Novak. That says a lot about what you know… or more appropriately, what you don't know."

Before I could respond, another figure appeared behind him. *Clara.*

"Really, Kiev? Chit-chatting with the redhead? I always knew you had the hots for her. Why don't you just go ahead? Take her right here if you want. It's not like her husband can stop you."

I'd already experienced being prey to conscienceless predators like

Lucas Novak and Borys Maslen. I was certain that they were no match for the red-eyed monster named Kiev. Still, I kept a brave face.

You can't let them faze you, Sofia, much less break you. Derek needs you now more than ever.

"You disgust me, Clara." Kiev said the words like she was the most despicable thing he'd ever laid eyes on.

She laughed—high-pitched and irritating to the ear. "Right. Please, Kiev, I see right through you. We both know the truth anyway. She's just a pastime. What you really want is *me*." She pressed her body against her brother's back, her lips touching his jaw.

Kiev looked like he was about to throw up. I, on the other hand, was confused, not to mention disgusted. I sat up straight, hoping to cover Abby's eyes.

Derek stirred on my lap. I was relieved that he didn't wake. Should Kiev try to take me, Derek would put up a fight, and as miraculous as his healing was, Derek was still no match for the Elder's children.

Clara looked at the little girl affectionately. "Hello, Abby. Did you miss me?"

To my surprise, Abby responded, "Yes, ma'am."

"Very good. Come with me then. We have a lot to talk about."

Kiev's lip twitched when Abby inched away from me, stood up and obediently walked toward Clara.

"Abby?" I frowned. "What's going on?"

Abby gave me an apologetic gaze—one that seemed to displease Clara, because she grabbed Abby's jaw and made the child look her in the eye. "Whose side are you on, Abby? Mine or hers?"

Tears streamed down the little girl's face. "Yours, ma'am."

"Good girl." Clara didn't miss out on the opportunity to give me a smug grin.

My heart dropped. *She's going to make Abby tell her everything Derek and I talked about.* I desperately tried to recall if Derek and I had discussed anything that could lead us or Abby into trouble, but my mind was blanked by panic and concern for a child I treasured deeply.

Clara held Abby's hand and tugged at the little girl to follow her. They began to walk away, but not before Clara placed a peck on her brother's lips.

Kiev's nose wrinkled, his stance tensed and his fists balled, but he didn't stop the vampire from doing as she pleased. He actually sighed with relief the moment Clara disappeared.

He caught me staring at him in question.

"You and her?" I asked, wondering if I had found his weak spot. "That's repulsive."

His jaw tightened. I saw a glimpse of humanity in him when he said, "My thoughts exactly."

"Then why do you let her get away with it? Can you not take her down? Put her in her place? If you hate it so much, why let it happen? Maybe you like it. You actually like it when your sister comes on to you."

"Shut your mouth before I shut it for you. Clara is *not* my sister. We're the Elder's children, but Clara... Emilia... all his spawns... *none* of them are my family."

"Then who is?"

"Whoever I want"—red eyes traveled from the top of my head to the tips of my toes—"for the moment."

I suppressed a shudder, fighting to maintain composure. *You've been around all sorts of disgusting creatures before, Sofia. You can handle this.* I stared at him, slightly mortified, but keeping my head held high, increasingly intrigued. I returned the favor and began to peruse him. *Strong, muscled, virile...*

My eyes met his and based on the way he was glaring at me, he didn't seem to appreciate the way I was studying him. To retaliate, he began hitting me where it hurt.

He set his eyes on Derek.

"You should've heard him scream in pain when I ran the knife against his flesh. Oh, and when the beasts came at him..." Kiev chuckled, delight sparking in his eyes.

I didn't even want to ask what *beasts* were.

Kiev's voice took on an almost nostalgic tone. "I never thought I'd see it myself... the fall of a legend. I honestly thought that Emilia was going to be his downfall, but he survived even that. I've got to admit that I like this better." He lightly kicked Derek's leg. "I like being the hand that brings him to his knees."

I'd gotten to him when I'd taunted him about Clara. His defenses had dropped. Now he was launching a counterattack. I managed to just smirk at him before nudging Derek. *Why aren't you waking up at all this commotion? You're not normally a heavy sleeper.* "Derek?" I muttered.

"He's fine."

I looked up to find Kiev rolling his eyes.

"He's not dead, if that's what you're worried about. So, enough of your moping, Lady Novak. Get up."

"No." I shook my head. "I'm not going to leave him here. I'm not going anywhere with you."

I was barely able to comprehend what happened next. Within seconds, his one hand was fisted over a clump of my hair, gripping it painfully. His other hand pressed against my back, pushing me against a wall, my cheek against the rough stone.

"My orders aren't requests, sweet queen. They're commands,

which you are to immediately obey."

I tried to hit him with my free hands, but he grabbed one arm and twisted it until I yelped with pain.

"I wouldn't exert myself too much if I were you. Not in this condition."

I had no time to wonder what he meant because he flipped me in one swift motion so that I was facing him, my back against the wall. His face was way too close to mine.

"Let go of me," I hissed at him.

"You're queen of The Shade, Sofia. Not queen of The Blood Keep. Your commands mean nothing here."

"What do you want from me?"

"I want you to come with me."

Derek lay motionless on the ground. He was clearly still breathing, but to still remain asleep even after his head had hit the ground when Kiev pulled me from beneath him was completely unlike him.

"Why isn't he waking up?"

"Damn it, I could snap you in half and still it's him you're worried about."

I slammed both my palms against Kiev's chest. "Why isn't he waking up?"

"I don't know, okay? Maybe his body is trying to cope with the torture he went through. I don't give a damn! I just know that I don't want to be here when he does, so you better come with me right now, Sofia, or I am going to make you regret it."

I froze. The threats meant nothing to me. What resounded in my mind was his slip-up. *I don't want to be here when he does.* Was I just fooling myself or did it seem like he was still afraid of Derek?

I didn't have time to ask because he began dragging me outside the cell.

"Let go of me!" I tried to pull away, but he was holding me by the wrist with such an iron grip I was sure my bones would break. "Let go of me, Kiev. I refuse to be treated like some child throwing a tantrum, being dragged to whatever hell you want to take me to."

Kiev stopped in his tracks, right outside the dungeon, his grip on my wrist tightening. "You want me to stop treating you like a child? Stop acting like one. I am lord of this castle—*your* lord. You will do as I say without resistance."

"Then get off me." I wriggled my wrist away from his grasp. "It's not like I can run away from you without you catching me. We both know that in both speed and strength, you overpower me."

He reached past me. I flinched when the cell door slammed shut behind us. I hated leaving Derek there.

"Promise me that nothing will happen to him in my absence."

"You are in no position to demand promises from me, Sofia." Kiev tipped my chin up with his curved forefinger. "But I must say, you are stunning when you exert your authority as queen of The Shade. Too bad that fact doesn't have that much pull here."

"Promise me and I will cooperate with you."

"I can force your cooperation and you know it. I might even enjoy your fighting back more."

I stood on my spot and just stared, raising a brow at him, bluffing confidence.

To my surprise, he said, "Fine. As long as you're with me, he won't be harmed."

I didn't like the sound of his preamble, but I was going to take whatever I could get.

"Very well then. Where are you taking me?"

He placed his hand on the small of my back and gently pushed me forward. "Follow me."

We walked through hallways with high ceilings and imposing pillars. Heavy velvet curtains coated with dust and cobwebs hung closed by every window. Everything about the castle was dark, foreboding and imbued with fear. Kiev led me into a room that looked like a laboratory of sorts.

"What is this place?" I grimaced, half-expecting Dr. Frankenstein to show up somewhere.

Kiev propped me on top of a desk. "Don't do anything stupid, Sofia. Sit still."

Within minutes, he was drawing blood from me through a syringe.

"What are you going to use my blood for?"

"You'll know soon enough."

"Where is Abby? Why would you take a child like her? What could you possibly want from her?"

Kiev eyed me for a moment, as if debating whether or not he should answer the question. To my relief, he did. "She's an immune. Just like you."

I felt the blood drain from my face. "How would you even know that? That only means that you…"

"Clara tried to turn her."

"She's just a child."

"As if Clara cares. Truth be told, I wouldn't be surprised if she's drinking the child's blood now."

"And you don't care that this is happening? Is there no humanity left in you?"

He began to chuckle. "Humanity? In me?" He pouted to mock me. "Is that what you're looking for, sweet Lady Novak? Are you actually trying to find some *good* in me? I'll show you what's good about me." He pressed his lips against mine. Invading. Intruding. Violating.

I tried to pull away from him but my struggles did me little good. When our lips parted, I gasped for breath—something he mistook as a gasp of pleasure. *This can't be happening to me. Not again.*

He gave me a smug smirk. "Good enough for you? You know, Sofia, if you ever tire of your mortal, remember that I'm waiting for you to give yourself to me. After all, without his power, Derek might be a lot less appealing to a young woman like you."

The idea that he was actually into me was sickening. I didn't know if I had it in me to fend off another Lucas or another Borys. "You disgust me," I spat at him. "I will always be Derek's. Always."

"Ah, yes." He smiled with genuine pleasure. "I must say it's beautiful to see the eternal love of Derek and Sofia Novak playing right in front of me. Riveting really. But I hate to say it, sweetheart. I doubt he'll want you after we're finished with you."

"What are you talking about?"

"I think it's time *I* start asking the questions. Don't you agree?"

"What are you going to do to me?"

"Why did you fall in love with him?"

"What does it matter to you?"

"Come on, tell me, Sofia. What exactly did you see in him?"

"Why are you such a monster?"

He seemed to tire of our questioning game, because he tilted his head to the side, ran a hand through my hair before grinning. "Mrs. Novak, believe me when I say that you haven't got the slightest clue just how much of a monster I am."

The moment the words left his lips, his fangs appeared and sank into my neck. At the same moment, he stuck a syringe into my arm, causing me to lose all consciousness.

Chapter 12: Derek

Nothing was left of The Shade. Nothing. War raged all around me as I stood at the center of a bloody battlefield. I couldn't make out the creatures that were fighting. Phantoms, all of them, but I was seeing my comrades fall one at a time.

First, Cameron, then Claudia, then Xavier... then Vivienne...

I wanted to scream when I saw her fall, but I couldn't. The pain built up inside of me until it balled into a magnificent force that caused fire to spark from my palms.

Anger. Fury. Rage.

I was unstoppable.

I hit anyone who came into contact with me. Someone had to pay for my sister's death. I was on a rampage, destroying everything in my path—indiscriminate and violent. I no longer knew who my allies were, so I determined to ruin them all.

Then I saw her.

My Sofia.

Beautiful as always.

Terrifying.

Covered in a thick black liquid, she smiled.

I couldn't think of anything more horrifying than seeing my innocent Sofia standing amidst a battlefield of phantoms, the liquid dripping from her head to her toes, flashing that eerie, delighted smile.

For a moment, I hesitated. Then I shook my head.

I said words more horrifying than the scene that surrounded me.

"She isn't my Sofia."

My eyes shot open, waking me from the nightmare. I couldn't breathe. I couldn't move. The nightmare had been plaguing me since our honeymoon began. A cold breeze swept across the dungeon. I was alone. I was terrified.

What are they going to do to her? I felt like I was about to lose my wife.

I took a long gasp for breath, refilling my lungs with air before jolting up in a sitting position. The cell was empty. My heart doubled its beat. My stomach twisted.

"Sofia!" I screamed at the top of my lungs. My voice bounced across the room in a mocking echo. "Sofia," I sobbed.

The idea that she could be going through what Kiev had put me through inside that torture chamber haunted me.

"What were you thinking, Novak? Why would you willingly become human again? Become weak again?" he taunted me as he ran the edge of the knife beneath my skin.

I shouted through the gag he'd stuffed into my mouth as I lay flat on my back on the steel platform he had me chained to. This was after he'd let loose the mutts. I didn't know what those creatures were, but they'd torn at my flesh before gulping generous amounts of my blood. I'd thought Kiev was going to let me die under their mercy, but he had other plans. Once he was satisfied watching the strange dogs maul me, he'd brought me to a dimly lit chamber where he took pleasure in taunting me as he tortured me.

His taunts escalated even as his methods became more torturous.

"What did you think was going to happen? You killed Emilia, crossed my father more times than can be counted, then you find the cure that would threaten our kind's existence in this world, and then you turn human. Did you really think you were going to get away with all that? Did you really think we would just let you live happily ever after with your precious redhead? What were you going to do? Buy a house with a white picket fence? Have children? Be normal?"

He grinned when he saw in my eyes that this was exactly what I'd wanted. It was what I'd always wanted—even before I turned into a vampire. Fall in love with a girl, raise children with her, live a happy, normal life. Instead, what I'd gotten was centuries of being a creature I detested.

"Why didn't you just kill her? Being around her, sensing how sweet her blood is, how could you have not bled Sofia dry? Where did you find the will?"

I glared daggers at him. A multitude of threats ran through my mind at the very thought of him ever laying hands on my wife.

"If you die, do you think she'll ever love again?" He stared at the dagger he was about to gut me with. He had a sparkle in his bloody red eyes—almost as if he wished Sofia would love him.

All I could do was snicker. The attempt made me groan with pain.

"Relax, Novak. Stop exerting yourself. I don't want you to die just yet."

I lay as still as I could, attempting to focus on Sofia, knowing that I had to survive that night. I couldn't afford to die. I couldn't afford to leave my wife behind. I had to protect her.

As I lay there, however, I knew that I wasn't who I used to be. The hours of torture Kiev put me through proved me weak. At the end of it all, I was convinced that I was completely useless to my wife.

I'm just too weak, *I told myself.* I'm powerless to defend her.

Those same words haunted me as I sat up inside the cell, terrified by the thought of what Sofia could be going through. I resented the words because I couldn't deny it. I stared at my palms, hating how weak I felt at that moment.

"What have I done?" I muttered, before realizing something was amiss.

I felt absolutely no pain. None. I checked my body, my arms, my legs. I ran my hands against my face. No wounds. Nothing.

How is that possible?

Lost in my confusion, I was completely stunned when a beautiful woman appeared inside the dungeon. She wore a white velvet robe with fur lining over a snowy blue gown. With silver hair and amber-gold eyes, she stared down at me.

It took several minutes before her presence fully registered in my mind. "W-who...?" I creased my brows and looked at the cell around me. "How?"

She gave no introductions or explanations. There wasn't even a greeting. All she said was, "You're coming with me."

I stood up, thankful that I was healed but mystified by it nonetheless. I shook my head. "Who are you?"

"I'm the Ageless, mother witch of The Sanctuary, and you're coming with me, Derek Novak."

"Wha... How do I know I can trust you?"

"You don't."

I frowned, taken aback by the bluntness. "What do you want from me? Why would you want to help me? What is The Sanctuary?"

"I came to get you out of here. I don't *want* to help you. I just know that I have to. You'll discover what The Sanctuary is if you come with me."

"I'm not leaving without my wife."

"You have to. If you stay here, mark my words, child, you *will* die. They won't harm Sofia. They need her. You, on the other hand…"

I wasn't used to being called a child, but if she was as her name implied, a five-hundred-year-old man was indeed a child compared to her.

"I can't leave Sofia here."

"You have a better chance of helping her outside of The Blood Keep than inside where they can torture you and make your powers regress."

"Huh? Powers?" My breath hitched as I tried to comprehend the words she was speaking.

"Your ignorance is astounding." She huffed impatiently. "Are you coming or not?"

"Where are we going?"

"The Sanctuary."

I only knew of one Sanctuary—the witch's temple back at our island kingdom. I definitely saw the benefit of returning there, where I had forces to command to free Sofia from the Elder's grasp.

"Sanctuary? You mean at The Shade?"

She scoffed at the notion. "No, child. The true Sanctuary."

I saw no other choice. Kiev would end my life if I stayed there. I was more useful to Sofia alive, though weak, than dead.

The moment I nodded, the Ageless grabbed my hand and within seconds, I was no longer at The Blood Keep.

I opened my eyes only to be blinded by a radiant sun. Once I had adjusted to the sudden change of lighting, I realized I was situated on the top floor of a towering building, standing on a broad white-marble verandah, overlooking a magnificent—almost ethereal—city.

A gentle breeze brought with it the fragrance of exotic flowers. For as far as my eye could travel, pure white architecture sprawled beneath me, with domed roofs studded with gems, glistening in the sunlight. The buildings were surrounded by lakes and green pastures. Not far in the distance came the crash of water. My gaze fell upon the crown of a waterfall, gushing down into a lush valley. An elegantly crafted bridge hung across the basin, allowing for passage.

One look at my surroundings and I could understand why anyone would call it true sanctuary.

Chapter 13: Aiden

Tense and irritated, I stood on one side of the large room they kept the rogue vampire in. I was infuriated that the witch and the vampire princess could go on and on about Derek with little thought to my daughter.

It's not that they don't care about Sofia. Stop taking things too personally, a voice of reason said, while the greater part of me was screaming, *How can I not take it personally? This is my only daughter whose life is on the line!*

Vivienne began tapping her foot on the marble floor in an attempt to control her temper. "Corrine said that they want the immunes. Sofia's life is not in immediate danger. Derek's is."

"We don't know what they want her for, Vivienne! Who knows what they can do to her?"

She glared at me and I began to wonder if I preferred this feisty leader to the mousy and pliable version of her that had existed not long ago. "I understand that, Aiden, but what would you have me do?" She spoke the words slowly, as if she was speaking to a child.

"Don't patronize me, Novak. We both know that you do not scare me one bit. So don't try to intimidate me either." I groaned. "We're getting nowhere. We're on the same side, are we not?"

"What do *you* think we should do about Derek? Do you agree to a trade?" Xavier butted in.

I mulled it over before shaking my head. "Opening the portal to a realm of original vampires seems like welcoming more trouble than we can handle. I think our best option is to ignore their trade proposal and just try to get both Derek and Sofia back. Of course, it's likely these Elders will try to open the portal anyway—with or without my daughter and son-in-law as bargaining chips."

"I agree with Aiden."

Arron. He was standing in the open doorway, looking more relaxed than all of us combined.

"There will be no trade. We cannot allow for the portal to be opened so easily." Arron said the words with a finality that was hard to ignore. "We're going to have to rescue Derek and Sofia from The Blood Keep. That's our *only* option."

"Are you mad?" Xavier eyed Arron from head to foot, wrinkling his nose in disgust. "We don't even know where The Blood Keep is!"

"Why would we even bother, Arron?" Zinnia stood up, her pretty face twisting with confusion. "Why should we care what happens to them? With Derek and Sofia taken, The Shade is without its ruler. We can do whatever we want with it."

Vivienne grimaced. "Silence this little fool before I rip her throat out and bleed her dry."

"Let's not get feisty," Arron drawled. "Zinnia is not privy to a lot of our organization's inner workings. The reasons are way above your pay grade, Zinnia, but right now, it is the hawks' priority to get Derek and Sofia as far away from the Elder as possible."

"How do you propose to do that, hunter?" Vivienne tilted her head to the side. "Do *you* know where The Blood Keep is?"

Corrine, who'd been silent the whole time, placed her cup on a wooden table. The thud diverted our attention to her.

"What's on your mind, Corrine? What do you think of all this?"

"Well, princess, I do have a way of finding out where The Blood Keep is." She eyed Arron from head to foot. "I don't trust him, but it seems to be the only recourse you have. At least, for once, you hunters and vampires actually agree."

I turned toward Natalie. "What did the Elder say about how we're to negotiate with them?"

"All I know is that they want the portal opened in exchange for Derek."

Xavier shook his head. "Vivienne, you can't seriously be considering not accepting the trade. Our number one priority is to make sure Derek is safe. Our loyalty is to him. The trade is the easiest way to ensure that he won't be harmed."

"Of course you'd be willing to have the portal opened," Zinnia muttered. "Why wouldn't you want more vampires coming in to help you?"

Both Vivienne and Xavier glared at her, but both decided to ignore her.

"I don't think we have a choice, Xavier."

"The Blood Keep is the Elder's territory. He is most powerful there. You know what the Elder did to your father, Vivienne. Do you really think we stand a chance against him?"

A muscle on the princess' jaw twitched at the recollection of the horrible way Gregor Novak had been killed. "I don't know, but we have to try, Xavier."

"It's done then. The hunters and the vampires will work together to rescue Derek and Sofia Novak from The Blood Keep with a witch's help." Arron seemed pleased with the results of our discussion. "Seems like we're creating history right here, folks."

I stared at him, wondering what his motives were. *What's so valuable about Derek and Sofia? Even though Sofia's an immune, she's still mortal. What do they have that the hunters need?* "What's in this for you, Arron? What's so important about Derek and Sofia that you want them away from the Elder?"

"I think we've all established how powerful a duo your daughter and her husband are, Aiden. Why wouldn't I want them away from the Elder? Besides, I would give anything for a chance to find The Blood Keep and destroy it."

I couldn't deny the allure of destroying a place like The Blood Keep to a hunter—especially someone as high up in the organization like Arron.

Before anything else could be asked, Sam and Ashley, two of Sofia's most trusted allies at The Shade, appeared in the doorway.

Sam's eyes searched for Vivienne's, while Ashley's searched for mine. Both spoke in unison. "We've got trouble."

"Yuri just attacked one of the hunters. It's chaos out there," Sam explained.

"He was trying to protect Claudia. Some of the hunters were apparently coming on to her," Ashley added in defense of the vampire.

I stifled a bitter chuckle when I saw Vivienne's and Arron's faces. *What a great way to kickstart this experiment of getting hunters and vampires to work together. Yuri Lazaroff, one of the most level-headed vampires I know, lost his cool and attacked a hunter. We're creating history indeed.*

CHAPTER 14: VIVIENNE

We arrived in what used to be the town plaza in the Vale to find a stand-off between the hunters and the vampires. Several of the vampires held hunters hostage while the other hunters had UV guns or wooden stakes pointed at the vampires. Several of The Shade's human citizens were standing in the middle of both sides, attempting to ward off a full-on fight. Gavin, Ian and Rosa—three of Sofia's most trusted among The Shade's humans—immediately caught my eye.

I walked right to them, Xavier, Aiden, Sam and Ashley following behind me. The way several stakes and guns pointed toward us as we walked by didn't escape my attention.

"What is going on here?" I demanded in as authoritative a tone I could manage. "Who started this mess?"

All eyes turned toward one side. Claudia hovered over a wounded Yuri, several stakes lodged into his body, one in particular barely missing his heart. Right behind Claudia was a dead hunter—heart ripped out.

"One of ours for one of yours, princess."

The words sent shivers down my spine.

Arron.

I slowly turned around to face him. By my comrades' faces, none of them were going to allow this to happen.

"A life for a life, Vivienne." Arron shrugged a shoulder. "It only seems fair."

"Who's going to tell me what happened here?" I screamed out.

Gavin stepped up. "The hunter"—he pointed at the lifeless corpse—"recognized Claudia from when she was held captive at hunter headquarters. He began taunting her as she and Yuri were passing by. Yuri lost it. There was nothing anyone could do to stop him."

"Your hunter went too far." I glared at Arron. "He had it coming."

"Nonsense. We had a truce. No one was to be hurt."

"My people have been harassed ever since you hunters took over the island. Enough is enough. None of us are going to take it anymore." I let my claws out.

Every other vampire surrounding us bared their fangs and extended their claws.

Arron didn't even flinch. He just smirked in response. "*Your* people, Vivienne? Is that what you think you monsters are? People?"

I was both offended and intimidated at the same time. I tried to recall the confidence and strength I'd had before the hunters had succeeded in breaking me.

Xavier's hand gently pressed against the small of my back. A show of support. I drew from his strength and tried to reach some form of calm.

What would Derek do?

Derek intimidated people by the sheer force of his very presence—one look, one frown, one growl. When that didn't work, he had brute force going for him.

I didn't have the kind of power he had and everybody knew it. I had to exert my own authority in my own way.

One thing Derek did that I could also do, however, was to not back down. I looked Arron in the eye and gave him my sweetest smile. "I don't care what you think we are, Arron, but trust my word on this. Push us too far, and we *can* be monsters. We've killed and bled for this island many times over the past five centuries. Don't think that we're not willing to do it again."

Arron calmly walked toward me. "You, princess? Is it not true that you have never shed blood? Didn't you tell us back at headquarters while we tortured you again and again and again that you have never even fed on a human? You were simply too innocent, too precious. Your brother went through great lengths to keep you from ever having to turn into the monster that he became, and now, he might just die under the hands of the Elder... all because you refuse to cooperate with us." The moment he was close enough, he pulled out a wooden stake and directed its point right to my heart.

Half a dozen vampires stood ready to attack him—Xavier included. I raised my hand to stop them. "Don't."

"Arron, enough." Aiden spoke up. "We need to figure out a way to work together. This isn't it."

"My men cannot work with these monsters until our man has received the justice he deserves." Arron pointed at Yuri with his free hand while the other pushed the wooden stake ever so slightly—just enough to press against my skin but not to break it. "I demand his life in exchange for the life that he took."

Nostrils flaring, blonde curls running amok, Claudia stood to her feet, her petite form not intimidating, but the manic look on her face showing that she would kill hunters—and vampires if needed—should anybody take even a step closer to Yuri.

I tried to remain calm, keeping my stare on the head hunter. "Go ahead, Arron. Push that stake into my heart and earn the ire of every vampire on this island. You *need* us. I don't know why exactly, but I know that you need us much more than we need you. If you didn't, we wouldn't still be alive, would we?"

Before thinking it through, I ran my claw across his left jawline, drawing blood. A collective gasp surrounded us and for the first time, Arron flinched. Rage flashed across his eyes along with a spark of orange color that seemed inhuman. I was taken aback.

What is he?

I could swear that my bluff hadn't worked and that it was going to be the end of me, but then Arron relented. "I guess you're stronger than I thought, princess."

"You have no idea what I would do to ensure that everything my brother fought for all his life will remain safe, so don't push me again, hunter. You are in our territory and if you don't want war, you will get your men to relent."

Arron's jaw tightened but he backed down. "You heard the princess. We are to work with them, not against them."

A wild commotion broke out, the hunters clearly not happy with their leader's pronouncement. Zinnia, in particular, seemed the most peeved.

"No way," she exclaimed, shaking her head, as she charged toward me. "A life for a life. That has always been the rule of a hunter. Hell, three lives of theirs for one of ours. They're dead already anyway."

Anger blazed in her eyes. The petite young woman drew a gun to point at me. She was about to shoot when Gavin pushed her to the ground, knocking the gun out of her hands.

"You heard your leader, little fool."

"Traitor," she spat at him. "You've betrayed the entire human race by siding with them."

"If the human race you're referring to are the hunters who have long since considered humans of The Shade dead, then yes. I'm indeed a traitor, but not to my own people."

"Vampires aren't people. I will never understand how you can be loyal to them."

"It's not these bloodsuckers I'm loyal to. Heck, I probably even hate a good handful of them, but I *am* loyal to Derek and Sofia. It's they who hold my allegiance. As long as they rule The Shade, it is home to us. We protect our home."

"Well, they're not here ruling, are they?"

"Zinnia, enough." Arron finally broke their spat. He nodded toward one of the hunters. "Calm her down."

Several hunters pried Gavin off of Zinnia, who was fighting violently against everyone who got in contact with her. The two glared at each other. Zinnia oozed hatred. Gavin, on the other hand, looked like she was just some mild irritation.

I felt a sense of pride over how resilient Gavin was. I also sensed guilt. Gavin had been born into captivity at The Shade.

It seemed we had reached truce. I had several of the vampires make sure that Yuri was taken care of. Arron told his men that anyone who did anything to irk a vampire would answer directly to him. Leaders were assigned on both sides, instructed to maintain the peace.

Arron, Aiden and I still had to decide how we were going to

rescue my brother and Sofia. We retreated to the Sanctuary for discussion. Everything had to go perfectly. We had to have the element of surprise on our side.

We had a plan, but I found myself restless. I took a long walk, finally ending up at a lake southeast of the island. I had no idea how long I'd been there before Xavier showed up.

"I thought you'd be here." His voice brought me comfort, let me know that I wasn't alone.

"Are we doing the right thing? I feel like something's wrong, Xavier."

He remained silent. I knew that he would have preferred to trade the opening of the portals for Derek, but I knew Arron and Corrine would sooner have us all killed than allow that portal to be opened. Still, I felt like I was gambling my brother's life and the risk was far too great.

For the first time in a long time, I felt like I couldn't trust Corrine. I knew she was hiding something from me. Motivations were beginning to get blurrier than I could deal with.

"What are you thinking about, princess?"

"I wasn't cut out for this, Xavier. I was never meant to rule."

Xavier shook his head adamantly. He grabbed my shoulders and forced me to face him. "Now that's a lie, Viv. You ruled this island for four hundred years while Derek was asleep. You kept us together. He didn't do that. You did."

"And look what I allowed to happen. Look at the mess Derek had to clear up when he woke up."

"No. You did the best you could under the pressure your father and brother put on you. Don't *ever* sell yourself short, Vivienne." He stared straight at me. "You were magnificent today. It was breathtaking seeing you stand up to Arron. It was beautiful to see you in your element—ruling like you deserve to, in a way only you can pull off."

I wondered why I'd never given Xavier the chance he deserved. He'd always been there for me. Always.

He was the one who'd stayed with me through all those nights I'd tried to recover from the torment I'd gone through under Borys Maslen's grasp. Xavier was the one who'd stood by me after my return from hunter captivity.

I loved him. Deeply. I had always loved him. And I knew he loved me. Everyone did, but I tried to pretend that he didn't.

Xavier bent down to press his lips against mine. I wanted that kiss desperately, but I found myself pulling away.

Pain flashed in his eyes, but if there was anything true of Xavier, it was that he was capable of quickly masking his emotions. He recovered quickly, smiling and most likely thinking of a joke, but this time, he wasn't able to think of one. So instead, he just gulped and asked, "Why?"

Tears began to stream down my face.

"Why can't we be together, Vivienne? I love you and I know you love me. Why can't we go beyond just being friends?"

"I…" My voice stuck in my throat. I sobbed as I tried to explain to myself why I was so terrified of being with Xavier.

How was I going to explain to him how a man's touch revolted me after what I'd been through under Borys? How could I ever allow him to carry the weight of all my issues? All my scars? He didn't deserve me. He didn't deserve this.

"Don't you love me, Vivienne?" Xavier asked.

I wanted to say no, look him in the eye and tell him that I didn't love him, but I couldn't bring myself to lie either, so I just stood there and trembled.

He didn't press me for an answer. Instead, he just brushed his hands gently over my shoulders and down my arms, holding my hands in his before pulling me closer and pressing his lips softly to my forehead.

I cried against his chest, finding comfort in his secure embrace. Xavier had been my one constant for the past five hundred years, and I couldn't imagine life without him. I'd never thought I could imagine anything worse than losing Derek, but I realized that I'd already survived "losing" Derek many times, yet I couldn't even begin to think of a life without Xavier.

"I will wait for you, Vivienne. I don't care how many centuries it takes before you're ready, but I will wait for you."

When those words—words I desperately needed to hear—came out of his lips, I knew that whether or not he realized it, I was his.

And almost out of instinct, I raised my lips to his and kissed him.

Chapter 15: Sofia

I woke on a bed with a red-eyed monster on top of me, taking a generous gulp of my blood. Nearby, a low growl came from some sort of animal. I couldn't see what it was because whoever was on top of me had my head at an uncomfortable angle, allowing him full reign over my neck.

As consciousness washed over me, my first instinct was to freeze, but then flashbacks of all the vampires who had violated me in this manner came back to me and something clicked inside my mind, and all I could think was *No. Enough.*

I jerked my head away from him. My flesh parting from his lips caused a loud slurp to bounce across the room.

Kiev groaned. "Don't deprive me, Sofia. You're a morsel too sweet not to partake of, and you know it. Even your beloved wasn't able to resist taking a bite." He steadied my head with a firm hand and once again sucked on my blood.

I scanned the part of the room that I could see considering the angle. I saw a vase on the bedside table nearby and tried to reach for it. His weight was on top of me and it was a struggle just to move but I was determined to not just lie down and take it. I wasn't going to become the victim again. Not anymore.

He seemed too wrapped up in drinking my blood to care what I did so I was able to get a hold of the vase. I slammed it over his head as hard as I could. The instant I did, red eyes—blazing with rage—looked down at me.

With my blood still dripping from the corners of his lips and one hand gripping a fistful of my hair, Kiev was a terrifying sight to behold.

I couldn't give in to my terror. *You have got to be used to this by now, Sofia.* I collected myself, grabbed a shard from the broken vase and stuck it into his neck.

Since he would heal immediately, especially with my blood running through his system, I was doing nothing other than annoying my captor, but I would make this as difficult for him as possible.

His surprise was to my advantage so I pushed his hand away from my head and bolted toward the door. To my shock, I came face to face with a creature whose fur was black as night, eyes shining bright yellow. It was a huge dog, taller than my waist when crouched on all fours, probably taller than I was when forced to stand on only two feet.

This must be the beast Kiev was referring to.

"Move one more step, Sofia, and you'll be the mutt's dinner."

"What is it?"

A fist grabbed a clump of my hair and pulled me right back to the bed. Kiev knelt over me, straddling my hips. His grip on my hair tightened, my scalp burning with pain. I yelped.

"It doesn't matter what it is. What do you think you're doing? Do you have a death wish, Novak?"

My lower lip twitched. All curiosity toward the creature faded away, because for a split second, I thought he was referring to Derek. I still wasn't used to being Derek Novak's wife. No matter what happened to us, no one could take away the fact that we'd gotten married, that we were a family. We had each other. I bit my lip at the thought of Derek's smile and his kisses. I could practically hear his laughter, and before I knew it, I smiled.

That took Kiev aback. His grip on my hair loosened as he took the shard I'd stuck in his neck out with his free hand. He stared down at me. I was intimidated by the anger on his face, but I couldn't keep myself from smiling.

"Crazy girl, why the hell are you smiling?" he hissed, his fist tightening around the clump of my hair he seemed determined to never let go of.

"Your eyes. They're red. Why?"

"I asked you a question."

"I asked you a question too."

"How does he stand being around you?"

"Why do you keep asking about my relationship with Derek?"

"Do you always answer questions with questions?"

I shrugged.

"You are one agitating woman. Do you know that?" He finally let go of my hair, staring at me like I was some sort of oddity he was trying to figure out.

"Agitating isn't usually the word used. Charming is the more suitable word I think." I pressed my palms against his chest. The way a muscle on his jaw violently twitched didn't escape my notice. I pushed him away from me. "Could you get off me now?"

He didn't budge. "I don't think you see the gravity of the situation you're in. Do you not realize how powerful I am?"

"I'll say it more slowly. Get. Off. Me. Now."

We had a staredown of sorts before he eventually looked away. He got off me, sitting on the edge of the bed beside me. He ran a hand through his hair, sighing with exasperation.

"Don't even think of trying to get away. The beast will eat you alive before you get anywhere near that door."

I sat up, my hand over my bleeding neck. The creature paced near the door. Its yellow eyes were fixed on me. Hungry. Eager to devour. I swallowed hard.

"What is it?" I repeated my question.

"I told you. It's a beast."

"What is a beast?"

"You ask too many questions."

I backed up on the bed, my knees propped up. I was unsure what to do. "I need something for my neck."

He bit into his wrist and offered me his blood to drink.

I grimaced. "I would rather bleed to death."

He growled at me, monster that he was, but he didn't insist. He grabbed a sheet and ripped it. He then began tending to the wound that he'd caused. The way he swallowed whenever he saw my blood intrigued me. I recognized that hunger in his eyes, that struggle to maintain control.

Maybe he's not as much of a monster as I thought.

"You know how to tend a wound." I was surprised by how gentle he was.

"You don't know me. Who I was…"

"Then tell me."

He looked at the bandaged wound with a satisfied smile on his face.

"You seem awfully proud of yourself," I said.

He narrowed his eyes at me. "What is it about you, Sofia Novak? How is it that you are so unaffected?"

Right. Me. Unaffected. I fought the urge to laugh. He held my future in his hands. He was capable of taking everyone and everything I loved away from me. *How could I be unaffected?* I remembered that I'd been in the exact same situation with Derek. Bothered by the thought, I pretended not to hear him.

I gave him a close look as he turned to face me—dark hair, handsome face with lines hardened by time and experience. He had a tired look about him, a stare that told me that those eyes had already seen more nightmares than I could imagine.

"You're right, you know. I don't know who you were or even who you are now, but I do know how powerful you are," I told him. "I'm married to Derek Novak. He was once the most powerful vampire of our time. I know power when I'm around it."

"And yet you don't tremble."

"Is that what you want? For me to shake at the sight of you? Do you really want my terror?"

A muscle on his jaw twitched. He remained silent for a couple of seconds. "The Elder turned my eyes this shade. Blood red. He wanted me to remember how much blood I've seen, how much blood I am accountable for, every time I look in the mirror. It was his way of reminding me that I can't escape from everything that I did. He wanted me to remember that I'm a monster."

I didn't know what to do or say. I wasn't sure how to handle bonding time with the Elder's son. Was I supposed to reassure him that he wasn't a monster when I saw one in him?

Or do I? This version of him seemed a lot more human than the monster who took me out of Derek's dungeon.

I tried to remember how my relationship with Derek had started. *Did I at any point see him as a monster? Was he? Was it just by instinct that I knew that there was good in him?* I accepted Derek in spite of all the atrocities he'd committed. Even after I'd learned about the history of The Shade, even after he'd ripped out another vampire's heart right before my eyes, I'd never seen him as a monster. I'd forgiven him. What was it about Kiev that was so different?

"Isn't he supposed to be your father?" I asked. "The Elder? Why would he do something like that? Why would he want you to always see yourself as a monster?"

"He's my father because he turned me at the most vulnerable point of my life. Beyond that, the Elder is the most cruel being I'd ever known."

"Won't you get in trouble for saying that?"

"Maybe."

The door swung open and we both jolted in surprise. The beast positioned himself to attack.

Clara appeared. She looked at the beast, grimaced, and ignoring the snarling creature, eyed her brother—in a way that was far from sister-like—before staring at me. "Having a little chat?" she asked. "I have to admit I'm disappointed. I was hoping to walk in on you acting on your attraction toward her."

Kiev looked agitated. "Why are you here, Clara?"

"Well," she purred as she sidestepped the beast and slunk toward her brother, running her hand over his torso, "I was getting the juiciest information from my little Abby"—she stared at me triumphantly, seeming to revel in my flinch—"when Father came and asked me to get you."

Fear flashed in Kiev's eyes, bright red turning into a dark crimson as he stood up. "Why?"

"We're taking a trip to The Shade." Clara snuck her hand beneath his shirt, her eyes focused on his body. "They refuse to cooperate. Apparently, they would rather cross us than save Derek Novak's life." This time, she looked at me, smirking.

It took me a couple of seconds to comprehend what she'd just said as my eyes widened in horror. *What on earth does she mean by that?*

That seemed to get Kiev's attention. He stepped away from Clara, pushing her hand away. "They actually refused a trade?"

"Apparently, they're that stupid. Not that I'm surprised." She rolled her eyes. She looked almost giddy. "We've been sent to punish them for their insolence and to open the gate ourselves."

My mind was reeling. *The Elder tried to propose a trade with Vivienne—Derek in exchange for something they want. What on earth could be at The Shade that's more important than Derek? What could possibly drive Vivienne to refuse? What does Clara mean by opening the gate?*

That Vivienne would think anything more important than her twin brother was beyond me. If she made that choice, there must've been a reason behind it.

What that reason was, I was too terrified to find out, but never had I been so afraid for Derek's life.

CHAPTER 16: AIDEN

We had a traitor amongst us.

"It must be Natalie. Who else could've informed them that we don't want a trade?" Claudia hissed. She was pacing the floor, her face healing from a fresh gash.

We had all been at the Port, gearing up to attack The Blood Keep, when the attack had happened. We'd left the Port to find what was left of the Crimson Fortress completely demolished by multiple explosions. It was a miracle the Port still remained intact.

I'd turned toward Vivienne. I was preparing myself to take the helm should she crumble and back down from leading. But she hadn't. Within minutes after the first explosion, she'd been pointing at people, barking out orders, putting protocol into place. After all, it wasn't the first time The Shade had faced war.

"Liana, Cameron," she barked at her best friend and her husband, "organize your team." She pointed out several of the other members of the Elite, teaming them up in order to lead their own teams. "Gavin, Ian, please take care of leading the humans. You know what to do. Xavier and Aiden, come with me. You guys too," she added, pointing at Sam and Ashley. "We need to protect the Sanctuary."

"And us?" Zinnia asked.

Vivienne looked her over from head to foot. "Where's Arron? I don't care what you do, idiot. Just prove yourself worth something more than empty threats."

I almost felt sorry for Zinnia as she looked around in search of her boss while the ground shook beneath us. I, too, was curious over where the head hunter could've gone, but I didn't have time to mull much over it, because Xavier had already grabbed me by the shoulders in order to speed our way to the Sanctuary.

We arrived at the Sanctuary just in time to see Corrine walking out of the temple, fists clenched, eyes blazing fire.

"Who the hell did this?" she screamed, casting a glare at all of us.

"I don't know," Vivienne responded. "I think it's the Elder's vampires attacking. Who could've told them?"

"Natalie hasn't moved an inch. It couldn't have been her." Corrine stopped between the two round pillars in front of the whitewashed edifice.

"Where is the portal, Corrine?" I asked, growing impatient.

Corrine hesitated to answer. I could understand that, considering how any of us could be the traitor.

"We want to protect the portal, Corrine. You have to trust us." Vivienne sounded desperate.

"It's..." Corrine took another step forward only to fly back, landing on the ground with a thud.

"What was that?" Xavier ran toward the building only to be thrown back just like Corrine.

"It's a force field," Vivienne blurted out as she looked at the Sanctuary in horror. "Only Emilia was powerful enough to do this."

"My sister had many tricks up her sleeve. After spending hundreds of years with her, I managed to learn more than a few of them." A red-eyed vampire appeared from behind the Sanctuary, a grin on his face.

Corrine's eyes widened in horror. "Kiev," she hissed.

He grinned, cocking his head to the side. "You know me." He seemed delighted.

"You're notorious amongst the witches and you know it."

He chuckled before turning his gaze toward me. "Your daughter's fine, Claremont. You need not worry about her. I'll take very good care of her... during her pregnancy."

My heart stopped. Before thinking it through, I drew my gun and shot him, trusting in my accuracy. The bullet hit the force field and boomeranged towards us, grazing Ashley in the arm. The young vampire began swearing loudly.

I couldn't think straight. "If you ever do anything to hurt Sofia..." I choked, unable to imagine what it was like for her being under the Elder's captivity while pregnant. I wondered if Derek even knew that she was having a baby. I wondered if *she* knew.

I knew for a fact that she hadn't slept with Derek until after their wedding. *She can't be far enough into her pregnancy to already have symptoms.*

"I told you. She's precious to us. She's carrying the spawn of a vampire-turned-human and an immune... Worth far more than father and mother combined."

Vivienne's moistened eyes met mine. We were both helpless and we knew it.

While Kiev was busy taunting us, Corrine was whispering

something beneath her breath. Within minutes, a whirlwind began to form from the sky, forming a funnel whose end was about to suck Kiev in.

Kiev looked up, laughed and snapped his fingers. The whirlwind immediately disappeared. "Nice try, baby witch, but very amateur. You should've just agreed to the trade."

Corrine smirked. "We both know a trade isn't possible."

Kiev flinched. "Really now?"

"You don't fool me, Kiev. Stop trying."

The expression on his face told us all that Corrine knew far more about him than any of us did. Vivienne's face hardened. I could tell that the same question that was running through my mind was running through hers. *What is Corrine talking about?* Clearly, she knew far more than any of us did.

"Corrine?" Vivienne croaked through choked breath. "What's going on?"

Corrine had a wild-eyed, almost manic, reaction in her face as she stared at Kiev. "You ruined Cora. If it weren't for you, she never would've become Emilia. I'm sorry, Vivienne, but this was the only way I saw to get this monster here and still keep the portal safe."

Kiev snickered. "Corrine, you really are like your ancestor. A naïve little fool."

I had no idea what was going on—especially with the witch the vampires seemed to trust with their lives. One thing, however, was clear. *Everyone* had an agenda of their own.

All this was made even clearer when Ian arrived, out of breath. He went straight for Vivienne.

"Arron's gone." he announced. "He abandoned the hunters."

I had no idea who Kiev, the red-eyed vampire, was, but he couldn't have been more right when he cast Corrine then Vivienne an amused look. "All hell's about to break loose, princess."

Chapter 17: Sofia

Five months. I haven't seen Derek in five months.

I stared up at the night sky, my arms spread wide on either side of me, so that my palms could reach past the embroidered blanket spread beneath me and touch the smooth grass. I wondered what it would be like to have Derek by my side, what it would be like to have his arms around me.

Over the past few months, I'd begun to love full moons. Those were the nights when the sky seemed to shine brightest. Those nights were no substitute for sunlight, but they were the closest thing to light that I had in a place like The Blood Keep.

Blood Keep. I grimaced at how appropriately named the Elder's territory was. *Even the name makes my skin crawl.*

I shifted on the blanket and rested my head on a satin-covered pillow. I was still a prisoner at The Blood Keep, but I was treated far better than Derek had been during our first days of capture. I recalled the last time I'd seen him, held him in my arms, kissed him. I missed him so much, and yet the thought that he wasn't in The Blood Keep, held against his will, ready to be tortured at the whim of our captors, gave me hope.

I recalled the night I'd found out that Derek was no longer at The Blood Keep.

"What have you done to Derek? Where is he? What have you done to him?" I pounded against Kiev's chest with all my might. I struck him, hit him, pushed him. He didn't budge. He just looked at me with that infuriating smirk on his face. "You promised me he wouldn't be harmed," I sobbed as I finally exhausted myself, my shoulders sagging in defeat.

"You done, Sofia?" Kiev asked.

I raised my eyes to meet his. I had every intention of showing him my defiance, but though it might have worked with the likes of Derek, I learned that night that the same thing wouldn't always work with Kiev.

Kiev was as unpredictable as anyone could get.

When our eyes met, Kiev struck me in the face so hard, I was thrown to the ground at least a couple of feet away from him.

"Mention his name again, Sofia, and I will make you bleed." The tone was almost seductive. He gripped me by the head so hard I screamed, my scalp burning with pain.

He was asking the impossible of me. How could I possibly last without speaking about Derek? "I want to see Derek," I insisted. "Now."

"Shut up!" He struck me again. And again. And again.

I thought he was going to kill me, but as he was about to deliver the fifth blow, the servant standing by the door took a step forward.

"Master," she breathed out.

"Stay out of this, Olga," Kiev hissed, his fist up in the air, ready to deal another blow.

She was young and beautiful. She reminded me of a porcelain doll, her eyes bright, her voice thin and almost baby-like.

"I'm only worried that you might cause her to..." Olga hesitated, fidgeting with her dress.

Clarity came over Kiev's blood-red eyes. He looked at me like I was dust turned into a precious diamond.

He dropped his hand and nodded. "You're right."

I was about to sigh with relief, but Kiev was far from finished. Instead he flexed his arms and cracked his knuckles. "Still, Olga, sweetheart, you know that someone has to pay for all the trouble Derek Novak put me through..." He turned to the young woman and before I could comprehend what was going on, he hit her.

"Kiev! Stop it!" I screamed.

He didn't stop until she was beaten to a bloody pulp. Kiev cuffed me to the bed when I tried to hit him on the head with the first object I could get a hold of.

When he was satisfied, he stood and pointed at Olga. "I can't hurt you, Sofia. What you carry inside you is too precious. Be thankful for that. Thus, whenever you displease me, it is Olga who will feel my wrath. And you'll know that you're responsible for her pain. Do you understand?"

"You're a monster," was all I could respond with, my mind reeling at what he was implying.

He chuckled, and then in a split second, his mood completely changed, as if the word 'monster' had triggered something in him. He began to cry and when he saw Olga's unconscious form on the ground, he gasped. "What have I done? Olga..."

He knelt beside her and forced her to drink his blood so that she would heal.

"Please don't cross me again," he pleaded and for a moment, I actually believed that he meant it, but I was confused by how he could be this violent man one minute and this whimpering child the very next.

I learned several things about my stay at The Blood Keep that night. Derek was no longer at The Blood Keep. That he had escaped was a hope I latched on to, something that Olga eventually verified. I also began to wrap my mind around the possibility that I was pregnant and that this was the reason I was so important to them. They wanted my child.

It didn't take long before nature verified this fearsome possibility for me. I was indeed bearing Derek's child.

Finally, I realized that Kiev wasn't just evil. He was stark crazy, and neither I nor anyone else was safe around him.

I knew then that I had to find a way to escape like Derek had, because I didn't want him to have to come back to The Blood Keep. Ever.

Five months into my stay at The Blood Keep, I was getting nowhere in my attempt to escape. Only recently had Kiev allowed me outside the bedroom he'd kept me in for the first few months of my captivity at the castle. All that time, I was heavily guarded. By a beast. *Beasts,* the vampires called them, but I'd been at The Blood Keep long enough to know what they really were—dogs turned into blood-sucking vampires. The dogs fed only on blood. They were twice their original size and they had the keenest senses an animal could possibly have.

One was always tailing me wherever I went. The only places I was allowed to go to were the gardens and my bedroom. All my meals were served in either of the two places. I couldn't get too far away without the giant, bloodthirsty mutt snarling at me.

Still, as far as I was concerned, an animal was an animal and the one that kept following me seemed likeable enough—if I ignored the fact that one wrong move I made would cause it to go berserk and drink my blood. I called him Shadow.

I looked around and found Shadow pacing the ground a few feet behind me. He didn't seem to be in a good mood.

"Hey, boy…" I nodded his way. He growled fiercely at me in response, reminding me of what had happened when I had dared approach the Keep's border. I'd ventured past the gardens and through the woods to the boundary line where the witch's spell of eternal night stopped, and day began. Shadow had tackled me to the ground as soon as I had got within fifteen feet of the border, first biting my shoulder, then aiming for my neck. If Kiev hadn't arrived to hold the beast back, I was certain it would have eaten me alive.

I rolled my eyes at the beast. "You're *never* in a good mood." I took a deep breath. *For crying out loud, I'm actually having a conversation with a dog. I must be getting desperate.*

The only people I was allowed to converse with were Olga and Kiev, although I could hardly call him a person. Olga was cordial enough, but she always acted like she was walking on eggshells around me. I couldn't blame her. Any mistake I made and she would pay. I wasn't exactly a safe ally for her at The Blood Keep.

I was often allowed to roam the castle's gardens, well-trimmed and beautiful. The gardens looked completely out of place in the Keep. Beauty didn't belong in such a place.

I flipped over so that I was lying on my stomach and propped my upper body up with my elbows. I watched Shadow pace like the brooding vampire that he was before he stopped to face me, his eyes hateful and full of hunger.

"So, Shadow, do *you* know where Derek is? Is he safe? Olga told me that he escaped. I have to believe that's true, that he's somewhere out there, doing everything he can to get to me."

Shadow's deafening growl told me that he was getting agitated by my friendliness. When he poised himself for attack, I backed down. "Fine. You don't want to talk. You don't have to be mad about it."

I felt the pressure to do for Derek what I hoped he was doing for me, to find him, but there wasn't much I could do at The Blood Keep. I was at the mercy of one person: Kiev, a man I could not understand at all.

Not wanting to think about Kiev, I sat up and retrieved the sketchbook I kept on my person at all times. I began thumbing through it. Every sketch it contained made my heart ache with longing. Every single one was of Derek.

I felt movement in my growing belly. I smiled as I began to stroke my stomach.

"Hello, little one. You're getting heavier every day." I trusted that my child could understand. Kiev had forbidden me to even mention my husband's name, but nothing could stop me from talking about Derek to my unborn child. "Your daddy would've loved nights like these. Stargazing. I'm looking at sketches I made of him. It helps me keep his face, his smile fresh in my mind. I miss him so much. I can't help but wonder what his reaction would be if he found out that you're coming. I bet he'd be really excited. I know he's always dreamed of having you."

I choked as I tried to suppress the tears, wondering what life would've been like had we lived a normal one. *Get it together, Sofia. You're bearing his child. You can't go through the whole thing depressed.* I knew little about pregnancy or children, but I had it in my head that my emotions affected my child. Having had Ingrid Maslen as my mother—I'd sworn early in life that I was going to be a good mother to my children. I determined to start as early as I could.

I began to hum a tune to my unborn child. The same tune Derek had hummed to me countless times. Our song.

Never had I wished for normalcy more. I was a pregnant teenager. I wasn't supposed to go through this alone. I needed my husband. I needed my family.

But this was the life I'd signed up for when I married Derek, and I could blame no one for that choice. Daily, I drew hope that I would be with him again, that this life within me was going to know how strong, loving, and wonderful a father Derek could be.

For now, I just need to keep myself together, stay alert and try to remain on Kiev's good side... for Olga's sake.

"Enjoying the breeze?"

Kiev's voice made my heart beat faster. I caught my breath. Chills shot up my spine. He induced sheer terror in me, but I wasn't about to show him that.

He sat beside me and shifted his attention to my stomach. "How's the pregnancy going? I trust the fresh air has been helping. Are you not getting cold?"

Based on the smile on his face and the uppity tone of his voice, he seemed to be in a cordial mood—a good sign.

"You seem rather pleased with yourself," I commented, maintaining a flat, civil tone with him.

"Hello to you too, Sofia. How was your day?"

"Devoid of sunlight. Yours?"

Just like The Shade, The Blood Keep was under an eternal night. No mornings. No sunshine. As much as I loved The Shade, I couldn't imagine raising my child never seeing sunlight. Suddenly, the house Derek and I had checked out back in California seemed like heaven.

"You didn't seem to mind the lack of sunlight when you were at The Shade." He grabbed the picnic basket I had with me. Olga had prepared the food inside the basket. Kiev thumbed through the food there. "This looks healthy. You haven't even touched it."

I wasn't thrilled about having him around, but it didn't look like he was going to give me a choice. "The Shade was home." *It was enough that Derek was there.*

"The Blood Keep is your home now."

Never.

He threw me a bag of sliced apples. "Eat."

I didn't want to irk him, so I took the bag and took a bite from one of the slices.

Most of the time, Kiev was kind to me—or at least he tried to be. I never did understand why. At first, I'd thought it was because of an attraction toward me, but he had made no advances on me since he'd arrived from The Shade.

I was dying to know what had happened at The Shade and what had happened to my husband—but the island and Derek were topics that were not to be broached if I wanted to remain unhurt, unscathed.

"Those sketches..." Kiev eyed the sketchbook I had on my lap. "They're all of him?"

I took another bite from the apple and chewed silently. My silence was enough of an answer.

"Why do you torture yourself this way, Sofia?" He reached for the sketchbook and began looking at the sketches. He seemed to get annoyed by it, because he eventually tossed the book back to me. "Forget him."

"That's never going to happen, Kiev, and you know it. Derek's not going to stop looking for me. He'll destroy this whole place if he has to."

Kiev's eyes flickered with anger. He grabbed me by the jaw. He gripped hard, enough to make me yelp in pain. "I would think that you already know better than that, Sofia. Your husband wasn't what he once was, and even at the height of his power, he was a slave to this place. Just like you are now," he said through gritted teeth. "Don't irk me further by talking about these daydreams of yours."

I glared at him, my sense of defiance and independence rising over my fear of him. Just to annoy him further, I looked him straight in the eye, and continued to talk about Derek. "He's going to come for me and you know it. He's going to hold my child in his arms and he's going to be a great father. He already managed to escape this place, didn't he? What makes you think he won't know how to return?"

Kiev frowned, his grip tightening. For a minute, I thought he was going to hit me, but then I was reminded of who was going to suffer for what I did.

"I'm sorry," I quickly breathed out. "I just... I'm sorry, Kiev."

"Olga's going to have a rough night thanks to you." He didn't seem pleased with the prospect, his fists clenching.

I wondered whether he was clenching them to defend Olga or to punish her. With him, I never knew. Most of the time, he seemed to really care about the young girl. I even thought it hurt him more to cause her pain than it did me.

"Don't hurt her. I made a mistake. It won't happen again."

He pushed my face away, my head jerking backwards. "Olga told me that you asked her where the food you're being given comes from. I want to know why."

I answered with a shrug. "I'm just curious. I have no idea where this place is. I was just wondering where The Blood Keep gets its food."

"Really? You're just wondering? You're not snooping around trying to figure out an exit from this place?"

I swallowed hard. "Like that's possible." I wrinkled my nose as I eyed the guard dog following me everywhere.

Kiev snapped his fingers and Shadow approached.

Shadow growled and snarled as he stepped toward Kiev. The animal wasn't that much of a fan of Kiev either. Kiev didn't seem to care. He bared his claws and dug their pointed ends into Shadow's fur, making the creature whimper, but to my surprise, it neither attacked nor cowered away from Kiev.

"Escape is not possible," Kiev said, "and we both know it, but I think you're crazy enough to try."

I grimaced, uncomfortable at seeing Shadow in pain. "Then you have nothing to worry about, do you?"

"You feel sorry for the beast?" Kiev's eyes sparked with curiosity.

"It has done you no wrong."

"If only you knew what it did to your husband when he was still here."

"So you admit it. Derek isn't here anymore? He was actually able to escape?"

Kiev just chuckled. "Don't get any ideas into that pretty little head of yours, Sofia. Olga's like a daughter to me, but I wouldn't hesitate to kill her should you even attempt an escape."

Like a daughter. I had to wonder what kind of relationship Kiev had with Olga. I couldn't wrap my mind around it, but it was perhaps one of the most demented, unhealthy relationships I'd ever seen. *This beats even Claudia's crazy.* Still, Olga meant something to him.

"You miss The Shade, don't you?"

"My heart aches just thinking of everything I left behind there."

"It may not be as you remember it. I don't see what you love so much about the place. It didn't look all that great to me last time I paid a visit."

Paid a visit? Is that all you did? I had a bad feeling about the state of The Shade at that point. "It's not the place that makes it home, Kiev. It's the people there... people I love."

I glanced his way. I was desperate for an ally, a companion, someone I could talk to who wasn't going to scare the life out of me—like Kiev—or wasn't trembling at the thought of speaking to me—like Olga.

"I'm about to give birth to my first child, Kiev. This is my first pregnancy. Would it be so bad if you brought someone from home to help me through this?"

"Am I not enough for you, Sofia?"

No, you're not. "Kiev, please..."

"Who do you have in mind?"

My heart leapt at the thought that he might be considering it. My first instinct was to request Corrine, but I highly doubted that Kiev would ever agree to bring a witch into The Blood Keep. She was simply too much of a threat. The next person who came to mind was Eli Lazaroff. Surely with all the knowledge he accumulated, he'd know a thing or two about pregnancies. Also, considering how pale and lanky he appeared, he wasn't much of a threat to anyone.

"I'm thinking of Eli Lazaroff." *Of course, he's also smart. Maybe he can figure out a way for us to get out of here.* "He could be a huge asset here, you know." I had to choose my words carefully. "Eli can help with my pregnancy. I'd feel so much more at ease with him around."

"You really want this, don't you?"

"Kiev, I need this."

"Just eat."

I took the last of the apple slices and bit into it. I was trying not to place any of my hopes on the possibility that Kiev would agree to bringing Eli into The Blood Keep. *Come on, Sofia. Why would you even want to endanger Eli this way?* I began to wonder if I had made a mistake even suggesting that Eli be brought to The Blood Keep. *I doubt he'll be very thrilled by the idea of being held captive here with me.*

"How did you know?" Kiev asked after I'd eaten my last bite—his eyes never leaving me while I was absent-mindedly finishing my meal.

"Know what?"

"That he had good in him?"

For someone who wanted me to forget Derek, I was surprised that Kiev would bring Derek up as a topic of conversation. He seemed strangely interested in how Derek had turned away from darkness and come to light. We'd had this talk before. I wasn't in the mood to answer, because talking about my love story with Derek only made me miss him more. Missing him more made me want to ask Kiev questions that made the red-eyed vampire want to hurt me. As much as I wanted to speak about Derek, conversations that involved him never ended without a bruise or two from Kiev.

I tilted my head to the side and drawled out my own question. "How did *you* know?"

His lips tightened. "Are we going to go at this again, Sofia? This questioning? Can you not answer my question like a normal person?"

Annoyed, I just stared at him and repeated my question. "How did you know, Kiev?"

"You stubborn little minx."

Stubborn little minx. I smiled, remembering all the times Derek had referred to me that way.

Seeing that I wasn't about to play this game on his terms, Kiev relented. "Fine. I'll play," he spat out. "How do I know *what*, Sofia?"

"How did you know I was pregnant? You seemed to know even before you took Derek and me here."

"We've had our eye on you ever since you left The Shade for your honeymoon. Your children… they're important to us."

"Children?"

"Twins. A boy and a girl."

"How do you know?"

"It's one of the things I learned from Emilia. How to tell if a woman is pregnant, what the child is going to be. It's always useful to know."

"Why?" The smirk on his face told me that I wasn't going to like the answer to that question.

"Let's just say that a pregnant woman is quite a scrumptious delicacy to our kind. I'm surprised the Elder hasn't tried to take your blood."

I'm surprised you haven't recently. I'd seen countless times the way he would lick his lips as he stared at the nook of my neck as if he was a man starving for months.

As if he could read my mind, he chuckled. "Don't think I haven't been tempted to drink from you, Sofia. The further along your pregnancy is, the more tempting it is to drink, but I can't give in, because I won't be able to restrain myself from bleeding you dry."

It's so strange how hearing that has become so commonplace to me. I thought back to the time when life had been simple and I was a teenager trying to cope with everyday normal things. Ben's face—his smile—came to mind. I hadn't seen Abby since Clara took her from the dungeon. I kept asking where she was but I wasn't given an answer.

Instead, I was told to relax and take care of myself. *Relax.* The idea sickened me. *Relax while I'm constantly afraid that you might have killed my husband. Relax, while Abby, who is practically my little sister, is in the hands of one of the most capricious and cruel vampires I've ever met. Relax while I bear two children who are in danger the moment I give birth to them.*

Relax while everything I love and live for is slipping away from me. Relax while I lose all control of my life. Relax, while I sit here trying to avoid a conversation with this red-eyed monster, who just confessed to craving my blood more and more every day.

Relax, Sofia. I repeated the words to myself over and over again. The only thing that got me through each day at The Blood Keep was the conviction: *Derek is coming.*

If not, I will find a way to get to him.

To my delight, when I opened my eyes after a long night's sleep, I found a familiar man sitting on a chair near my bed, waiting for me to wake up.

"Hello, my queen. I was told you requested my presence."

Eli Lazaroff.

Chapter 18: Derek

Five months. I'd been at The Sanctuary for five months. I knew nothing about what was happening back home at The Shade. Even worse, I knew nothing about what had happened to my wife at The Blood Keep.

During my time at The Sanctuary, I was given spacious living quarters on the top floor of what seemed like the tallest building in the city, where servants sought after my needs. I tried to converse with some of them, but none of them ever spoke to me. I didn't even know their names. Whenever I addressed them, they ignored me. They seemed to hate me, though I wasn't sure why.

The only people who talked to me were the Ageless and Ibrahim, the warlock assigned to mentor me. And I wasn't allowed to leave my quarters, except for when I was training.

Five months had revealed things about myself that I never thought possible. I had my strength back—probably more than I'd had when I was a vampire.

My ability to heal was back. Though it didn't happen as quickly as when I was a vampire, whenever I healed, I was stronger than before I was wounded.

My agility was also back. Again, not the same speed as I'd had when I was a vampire, but definitely far quicker than a human was supposed to be. My heightened senses had also returned.

But what the vampire curse had suppressed all these years was something beyond my imagining—fire. I had the ability to conjure fire. I didn't know how. I didn't know why, but I did. What I didn't have was the ability to control it and since the witches had introduced me to this ability, ever since the first time fire came out of my fingers, harnessing the power had proven to be difficult.

Whenever I asked where all these powers came from, I was given a cryptic answer about Cora investing much of her power in me. It was no secret that during my four-hundred-year slumber, Cora had placed some sort of spell on me that made me more powerful. Maybe she'd been channeling power from The Sanctuary to me all along.

I'd never understood why the Ageless allowed it if she knew that Cora was doing this, or how she couldn't have known considering how powerful she seemed to be.

All I knew was that once a witch's power took over a human being, it did things to that person, and since I was a vampire when it happened… it had placed those powers in a state of preservation so that when it came out, it came out in uncontrollable bursts.

The witch and warlock tried to help me take control of the power, making me spend most of my time in their realm trying to do something that even they didn't seem to fully understand.

I was standing in the midst of a wide open field surrounded by small lakes, staring at a round target—one I wanted to destroy simply because I was tired of being held captive in the witch's realm.

"Relax, Derek," Ibrahim said in his deep, soothing voice. "You won't be able to harness your power unless you learn to calm down."

"Calm down?" I uttered through gritted teeth, sensing heat creep from the blades of my shoulders down to the tips of my fingers. "I want to see my wife!" A ray of fire burst out of my palms, burning not only the target, but everything else in its path.

I tried to control it, but I couldn't.

"You have to control your rage!" Ibrahim screamed through the chaos, standing behind me, making sure that he was out of the fire's way.

"The vampire's curse kept you cold," was the Ageless' simple explanation and nothing else was said after.

That morning, under the blazing heat of the sun, I was half-wishing that I was a vampire again, because nothing I knew to do could make me calm down. The fire was beyond my control.

I shut my eyes and tried to imagine Sofia. Five months was far too long to be away from my bride. I was afraid I would forget her face. I was afraid that... I couldn't even think about it. Tears began to brim my eyes as visions of her smile, her laughter, her warmth came to me. Her soft kisses back at the dungeon haunted me—the memory, just like the kisses themselves, was both sweet and painful at the same time.

So wrapped up in cherished memories of my beloved, I lost track of what was happening around me and I found myself kneeling on the ground, sobbing.

"That's it. That's how you do it." Ibrahim sounded beyond relieved. He'd probably been afraid that I would burn The Sanctuary down. "You need to learn control." He snapped his fingers and a strong, cool wind blew the fire away before it could spread.

Just then, the familiar form of the Ageless appeared from the horizon, walking toward us in a slow, steady stride. Sympathy flashed in her eyes when she saw me but that quickly disappeared when she addressed Ibrahim in a curt tone. "How is he doing?"

During my stay at The Sanctuary, it had become increasingly clear that the Ageless was their leader, that she was a mother of sorts to their kind. Beyond that, she was perhaps the most powerful among them. It had become commonplace to see Ibrahim speak to her with reverence.

"It's proving a little challenging, but there's improvement."

"Why must I stay here? Why can't I train elsewhere?" I snapped at her.

"And have you burn down half the human realm in the process?" Ibrahim laughed wryly, in an attempt to break the ice.

He failed.

The Ageless and I were both glaring at each other. "You know why, Derek." That infuriating tone made me feel like an idiot. "You need to learn to harness your power. You're useless to all of us until you learn to control and manage your strength."

"Do you know where my wife is? What has happened to her?"

"We have time. You need not worry."

"Time? Time for what? Where is she? Do you know?" I was feeling the rage building up again. I breathed a couple of sighs to keep my temper in check. As a vampire, I'd usually let my temper run amok, but this time, I couldn't afford to let that happen. "You've kept me from Sofia for five months. She's my wife. How can I not worry?"

"I'm sure she's safe. If they did anything to her, we would know and we would tell you."

"Right," I scoffed, "because you witches are all-knowing and all-useless."

"Useless?" The Ageless' nostrils flared. "After everything Cora did for you, I would think you'd be the last person to say something like that. You owe your power and your very existence to our kind."

I got up on my feet. "I owe her a lot. But did you also know what she did to me? What she put me through at The Blood Keep?"

"I've heard. She'd never thought being a vampire would inhibit her powers. Had she known, she never would've agreed to the Elder's deal. Cora was always independent. The centuries she spent under the Elder's control were hell to her... until you ended it. We are grateful that you ended her misery. You knew Cora and how beautiful, powerful and kind she was before the Elder corrupted her and turned her into Emilia."

"And yet you did nothing to stop her from getting corrupted."

Pain sparked in the Ageless' normally blank gaze. I'd been so caught up in my anger that I'd missed the hint of affection that came with the way the Ageless spoke about Cora.

"What was Cora to you anyway? You cared about her, didn't you?"

"She betrayed us. She should've been loyal to our kind, but she chose to be loyal to whatever feelings she had for you. Everything you are now, you owe to her. She destroyed herself in order to make you indestructible."

"So I'm right. You did care about her."

"She was powerful. Had she remained the Ageless, she would've been unstoppable, far more powerful than I am now. Everything I know, I learned from her, and my powers have been growing ever since, but she gave all that up. For you. Frankly, I don't understand why." She eyed me, unimpressed.

"You could've stopped her." Despite what Cora had turned into, I couldn't deny the guilt that I felt at the thought of the beautiful witch. There was once a time when I'd seen Cora as my best friend. I hated that her life had had to end the way that it did. "You probably should've stopped her."

"Yes. Maybe I should've. But I didn't. I reasoned to myself, out of my own love for her, that she had a choice and she'd made it. I told myself that we had to let things unfold naturally, that we cannot interfere just to undo one disastrous choice or save one life."

"And yet you saved mine. What makes my life more important than hers?"

"Your life isn't more important than hers. As I said, she made her choices and she had to live with them."

My jaw clenched. There was nothing I could do about what happened to Cora. Past was past. I couldn't change it even if I wanted to. What I did know was that Sofia needed me. Regarding my wife's fate, there was still something I could do.

"How about Sofia? Is my life more important than hers? Why doesn't she get to be saved?"

"They won't harm her. You have time."

"How are you so sure of that? She's at The Blood Keep! Captive! My wife doesn't belong there!" I could feel the heat rising again. Part of me wanted to unleash the fire and burn both the Ageless and Ibrahim to a crisp. Part of me understood what they were saying. The power I had was beyond my comprehension for now and I couldn't go back to my world without understanding it. The greater part of me, however, just really wanted to hold Sofia in my arms.

A lump formed in my throat when I remembered the dream—the same dream I'd had every single night since I married Sofia. The idea of us turning against each other was sickening, and the longer I was away from her, the more possible it seemed.

The Ageless looked at me with her typical glare, not a single hint of empathy or sympathy in her eyes. Silver hair glistening, she was as fascinating as she was terrifying.

"We can't keep going over this, Derek. Trust me when I say that we have time. You want to see Sofia, I get that, but you will risk your life—and many others' lives—if you go looking for her while you're still not ready."

"You didn't answer my question, witch. Why do I get to live?"

"Because—thanks to Cora— you are now the man powerful enough to help restore balance between the realms."

"What realms?"

"You already know of two—ours, the witches' realm, and yours, the human realm. There are two others—that of the vampires and that of the Guardians. Two realms at war with each other. We exist to maintain the balance between the two."

"We? Humans and witches?"

"No. We... witches maintain the balance. Humans are like currency—the immunes being of highest value. The vampires are hoarding too many of the immunes."

"I was a vampire. I didn't care about the immunes."

"Really, Derek? You didn't care about the power that you sensed whenever you drank Sofia's blood?" The Ageless didn't say it as a taunt or a challenge, just as a fact. "I'm not talking about your kind of vampire. You are mutations of the original, weak compared to them. The Elder is the first vampire who entered the human realm. You are his creation, but the Elder is just one among many—one among the original vampires."

"Ok. Restore balance. How do we do it? Let's just get it done."

"Don't be an impulsive fool, Derek. You know you're not ready."

"You don't understand!" I turned towards Ibrahim. "*You* keep telling me to calm down, to relax. You say that's the only way I can control…"

Fire once again burst from my palms and it took all of me to redirect my body so that the flames didn't get to my trainer and the Ageless. I screamed as ray upon ray of burning fire erupted from my body, evaporating the tears before they could fall from my eyes.

The Ageless mumbled a couple of incoherent words and within seconds the fire was gone, but I was still burning with a reality I knew to be true—a reality that the Ageless could never comprehend as she stood over me and with her stoic countenance reinforced her point.

"I think we can all agree that you are not ready." She turned to Ibrahim. "Continue the training."

Ibrahim stroked his dark goatee and sighed. "Tough break, Derek, but her word is law."

I shook my head. "I can't stay here, Ibrahim. What you don't understand is that I was *never* able to control my temper or my power. Not on my own. Not until Sofia came into my life."

"She will be back into your life the moment you gain control. It can be done."

"Damn it, Ibrahim. Don't you understand? The longer you keep me away from her, the more I lose control. I need to at least know that I'm getting closer to her, not farther." My teeth were gritted, my fists clenched, as I stood to my full height. I was fighting with every inch of my life to keep the fire from bursting out of my exhausted body once again.

Spent and desperate, I told him the one truth they couldn't seem to grasp: "Sofia *is* my calm."

Chapter 19: Aiden

Five months. It'd been five months since the Elder's children had attacked The Shade and taken over, five months since the portal had opened. I knew nothing about Sofia or her pregnancy. There was absolutely no news about the fate of Derek.

As far as The Shade's leaders were concerned, we were all in the dark.

We all feared that both were gone, but none of us had the guts to say it out loud. I, for one, was certain that my daughter was alive. I convinced myself that had anything happened to her, I would've known. I felt it in my gut.

Sofia is alive.

I had been given her bedroom at the Catacombs. After the Elder had attacked The Shade, the Black Heights was the only intact establishment at the island. Everything else was ruined. Apparently, destroying an entire mountain range wasn't thought beneficial. We still had the Catacombs and the Cells.

I heaved a deep sigh as I stared at the ceiling of her room. I'd left it mostly untouched. I wanted to sense her presence lingering there. I shifted on the bed in an attempt to make myself comfortable. I muttered a prayer for her, hoping to God that she was all right. I was never a man of faith, but at that point, I was desperate enough to believe that a Higher Power would somehow let her know that she was in my thoughts.

Everything's going to be all right, I told myself, only to scoff at the notion. *Nothing is all right.*

Every time I closed my eyes, I saw terrifying red eyes looking directly at me. I saw his sneer. I saw the manic look on his face as he stabbed Natalie Borgia in the kneecap, smiled at her scream, watched the wound heal only to stab her again.

Natalie had died for betraying the Elder the same day the Elder took over The Shade. In the back of our minds, we'd known that the Elder wasn't just going to stop at opening The Shade's side of the portal. We were right. They wanted full control.

On top of Natalie's death, three hunters were also tortured and killed. None of us understood what was going on with Arron, and why he would bail like that when he seemed so adamant that the portals not be opened, but one thing was for certain: in the world we were entangled in, we couldn't trust what we did not understand.

After they were done punishing those who had crossed them, Kiev had burned the Sanctuary down. Though we never found her body, we'd concluded that Corrine had met her death within its walls. Unless she used some sort of magic in order to escape, just like the temple, she was nothing but a pile of ashes now.

Along with her demise, we were certain that the protection over the island was going to disappear, right along with its endless night.

We were mistaken.

Kiev grinned at our cluelessness. "Don't worry. The Shade will be safe as long as you comply with our demands." He grabbed a clump of Vivienne's hair and dragged her to the ground. He seemed to know how much her struggles to break free from him were killing Xavier, because he glared at the vampire before announcing to us what the Elder had planned for his new conquest. "Your princess here will remain in power, but she is, of course, to do as the Elder instructs. Without question. Remember that the true rulers of this island are still within our grasp. One error from Princess Vivienne here and we won't mind killing Sofia's offspring right in the womb. Besides, cross us once and we won't hesitate to end The Shade's endless night, let the sun out and burn every vampire here. Will you comply, princess?"

Vivienne's eyes betrayed how revolted she was by him, but we all knew she wasn't being given a choice. She *had* to comply. She was the Elder's puppet and anything she did that displeased the Elder was to receive "just" punishment—Natalie's torturous death was the public example.

I was expecting Vivienne to wither away, to return to the empty shell she'd become after what we put her through at hunters' headquarters, but the strength and defiance never left her eyes. I wondered if Xavier had something to do with that, but whoever was to thank, I was more than grateful that she still had fight in her.

We needed her to be strong. She needed to be strong. She couldn't give up, especially now that she, just like the rest of us, had just become a pawn in the Elder's game.

After proclaiming her as the ruler of The Shade, Kiev, Clara, and the Elder's minions left for The Blood Keep and it seemed like we could do as we wished. The first thing Vivienne did was to make sure that all those who were lost would be honored. Hundreds of bodies were buried in the days that followed. Gavin's family—his mother, Lily, his brother, Robb, and his sister, Madeline—among them. Rosa, one of my daughter's dearest friends, had also met her end.

I could only imagine how heartbroken Sofia would've been to find out about the loss.

A memorial service was held to honor the dead's memory. At that time, it didn't matter what any of us were—vampire, human or hunter. We became one in our grief.

I was standing beside Zinnia during the candlelit service, listening to the sobs and the cries, the broken hearts, grieving the loss of loved ones. Zinnia was deathly silent for most of the service, except for one haunting moment when she whispered to herself in a voice so low she probably thought I wouldn't hear, "The vampires cry as if they're human. Who knew they could be capable of grief?"

Despite all the walls the young huntress had made to convince herself that devoting her life to killing vampires was a life worth living, she was beginning to see that misery existed on both the vampires' and the hunters' sides. Both had suffered loss.

Still, the solidarity that came out of our grief didn't last long. The hunters still hated the vampires and the vampires felt the exact same way. Especially considering that blood was scarce, tensions were beginning to rise.

Any thought of leaving The Shade ended when after a handful of hunters attempted to escape, Clara arrived, bled each hunter dry, and with a bloody mouth and a blood-curdling grin, announced that anyone who tried to leave the island was going to answer to her.

"We have plans for you little hunters," she said to those who remained at The Shade. "You didn't think that you could just get away with everything that you did to us vampires, do you? No, each of you is going to pay very dearly for all the vampires you killed."

Her words were a bone-chilling clue to what the Elder had planned for his captives.

In the months that followed, the Elder's minions began bringing their captives to The Shade. It seemed the Elder saw the island as his very own Alcatraz. Vampires from other covens—most of them opponents of the Novak clan—began to occupy The Shade.

We weren't told how to handle their arrival. They were just dumped at The Shade and it was up to Vivienne to figure out what to do with them.

Protecting the humans began to be a challenge the more outsiders were brought to The Shade, but we had control of the Black Heights—and both the Cells and the Catacombs within it. All outsiders were simply kept outside of the cavernous mountains.

As for the portal, none of us knew what had become of it. We weren't given any information on whether or not anyone had crossed through any of the realms.

I really didn't care until Vivienne showed up outside my bedroom one night.

"I'm sorry. I just… I can't sleep," she explained when I found her standing outside my door.

As if I'm the person you always go to when you can't sleep. "Neither can I," I admitted.

"Can we talk?"

"Sure."

Intrigued, I stepped out of the bedroom and we both made our way to the living room. We made ourselves comfortable on separate couches before the vampire heaved a deep sigh.

"What's going on, Vivienne?"

"It's been months, Aiden. Do you think they're still alive?"

"I have to believe that they are. Sofia is important to them. They won't just..." I thought of my teenage daughter going through her first pregnancy. Possibly alone, a captive of a psycho freak like the Elder. I found myself unable to breathe. I hated that I couldn't be with her. Sofia was strong, but I was her father and she'd been away from me for so long. I was never going to forgive myself for not being there for her through this.

"Do you think they're together? Do you think Kiev is telling the truth? That Sofia is really pregnant? If she is, then they would keep them together, wouldn't they? I..." Vivienne probably realized that it was pointless throwing her questions at me because she just stopped. "I'm scared, Aiden."

"I am too," I admitted, finally realizing why it was me Vivienne had come to. Of all the people in The Shade, only I could understand Vivienne's fears regarding Derek and Sofia. I hadn't wrapped my mind around the idea until that moment, but whether I liked it or not, since my daughter had married Derek, the Novaks were now our family.

In an attempt to appease both her and myself, I said the words that became our glue that held us together for the days to come.

"Sofia and Derek are strong and resilient. They'll make it. Now, we have to do them proud and stay strong and resilient too. They can't return to..." I gestured towards our surroundings. "This."

Vivienne stared directly at the space in front of her. "We need to rebuild The Shade."

I shrugged. "How hard could it be? You did it in..." I paused in wonder "How long *did* it take you to make The Shade what it is?"

"Five centuries."

I couldn't keep myself from scoffing. "Great. We're attempting the impossible."

Hope and determination sparked in the blue-violet eyes of The Shade's princess. A smile formed on her face.

"Impossible never stopped us before."

Chapter 20: Sofia

Eli Lazaroff and I had never gotten the chance to bond throughout my stay at The Shade, but the moment I saw him at The Blood Keep, he became my best friend.

"Eli?" I blinked several times to make sure I wasn't just seeing things.

"In the flesh, my queen." He nodded stoically as he scanned the room, his eyes settling on Shadow, who was seated by the door, busy lapping up a bowl of blood. Eli showed no trace of fear over the magnificent creature. On the contrary, he seemed quite taken by it.

He probably wants to poke it and study it. Curiosity might just kill Eli Lazaroff if he does that. I stared at him for quite a bit, still uncertain if he was some sort of apparition. I couldn't explain how my heart was swelling with joy just to have a comrade, an ally at the castle.

I jumped off the bed and threw my arms around his neck. As I hugged his tall, lanky build, I began to sob against his chest, giving in to the emotions I'd been suppressing over the past months.

Eli stood stiff against my embrace. He clumsily began brushing his one hand over my hair as he cleared his throat. "Your highness, I... I'm sorry."

I pulled away from him, not wanting to make either of us uncomfortable. "No, Eli, *I'm* sorry. I just... you understand. You're the first person from home I'd seen in months, and..."

"I understand, your highness." He nodded sympathetically.

"Please. Call me Sofia." I pulled him toward one of the couches near the window of the finely-furnished bedroom. I sat beside him, eager to hear about home, but also dreading what he could tell me. "How's The Shade? How's Derek?"

He lifted his black-rimmed glasses over the bridge of his nose and creased his brows. "What do you mean? Isn't the king here with you?"

I tensed. "You mean he isn't at The Shade?"

Eli shook his head. "We haven't seen either you or him since you both left after your wedding, and now..." His eyes focused on my stomach, a mixture of concern and excitement in his eyes. "I never thought I'd see the day when a woman would be carrying Derek Novak's child."

"Children," I corrected him, albeit absent-mindedly. *If he isn't here and he isn't back home, where is he?* I was tempted to think the worst, but I couldn't allow myself to do that. "Eli, is there a way we can find out where Derek is?"

Eli shook his head. "Not from here, we can't. Unless you can convince your captors to allow you to have your pregnancy at The Shade. Your father is concerned for you."

A lump formed in my throat at the mention of Aiden. *What I would give to be in his embrace right now...* It dawned on me that Kiev had more cards against me than I had initially thought. If he could get Eli at The Blood Keep in a span of mere hours, I had to assume that they had control over The Shade.

"What's happening at The Shade, Eli?"

I was nowhere near prepared to hear his answer to my question. All the lives lost, all the destruction left behind... by the time he was done, I was in tears.

I thought about the young lives that had been taken—Rosa, Lily and her children. Even Natalie, whom I knew more from Derek's stories than anything else, left a hole in my heart when I heard about her sorry demise. It took a while before I was able to choke down the tears, but I knew... I sensed it somehow. I changed that morning. More than grief and sorrow, I felt something else... an emotion I wasn't quite familiar with began to creep in. Hatred.

I wasn't even sure exactly what it was that I hated, but I knew that its seed had taken root in my core as I began to sob uncontrollably. I was exhausted by the unfairness of it all, and try as I did to deny it, I felt like it was all my fault. Countless what-ifs began to plague my mind as the faces of those who had passed away during the Elder's attack began to eat away at my teetering grip on my own sanity.

I wondered if Derek knew what had become of The Shade. I tried to comprehend why it was so important that they did not allow the gates to be opened.

"It seems that in our world," Eli concluded, "if you want to survive, you can't go about it without sacrificing the lives of other people."

I couldn't think of any objection, not when so many lives had indeed been sacrificed for my sake—for the sake of The Shade. I longed so much to have Derek with me at that moment, hear his deep voice remind me of the beauty in this world, but at that moment, the sense of loss kept me from even visualizing him in my mind.

Derek, where are you? We need you. He was alive. I had to believe in that. But at the same time, we had to make our move. We couldn't just wait for Derek to save the day.

"Eli," I said breathlessly. "Is there a way we can escape from here?"

Eli tightened his lips, a muscle on his jaw twitching as he gave the question some thought. "I'm sure there is, Sofia. There's always a way, but I have to ask… if we do succeed in escaping, where do you intend to go? The Shade is also occupied by the Elder."

I had no ready answer to the question.

Eli swallowed hard whenever he looked at me. It hadn't registered to me that I was in that bedroom with a vampire until that moment. *He must be craving me too. That's why he's acting so strange.*

"I want my children to experience sunlight, Eli."

"What are you saying?"

"If we manage to find a way to escape, we'd have to do it in sunlight. It will buy us time from the Elder's vampires pursuing us."

The color drained away from Eli's face. "You're serious?"

I nodded. "It would mean us escaping to the human world. We'd have to go to the hunters. It's our only chance."

"The sunlight will eventually kill me."

I shook my head. "You won't die if you drink my blood first."

"You're suggesting that I take the cure?"

"I'm not forcing you to do this, Eli. It's not a command or anything. I know the consequences of turning human. I saw what it did to my husband, how vulnerable it made him, but…"

Eli nodded as he digested the information. "Very well then. Let's figure out a way of escape. You've been here longer than I have. Do you have an plan in mind?"

I shook my head. "I was hoping you could help with that." I looked out the window overlooking the gardens. "The only places I'm allowed to go to are this bedroom and the gardens. I doubt the servants I get to interact with will ever have the guts to help us escape. You, on the other hand… Maybe you can volunteer to help the servants grow crops. There must be a loophole we can use to our advantage somewhere in that information."

Eli stood, clasping his hands behind his back. "There's not much to hold on to, Sofia. No one has ever been able to escape this place."

"Except for Derek."

"How do you know that he was able to escape? How are you so certain?"

"Because if he wasn't able to escape, then he's most likely dead, and that's a reality I won't be able to live with. He's alive. That means he is *somewhere*."

Eli seemed dubious, but he nodded.

I could see the hesitation and the fear in his eyes, and I had to wonder about how selfish I was bringing him here, but I didn't have much of a choice. Five months was already way too long and I still didn't have a plan. I was hoping that they would give Eli a little more leeway than they gave me. "Eli, you are the smartest person I know. You were invaluable in building up The Shade. Prove how invaluable you are to the people here and we might just have a way out."

Eli smiled. "I know who I am and what I can offer. That's not what I'm worried about." He gulped, his eyes on my neck.

I took a short breath. *He's craving my blood.*

As if reading my mind, he threw me an explanation as he began pacing the floor. "If I need to turn to a human just to be able to escape… Once I drink your blood, Sofia, I'm not sure I can stop."

"You can," I said with a curt nod of determination. "You will, but before we worry our heads over the consequences of you drinking my blood, we have to think of a way to escape first."

Eli nodded shortly then stopped his pacing before furrowing his brows. "You say that the only places they allow you to go to are this bedroom and the gardens, correct?"

I nodded.

"How do they make sure you stay within these boundaries?"

I pointed Shadow's way. "Once, I tried to go where I wasn't supposed to and well, let's just say that Shadow has already had a taste of my blood."

"Shadow? That's his name?"

"That's what I decided to call him. He doesn't really answer to the name. He just answers to Kiev snapping his fingers. Kiev calls them *beasts*."

"Them? You mean there's more?"

I nodded. "More than I care to count. All over The Blood Keep, but Shadow here is tasked to guard me. He has my scent and everything. Kiev told me that Shadow would be able to track me down even if I were miles away."

Eli stared at the beast for a good long while before he gave me a determined nod and said the one thing I desperately wanted to hear.

"I think I know a way out of here."

Chapter 21: Derek

No matter what I did to convince Ibrahim that there was no way I'd calm down as long as I felt far away from Sofia, he didn't budge.

"I understand." He would shrug and shuffle his feet. "But the Ageless has spoken."

While I understood how easily the power the witches had could be abused, I didn't understand their blind submission to the Ageless. I didn't understand how they could just sit on that power when they could be an agent for good.

However, I had to accept that to reason and argue would be futile, so I had to settle for the next best thing: music. Whenever I returned to my quarters, I would go directly to the guitar they'd provided for me and strum the song I'd hummed many times to Sofia. It was a wordless song that was ours, one that helped make memories of her more vivid.

As time went by, it felt like I was losing control more than I was gaining it. I resorted to using wooden utensils, because I'd already seared my lips and tongue more times than I could count with the heat that was coming from my palms.

I would never gain control of the power—not without her. The prophecy still stayed true. We were strongest together and we were weakest apart. I couldn't believe that I'd doubted it even for a moment.

Music and memories got me through every day, but my patience was wearing thin and my training with Ibrahim was getting nowhere. The warlock having already given up on me, I was summoned to the quarters of the Ageless.

She lived in a palace made of pure white marble and studded with red rubies. I was brought inside and through a series of halls, gardens and brightly-lit rooms. I couldn't help but contrast the place with the Elder's castle. The palace was to light as The Blood Keep was to darkness. It felt like hours before Ibrahim and I finally arrived at a courtyard, beautified by a variety of strange-looking flowers and plants. The Ageless was standing in the middle of a sand circle, located at the center of the courtyard. Her eyes were closed and her face was turned toward the heavens, a peaceful look on her beautiful face.

With the sunset serving as her backdrop, she looked nothing short of heavenly.

Ibrahim cleared his throat to get her attention, but whatever she was doing, it seemed she wasn't going to stop for anything. We just had to wait our turn.

Ibrahim motioned for me to follow him toward a gazebo where we sat to wait for the Ageless to be ready to meet with us.

"So you've finally given up on me," I told Ibrahim, almost in an accusatory tone. "Didn't I tell you that I wouldn't be able to control myself? Not without Sofia?"

"I didn't give up on you. I'm simply taking extreme measures in order to get you ready. Yes. You told me many, many times."

"And you've finally decided to listen? What exactly are these extreme measures, Ibrahim?"

"You'll find out soon enough. What you should know right now is that we're running out of time. If you really want to save Sofia, you need to cooperate with us."

My pace quickened. "Why? What's happened to her?"

Ibrahim remained silent.

My jaw clenched. "Ibrahim, at some point, you people have to trust me. If this is *my* mission, then I need to know what I'm up against. You can't keep me in the dark forever."

"I know," he nodded. "That's why we're here. We're going to try to convince the Ageless to trust you."

My eyes lit up. "Really?" I couldn't hide the relief from my voice.

"Don't get excited just yet. Odds are that she isn't going to agree. Understand, Derek, that your kind—whichever kind you belong to, vampires or humans—haven't really given us much reason to see you as trustworthy."

I didn't respond out of a fear that I would say something I'd eventually regret. I was perhaps being unreasonable, driven by my desire to be with my wife, but I hated how condescending the witches were to other kinds. For some reason, I couldn't bring myself to trust them—not when they had remained in their high and lofty sanctuary while the rest of us suffered in our own realms.

"My meditation cannot be interrupted," the Ageless explained, appearing before us. "While I am sorry that you had to wait, I can't say that I feel too bad. Do tell me. Why have you come?"

Ibrahim and I looked at her, breathtaken by her beauty. I was about to stand up but Ibrahim motioned for me to wait. I wasn't pleased that I was once again being left out of the important conversations, but I'd been at The Sanctuary long enough to know that I had no real influence there.

So this is what it feels like to be a pawn, just a piece someone's pushing around in order to win a game.

The Ageless and Ibrahim took a walk along the stone pathway that lined the courtyard. I watched as they got into a serious discussion about my fate.

It felt like forever before they finished their little stroll and returned to the gazebo.

Ibrahim seemed rather pleased with himself by the way he smiled at me. The Ageless was, as usual, devoid of any expression.

"Your mentor says that it will do you good to know the severity of your mission, how important it is that you do not mess this up. I will allow you to communicate with Corrine."

My breath hitched.

"Be warned, however, that you're not going to like it."

I swallowed hard and nodded. I had no idea what to expect. Dread came over me.

Once I finally got to speak with the witch of The Shade, I realized that nothing could've prepared me for the revelations that she unveiled during our conversation.

I didn't know what effect Ibrahim and the Ageless were expecting the conversation to have on me. Perhaps they thought that finding out about what was happening back home would motivate me to work harder. My conversation with Corrine had the exact opposite effect on me. After finding out what had happened to The Shade, I was more determined than ever to return home.

My people need me. Sofia needs me. I'm turning into hell personified and for the life of me and everyone I love, I need to get the hell out of here.

Chapter 22: Vivienne

Xavier, Cameron and Liana stood around the wooden table inside Sofia's quarters, now converted to our center of communication. Yuri and Claudia were standing next together, leaning on the wall near the table, seemingly preoccupied with each other. Aiden sat comfortably on the couch nearby, legs crossed, listening in on our conversation.

I, on the other hand, was pacing the floor, hands clasped behind my back. I had just told them that I wanted The Shade rebuilt in time for Derek's arrival.

"Rebuild The Shade." The words rolled out of Yuri's mouth as if it was a marvel he couldn't wrap his mind around.

"We don't even know where Derek is or if he is…" Cameron held his tongue, casting a guilty look at his wife, who was glaring at him to stop talking.

"Derek is alive," I said. "His return hinges on a *when* and not an *if.* My brother is coming back with his wife and child and when they return, they cannot arrive to this."

I could feel Xavier's stare on my skin. He knew me more than anyone else in that room did, even my best friend, Liana, so even if I could get everyone to accept my bold statements, he could see past my bluff.

"You do remember what we had to do just to build the Crimson Fortress alone, don't you?" Claudia spoke up, her stare fixed on Yuri as she playfully fiddled with strands of his hair.

She seemed back to her old self, flirting and treating everything like they didn't matter, even though all of us knew how much the island had begun to mean to the feisty blonde vampire.

"Are we really willing to do that again?" she challenged, pouting as she did. "All those lives…"

The hundred-foot tall, thick walls that lined The Shade had been built on the shoulders of human slave labor—mostly hunters, sent by their order to destroy us. They were prisoners of war and we owed the establishment of The Shade to their capture. It had taken almost a hundred years to complete and a lot of human lives—more than we cared to admit. The rest of the establishments on the island—ruined by the recent battles—had taken centuries to complete and develop.

Unless I expected my *human* brother to return in at least a century, there was no way we could finish rebuilding The Shade in time for his arrival.

I swallowed hard. I wasn't exactly thrilled over the idea of having to explain our choices to Aiden.

I was relieved when Xavier spoke up. "It doesn't have to be that way again. We have the technology to…"

"And how are we going to get the kind of technology we need when we are forbidden to leave the island? We have to accept that our ruler will return to a dystopia, and there's nothing any of us can do about it." Cameron, a carefree and happy person, was more distraught than I'd ever seen him.

Liana gently ran her hand over her husband's arm. I could tell that she was trying to keep away the tears. We hadn't spoken much but I knew that the trouble The Shade was experiencing was taking its toll on their marriage.

I looked at all the faces surrounding me. *It's taking its toll on all of us.*

"I don't care what Derek comes back to." Xavier broke the tense silence. "This is *our* home. We've all known Derek for hundreds of years. We know that he won't care that The Shade was ruined. It will break his heart, yes, but he will understand. What he won't understand is if we do nothing to pick ourselves up after all these tragedies."

"He's right," Yuri agreed, his eyes on Claudia, who seemed curious to hear what he had to say. "If we're going to rebuild, we're doing it for ourselves, for our own healing. You all know how loyal I am to Derek, but we need to stop doing everything *for* him and learn to start doing things for ourselves, for our home, for this kingdom. Derek is our ruler, but he isn't The Shade."

"That sounds patriotic and inspiring and all," Aiden said, "but the dilemma still remains. How are we going to rebuild?"

"I wish Eli were here." Never more had any of us felt the absence of Eli than we did at that moment. "If there's anyone who could think of a way, it's him."

Yuri winced at the mention of his brother. Kiev had come without explanation and just demanded Eli go with him. There hadn't been much we could do to stop him. Yuri had tried to fight back, but nothing came of it.

I blew out a sigh. Rebuilding The Shade without either Derek or

Eli seemed impossible.

"Can we really do this?" Claudia voiced what we were all thinking. "Without Eli's brain and Derek's brawn?"

"Yes. We can. They would want us to." Yuri pushed. "The way I see it, this is a way for us to start anew. If we're going to rebuild, we might as well forget what it once was and dream of what we want it to be. That's where we are going to start. What do we want to see in the island?"

His suggestion awakened something in me—something inside that was already on the brink of death. Hope.

"That's a step toward the right direction," Aiden approved. "But if you're going to create a vision of what the island ought to be, I think it's time we hear what the humans have to say, because for all we know, when Derek arrives, the question of who will take the cure will be back in play. You might as well start thinking of living on the island as humans, and not as vampires."

A tense silence filled the room. In the chaos of everything happening, the cure had completely left my mind. I had been so preoccupied by running the island that my own dreams of living a normal life—maybe with Xavier, should he choose to take the cure—had taken a backseat to everything that was happening around us.

"Aiden is right. If we're going to do this, we have to do it with our human allies."

Claudia rolled her eyes. She opened her mouth and I was expecting to hear an objection, but was pleasantly surprised to hear her say, "I'll go find Gavin. Expect the annoying blue-haired hunter to be with them. She's like their pet or something."

The way Aiden grinned at the mention of Zinnia didn't escape my notice. I hated the little minx. She was like a pest I couldn't get rid of, but for some reason, Gavin seemed to be able to tolerate her.

While Claudia and Yuri left to get The Shade's human leaders, we went about discussing plans for The Shade. When they returned, Gavin and Zinnia weren't with them. Instead, Clara stepped into the quarters, followed by a posse of the Elder's vampires.

I tensed. *This can't be good.*

Clara looked around. "I'm thinking these are the best quarters you have available since we destroyed everything else?"

No one responded. Instead, she was met with hateful, questioning glares.

She seemed unfazed. "I want this place cleared out. In fact, I want this whole level cleared out. Whoever is staying here"—she gave me a quick look over from head to foot then back—"I'm assuming it's you… you'll have to move to another level. Make sure this is done by the end of the day, princess."

"May I ask why?" The words came out low and clipped, escaping through gritted teeth.

"Just do it. All you need to know is that this time tomorrow, the *real* vampires take over." Fear flashed in her expression. "They will want food and drinks. Or their version of it. And, of course, plenty of entertainment."

My heart fell. All hope I had of creating a new vision for our home melted away. Her words were clear enough.

The Elders were coming to take over The Shade and the horrifying reality sank into me, as well as my companions.

We were their food.

We were their drinks.

We were their entertainment.

Chapter 23: Sofia

I lay flat on my back on the queen-sized bed. It was late into the night, as evidenced by the chimes of the antique clock on one wall of my room. I fluffed up the pillows in order to prop myself up on the bed. I stared at the pendulum swinging from left to right. Almost hypnotic.

Twins. I smiled. A bittersweet one. *A son and a daughter.* I couldn't wait to hold them in my arms and be to them the mother I'd never had. I stroked my tummy gently, trying to hold back my own tears.

An image of my children crossed my mind. Wishful and almost nostalgic. I could almost hear their laughter. For some reason, I saw them building sandcastles on a beach, the sunlight kissing their skins, their bright eyes hopeful and trusting. I imagined Derek's hand on mine, squeezing so tightly, I could practically feel it.

Dreams of the future, of what could be, were the only hope I could cling to.

"We're going to be all right. We're going to be with your father someday. A family." I said the words hoping that I would believe them.

I longed so much for the images to be true. I thought back to the house Derek had wanted to purchase in California and suddenly, the thought of being a family with him and our children—away from The Shade, away from The Blood Keep, away from *this*—became the most enticing thing my mind had ever dared entertain.

They had come unexpectedly, but I wanted my children and I knew Derek did too. We'd dreamed of this. Yet, despite my anticipation, their arrival was also met with dread.

I have to figure out a way to get out of here before I give birth. My children cannot be born at The Blood Keep. Thoughts whirled over what the Elder could have planned for my children. Kiev's words still echoed in my mind.

"Your children… they're important to us."

I dared not imagine why, but I knew that whatever they had in store for the twins was something neither Derek nor I could ever wish for our children. I wondered what made them so important. The answer came from the part of me that had a firm grip on uncomfortable truths.

They're the children of an immune and an ex-vampire. That makes them special enough to poke and prod and test. I didn't want to think about what they could be capable of. I didn't even know if I wanted to find out.

Eli's plan of escape was pure insanity, but we'd been working on it for the past few months. We both knew that we only had one shot at an escape so we couldn't risk being haphazard about our strategy.

According to Eli, the *beasts* were a product of the vampire coven in The Underground—the same one Natalie had reported that the Elder had annihilated because of their loyalty to Derek.

"We had close ties with The Underground," Eli explained. "Vivienne once sent me there in order to help them stabilize their community. One of the projects I helped them with was the creation of the beasts. Stray dogs that they took from the streets. We turned them into vampires. We didn't think it would work at first, but… here we go. Fierce creatures they are, and only trainable by a vampire."

Eli knew how to train them, and so he began to secretly train Shadow during the few times that Kiev allowed Eli and I to enjoy each other's company. Kiev reasoned that the only reason he'd allowed Eli to join me was because of the babies. I didn't care why he allowed it as long as he did, because apart from our need to discuss our plans for escape, I found Eli quite an engaging conversationalist.

Still, our conversations were few and short, since he had to put his focus on gaining Shadow's loyalty. "They're wildly unpredictable creatures when they're not loyal to you, but once you gain their loyalty…"

After two months, Eli was able to control Shadow.

And thus, our crazy idea was for both of us to go into The Blood Keep's boundaries at a time when it was day on the other side and ride Shadow out of The Blood Keep.

"Do you think it will work?" I asked Eli.

He nodded. "I'm hoping it will. It's all we can really do." He must've noticed the expression on my face, because he asked, "What's the matter? You're scared?"

"I'm afraid of what Kiev might do to Olga. He warned me that should I try to escape, he will kill her."

"Do you think he'd do it?"

Yes, my mind said, but I responded with what I wanted to believe in. "No, she seems precious to him." I justified my willingness to put her neck on the line with my desperation to escape. I was doing it for my children.

For Eli. For Derek. For The Shade.

Maybe Olga is the necessary sacrifice, *I told myself, hating that I would even consider sacrificing another person in order to save myself or even the ones I loved.*

I lay there, mulling over the decision I'd made, telling myself that I had no other choice. Eli and I were going to escape in a week. I was already in my third trimester. We both knew that I could give birth any time, but I'd insisted that we go through with it. As far as I was concerned, the fact that I was going to give birth soon was the primary reason we had to get out of there.

I had no idea that coupled with my growing hatred toward everything going on around me, everything beyond my control, my willingness to put Olga's life on the line to save my children was enough of an opening to allow the darkness a foothold in my life.

Olga's face was still etched in my mind when a cold wind began to sweep through the bedroom. The dim lighting allowed me to see everything in the room. Shadow began to cower and back away into a corner, fright traced in his bright yellow eyes. I scanned my surroundings. I couldn't see anyone there, but I wasn't alone. A thick, dark presence was with me, drawing near me.

Touching me.

I screamed when pain unlike anything I'd ever known coursed from the tips of my fingers to the nape of my neck. It only lasted a couple of seconds, but the torment felt like it lasted an eternity. Tears were rushing down my cheeks as I tried to catch my breath. My first instinct was to clutch my belly, fearing that whatever just happened could have somehow hurt my children.

"I love hearing you scream."

It was the strangest thing. I didn't actually hear the words, or at least I didn't think so. They were almost like thoughts being inserted into my head from an outside entity. One that I could not see. I couldn't control my trembling.

"You fear me," the presence stated. "Good."

"Who are you? *What* are you?"

"I've been waiting to meet you. Queen of The Shade, the woman who stole Derek Novak and my daughter, Emilia, away from me. You've ruined so many of my plans, Sofia Novak. Now, I can pay you back all the trouble you've caused me."

"You're the Elder."

My body was yanked forward in an upright sitting position in the middle of the bed before my head was violently jerked backwards, my scalp burning with pain, as if someone were pulling at my hair. I couldn't feel his touch. I didn't even know if he had fingers, hands or arms, but I could feel the pain coursing through me.

My hands were still gripping my tummy as I screamed when blood began to ooze from a shallow cut that formed on my jaw line.

"Don't worry. Nothing I do to you will harm your children. I won't cause them any pain. At least not yet. But you, however…"

Something struck me, as if I'd been whipped, and I arched my back in agony, blood seeping through my clothes.

"I've been waiting for this. I never could come to you before. You were so protected by your own light, but now… now that The Blood Keep's darkness has managed to get to you, I have a foothold on you. I love how your slender form trembles. That's right, Sofia. Be afraid. You've got everything to fear now that you're in my presence."

Another lash formed on my back, drenching my clothes with blood.

"Please…" I sobbed. I was about to beg, but I held my tongue. I refused to give him the satisfaction.

"Your husband was supposed to be mine. I created him, after all.

He is my descendant, as is every other vampire you hold dear. They're all mine, but people like you... you ruin everything. Your beauty sickens me. But worry not, child, when I'm done with you, you'll be ugly beyond imagination. Derek won't even be able to stand looking at you. Mark my words, young one. I'm going to make you pay ten times the trouble you've caused me."

His threats were cutting me to the core. I wanted to believe they were empty threats, but something told me that the Elder had the power to do whatever he wanted with me. I wanted to fight back, to defend myself, to somehow get back the light I once held within me, but I couldn't.

How do you fight a presence you can't see? How do you once again spark a light that everything around you is determined to extinguish?

"I can sense your surrender. I'm disappointed. Well, almost. You've no idea the pleasure it brings me to see you in this state. My prisoner. Helpless. Away from everyone and everything that you love."

I clung to the fabric of my night shift over my stomach. He laughed. "Do you really think you'll be able to hold those children in your arms? Be a mother to them? How would you even know the first thing about being a mother when you've never even had one? Camilla Claremont was mine. I enjoyed seeing her transform into the wickedness that was Ingrid Maslen. Now, before I leave you, let me give you a picture to dwell on until we meet again."

Something I couldn't see coiled around my head and suddenly, I was at the beach, watching my twins build sandcastles, my husband holding my hand. I was living the image of laughter and mirth that had been playing in my head before the Elder arrived. Dread swept over me, because even my imagined refuge was about to be ruined.

A wave washed over the sandcastle the twins were building. Tears were streaming down their faces as their eyes searched for me. I was standing from a distance, desperate to come to their aid, but while Derek ran to them to save them from another wave that would crash against the shore and sweep our children into the ocean, I couldn't move. I couldn't help them. Derek tried to get them, but the waves sucked them into the sea. Derek screamed in horror, echoing my own cries as he plunged into the ocean to try and save the twins.

Everything came to a standstill as my husband disappeared under the water. Just when I thought that I'd lost him, I gasped with relief when he emerged from the ocean. I searched his arms for our children, but found them empty. He swam to the shore and rose to his feet, shoulders sagged in defeat. Tears were streaming down his face, a picture of abject dejection as he trudged his way through the white sands. He knelt on the ground, distraught—a father who'd failed to rescue his own children.

"Derek..." I gasped, barely able to breathe. As if hearing my uttering, his eyes met mine, hatred oozing from his countenance.

In an instant, he was standing right before me, fire dancing in the back of his eyes.

I swallowed hard. Never before had he given me such a look. I repeated his name, trying to touch him, but he pushed my hand away.

"I blame you," he said through gritted teeth. "You're the reason they're gone. *You* ruined everything."

I gasped. He might as well have ripped my heart out of my body. It would've been less painful. I was too shocked to formulate words, so I just stared into those bright blue eyes that once looked upon me with such love. Not anymore. In its place, there was nothing but resentment and spite.

I was relieved when the love of my life disappeared into thin air. I couldn't bear him looking at me that way.

I was at a loss for words, panting as the image faded away and I was back at The Blood Keep, fully aware of my surroundings, in the presence of the invisible one, the Elder, who held my very life in his hands. He chuckled—an expression without the slightest bit of pleasure. Just pure sadistic hatred.

"That, dear Sofia," he said with words that could be felt more than heard, "is the future you can hope for. If you ever think you can live a normal life with your children and the love of your life—a *normal* family—think again. You're mine now and there's nothing you or Derek Novak can do about it."

I wasn't able to breathe out the tension building up inside of me until the Elder's presence left my bedroom, leaving behind him the outward chaos left by a cold sweeping wind and the inward turmoil of a nightmare. Once I was alone in that bedroom, still feeling the pain of the torment he'd put me through, I knew for a fact that I would do anything to get away from the Elder and the fate that he displayed before me.

Anything, I determined. I stared at the giant beast that was to be my only means of escape and winced. Eli's escape plan was insanity, all hinging on whether he had been successful in gaining Shadow's loyalty or not, but I knew I had to take the risk.

Something in the expression on Derek's face, now etched in the back of my mind—the hatred in his eyes—rattled me. *You need to take a risk, Sofia. You have no other choice.*

I began to sob, because in spite of the revelation that the Elder had had a hold on me the moment I gave in to my hatred, I still didn't change my mind.

"I'm so sorry, Olga," I said between sobs.

I felt like whatever light, whatever good, I had in me was slowly slipping away, replaced by hatred, bitterness, fear and exhaustion, and there was nothing I could do about it.

The Sofia who had married Derek was gone. In her place was me. Me and my darkness.

Chapter 24: Derek

I thought that I was going to speak with The Shade's witch through some sort of communication device between the realm of the humans and the witches. I was wrong. The sultry, olive-skinned brunette was brought right to me at the Ageless' gazebo.

I was so relieved to see someone from home, I reached for her and drew her into a tight embrace. "You have no idea how happy I am to see you."

She tensed against me. She sounded breathless when she said, "Hello, Derek."

Her voice was devoid of its sharpness. The witch, who had never once flinched even at my biggest fits of rage, was trembling as I stepped away from her. She couldn't even look me in the eye. She was standing before me, fists clenched, tears threatening to fall from her eyes.

"Corrine? What's wrong?" A million questions were running

through my mind, but for some reason, the only question I was able to blurt out was, "Did you just arrive?"

She opened her mouth, but save for a restrained squeak, no sound came out.

She was putting me on edge, causing a build-up of heat on my body. I breathed a couple of sighs, thinking of a way to somehow calm down. "For your sake, Corrine, you better say something before I do something I regret. Are you going back to The Shade? When? How?"

Her gaze was listless. Even my threat didn't seem to affect her. Instead, she just bit her lip and shook her head. "I'm not returning."

"What do you mean you're not returning? Who's keeping the spell over The Shade? What has happened to the island?"

"The Elder has taken over The Shade. His witches are keeping the spell going."

"No..."

"I'm so sorry. They think I'm dead. Kiev burned the Sanctuary down. I barely escaped to this realm before... everything was lost."

I was trying to make sense of the words, but it all came as a confusing of pile of questions. "What? No... How? When? Sofia... how is Sofia? And Vivienne..." My breath hitched. A thousand horrifying implications ran through my mind.

"The Elder still has Sofia. I haven't seen her since you two left for your honeymoon. I think she's..." Corrine stopped, casting a glance at the Ageless who gave her a stern glare.

"You think she's what? What has happened to my wife?"

"I don't know."

"You're lying. Why are you lying?" I grabbed her by the shoulders at the same time as a wave of heat went from my shoulder blades to my palms. My touch burned her skin and she screamed in pain.

The Ageless intervened by casting a spell on me, effectively throwing me to the ground. Only her spells had any effect on me when the power took over and I lost control. This time, however, as I crouched on the ground and tried to get up, even her cooling spell did little to quench the heat emanating from my body.

Tears would have fallen from my eyes, but they quickly evaporated due to the heat that I was exuding.

"What's happening to him?" Corrine gasped as the Ageless healed her shoulders of the burns I'd inflicted on her.

"He's losing control. Without the vampire curse, the powers your ancestor bequeathed to him have been unleashed. Even *we* don't know the full extent of his capabilities and now it's all coming out."

She had basically just admitted that even they had no clue how to harness my power. *So all this time, they've been playing trial and error with me, experimenting with different methods to try and bring my powers under control. They have no idea what they're doing.* The thought drove me to the brink of insanity. I screamed my agitation out and with the piercing shout came torrents of fire shooting out of my palms.

"Mistress," Ibrahim gasped. "He's beyond control." He was trying to cast a cooling spell on me, but his attempts failed. No wind or ice or water cooled me down.

I saw stark terror in the eyes of my mentor as the wizened warlock realized that nothing he did could restrain the power that was escaping from my exhausted body. I was about to implode and nothing seemed to be able to stop it. Giving up on trying to stop me, he formed a force field around himself, the Ageless and Corrine in order to stay safe from the red-hot flames darting out of my palms.

The Ageless glared at Ibrahim first and then looked at me like I was a child who had just disappointed my parents severely. Her calm was unnerving. She didn't seem to be fazed by anything at all. I could swear she muttered a few curses before shutting her eyes and mumbling incoherently. She began to float from the ground and within minutes, a whirlwind appeared, quenching the flames I'd just created, saving her palace from sure destruction.

She might have quenched the fire I'd created, but she hadn't stopped the source. No matter how I tried to control it, the fire was building up inside me, threatening to escape.

"Take control!" she screamed at me. The pressure only increased the build-up of fire within me. To my shock, she lunged forward.

"No! Don't come near me!"

The warning went unheeded. She was coming at me at full speed, her widened eyes letting me know that she knew that what she was asking of me was impossible.

"You can claim control." This time, her tone was calculated and controlled. Desperate.

"I can't!" I managed to scream out as charring red fire began to flow through my veins, forming outside my fingertips.

She gulped just before reaching me. She pressed her palms against mine and stared right into my eyes. I wondered if she knew whether what she was about to do would work. I couldn't help but admire that she did it anyway. An ice-cold sensation seeped from her skin to mine. She was neutralizing my fire with her ice, creating a warm energy between us.

"I can't..." I seethed. "I can't..."

For a moment, I thought she was going to give me another pep talk. They kept telling me that I could take control, that I could get myself together and harness the power. Instead, to my surprise, the Ageless nodded, her eyes glazed over.

"I believe you."

"Sofia. I need my wife. If you don't bring me to her or bring her to me… if you keep at this, I swear… I don't know if I'll be able to keep myself from burning your realm down."

Her eyes flickered and she slowly nodded. "I think what's best for you is to stay here, Derek, but we have interfered with your life long enough. Remember, however, that should you choose to leave, the consequences are on you. If your lack of control destroys Earth, then there's no one to blame but you."

I clenched my fists, wondering to myself—like many times before—if I was indeed doing the right thing. Convinced that I was, I nodded. "I need to get home."

"The Shade—or what's left of it—is waiting for you. Corrine will take you there."

Corrine's eyes widened. "I can't go back. I don't want to. Please."

"You will take Derek through the portal and you will not return until his mission is complete. He will need your powers to neutralize his."

"Please," Corrine begged, making me wonder what on earth could've possibly broken the woman's spirit. The witch cowered in front of no one. To see her so shattered made for a fearsome omen of what I was about to see.

The Ageless, however, was unmoved. The silver-haired vixen's shoulders sagged. "There is no other way, Corrine. He will ruin The Sanctuary if he stays here. We can't help him anymore. You can. Take him back home."

I was relieved, but I was also confused. The witches were supposed to be the agents of good—maintaining balance, or so they said—but if there was one thing my stay at their realm had taught me, it was that I couldn't trust them.

Just like all the other realms, they were looking out for themselves and no one else.

I had no idea what had happened to The Shade, how ruined it probably already was, but one thing I knew for sure was that no matter how magnificent the witches' realm was, it could never be the kind of paradise my true home was to me.

Chapter 25: Aiden

Clara left after promising that she would return "to see us entertain the Elders". I had no idea what she was talking about, but I didn't need Eli's genius to know that we were being set up for trouble.

I slammed my fists against the dining table we now circled. "What do we know about these creatures?" I asked, terrified by the thought that it was one of these "original vampires," these "Elders", who was holding my pregnant daughter captive.

Vivienne shook her head. "None of us have ever been in the presence of the Elder. We were never sure if the Elder was even real, but in hindsight, maybe the Elder had something to do with Derek turning over to the dark side." I could tell by the expression in her eyes that whatever version of Derek had existed at that time, she hadn't liked it.

"That was Derek at his worst, his darkest," Xavier explained. "We were loyal to him. We loved him. He was our leader. But we all feared him."

I didn't need to know exactly what he'd done to get a picture of just what sacrifices were made to secure The Shade. I knew my history as a hunter and I knew the thousands of lives that were claimed before The Shade disappeared from the maps. Many companies of hunters—brave warriors—had been lost at the island.

The man my daughter had married was notorious for a reason. That was never a secret to me.

"He *never* said anything about the Elder? Ever? There must be something—anything—that we know about this creature. Even just tall tales and rumors."

Vivienne shrugged. "As I said, none of us were even sure that the Elder existed until recently, when he started manifesting himself."

"I've encountered him," Claudia spoke up. "Once. A long time ago."

All eyes turned toward the blonde vampire.

Claudia shifted uncomfortably on her feet, almost as if she were afraid we would hurt her.

"You've *seen* the Elder?" Yuri asked. Clearly, even he had never heard of this before.

Claudia shook her head. "No. I don't think anyone ever has. Not even his children. He is a presence sensed. He is absolute coldness seeping into your bones, freezing you. He is pain. He is fear. I…"

Her eyes were wide with horror. I could only imagine what was going through her mind.

Vivienne was getting impatient. "How did you come to have an encounter with him? Why would you even want to go to him?"

"I never went to him, Vivienne." Her voice came with a hiss as she uttered Vivienne's name. "You don't go to the Elder. He comes to you. When he pleases, and often times, he does it to draw blood. I don't understand it, but he seems drawn to the darkness of one's soul. We all have it, I think, and that's what usually draws his presence."

"He sounds like the devil himself," Xavier muttered.

"He might as well be," Claudia said softly, swallowing hard. Her eyes turned toward Yuri. She was crying out for him to reassure her, to let her know that despite what she was about to reveal, he would still love her.

Yuri had become one of my friends at The Shade, and I knew without a doubt that no matter what, he would still love her. Deeply. Nothing was ever going to change that.

An ache formed in my heart at that realization, because in Yuri and Claudia, I'd always seen myself and Camilla. I found myself wishing that they could survive whatever was to come. I wouldn't have wished Camilla's fate and mine on anyone.

"It's all right, Claudia," he assured her. "Tell us everything."

"It was me whom the Elder came to in order to get to Derek. He instructed me on how to conjure the darkness in Derek. The first time the Elder came to me was the worst night of my life. I've seen evil in many of its forms, been a victim of it. I've even been evil myself, but nothing compares to the Elder. I don't think Derek ever forgave me for bringing the Elder into his life. I…"

A bitter smile formed on Vivienne's face. "I'm sure he has, Claudia. If he hadn't forgiven you, I doubt you'd be alive." She stood to her full height and nodded in resolution. "None of us are strangers to the atrocities that happened here at The Shade. That's the past. Let's leave it there. What we need to deal with now is that a force that is completely unknown to us is about to come to our home. The Elder isn't just a myth like we once thought he was. He exists and he is not alone." Vivienne shuddered as the implications of what she was saying sank into her—into all of us.

"We'll survive this." Liana spoke up. "We have to. I want that cure, Vivienne." She turned to her husband and clutched his hand. "We're so close to being human again, living with a family. Normal. Mortal. And Sofia... if she really is pregnant... Derek and Sofia are family to all of us. We're family. We've made it this far for the past five centuries. Together. We need to get through this the same way. Together."

I was taken aback by what she said. I'd known that Derek wanted the cure in order to become human and be with Sofia, but it had never dawned on me that any of the other vampires wanted it as badly as he did.

With Anna, the only immune apart from Sofia, having been taken to the hunters' headquarters soon after Derek and Sofia had left, there was no way any of them could take the cure for themselves. For some reason, the cure made the stakes higher. I looked at every person in that room—all of them vampires—and found myself perturbed that I honestly saw each of them as family.

I'd be a fool to still think of myself as a hunter, I thought, *but then again...* I thought of Zinnia and Julian and other comrades I'd made as a hunter, and I saw them as family too.

Liana's pep talk seemed to have the desired effect on all involved. I had to give it to these vampires. They were resilient. Practically unbreakable.

"We'll make it." Cameron nodded.

"You don't look convinced, Vivienne," I said.

Vivienne forced a smile. "All I know is that if any of us are going to make it—together or otherwise—we need to know what we're up against. Claudia, we'll need you to tell us in detail everything you know about the Elder. Your encounters with him. What he did.

What he put you through. That may be painful to relive, but it's necessary for us to know."

Claudia nodded. "All right. I'll try to remember."

"Good, but before that, Yuri, I need you to look through all the texts your brother has kept over the years. All the information about the original vampire. Legends, stories, rumors... I don't care what it is. Find it. Ask Ashley to help you out. She's already worked with Eli before when they were trying to figure out the hunters." At that, Vivienne gave me a side glance, almost as if to apologize.

Yuri immediately went about the task, digging through the many resources his brother had collected over the past five centuries, leaving us all to hear what Claudia had to say.

"When the Elder comes, he will always make you bleed," Claudia started. "An encounter with the Elder will always leave you in pain after." She detailed how the Elder inflicted pain. The mystery of his invisible presence. She told us everything she knew.

"Okay," I drawled after she was done. "We know what he is like. Now what we need to figure out is how to fight back. What are his weaknesses? How do we destroy him?"

Silence crossed the room as we all hung our heads to dwell on the reality we were facing: *How on earth do you fight a creature that you can only sense, but never see?*

Chapter 26: Vivienne

I was perched on an overhanging plateau at one side of the mountain range that was the Black Heights. I had to get away from everyone at the Catacombs, try to gather my thoughts together, find a dose of peace that could get me through the night.

I stared at the view ahead of me. Far into the distance, where the night of The Shade stopped and the day of the rest of the world was about to start, the sun was rising. It would only be a few hours before the Elders arrived.

"Vivienne?" A familiar, warm, soothing baritone spoke from behind me.

I was both relieved and shaken to have him around. Xavier had over the past months awakened my desire for him in so many ways that his very presence scared me. I was pleased to have his company, but I was also afraid of the effect he had on me.

"What are you doing here?"

"I was looking for you. I know this is one of the places you go to when you want to be alone."

I smiled, sensing him approach from behind me. "You keep stalking me, Vaughn."

"I would think you'd be used to it by now, Novak." The tips of his fingers brushed against my shoulders, then down my arms. "Vivienne... You're trembling. You're scared."

"Aren't you?"

"Cameron and Liana are right. We've made it through a lot together. We can make it through this."

"I want to believe that we can make it, but we don't even know what we're up against. All that talk about unity and togetherness sounds great, but the Elder is a threat just on his own. To think that there are more of his kind..." I heaved a sigh. "Yes. Liana is right. We need to make it through this together, but we also have to look at this with a dose of realism. Xavier, we are an Elder's creations. Mutations of the original. We are just watered-down versions of that particular Elder's power. Who knows what the others are capable of? The information Claudia revealed and Eli dug up... they're threadbare clues to what kind of creatures these things are. How do we fight that?"

His cold breath touched the back of my neck, his forehead pressed against my head, his hands brushing up and down my arms. No matter how cold we both were, he made warmth climb from the pit of my stomach to the top of my chest.

"You always worry about things that are beyond your control, Viv. You worry too much."

"I can't help it." I frowned. "And you? You worry too little, Xavier."

"The way I see it, these Elders are coming. Nothing we can do to stop it. We might as well cherish these last few moments we have, these times when we're still free from their hold. I think it's what Derek and Sofia would've done."

"Really? You don't think my brother would've had some sort of plan concocted by now? An escape... something?"

"An escape to where? Derek has done a lot of great things, but I don't think even he could've found a way out of this one. Stop being so hard on yourself. Besides, Derek isn't here. And you're not Derek. Stop trying to be him. Do you see any of your subjects complaining so far? Vivienne, you've been keeping us all together since Derek and Sofia left."

I spun around and pushed him away. "I hate you."

"Hate me?" His eyes widened, his ruggedly handsome face twisting in confusion. "Why?"

"For being so calm! You're always so cool and collected and..." I had no idea what was happening to me, but tears were beginning to fall from my cheeks. "You remind me of who I used to be before the hunters got me."

His eyes cleared when he realized what I was telling him. "I remember." He nodded with a bittersweet smile forming on his lips. "Nothing seemed to faze you. Your father and Lucas... they would be in a panic, but you... I used to wonder if anything could ever shake you. You were the very picture of fortitude at that time— exactly what The Shade needed."

I raised my eyes to his, the terror and dread that I felt being shoved to the back of my mind by his mere presence. I loved him. Always had. The way he was looking at me at that time unnerved me. I wished I believed in myself as much as he seemed to believe in me.

"How can you look at me that way?"

"What way?"

"Like you think I'm amazing."

He grinned. His mouth opened to reply, but instead of words, I found myself being pulled to him, his lower lip caught between mine. I slightly bit into his lip. He groaned and pulled away, but the naughty expression on his face—the hunger behind his eyes—told me that this encounter was far from over.

"You love me, princess. Admit it." His grip on my arm tightened. He wanted to hear me say the words. He was desperate for it.

My lips trembled. I could find no reason not to say it, so I didn't understand why the words wouldn't come out of my lips. "I… Xavier…" I had no idea what terrified me more—the coming of the Elders or baring my heart completely to the man I loved. Xavier made me feel vulnerable. "You said you'd wait until I'm ready."

"And I'd do that, Vivienne. You know I would, but…"

I pressed my lips against his to silence him, hoping that if I couldn't express what I felt for him in words, he would understand that I loved him through my actions.

Still, even as I reveled in being held in his strong arms, I could tell that I would regret not telling him. Especially when a cold, foreboding wind began to sweep through the island.

That meant only one thing.

"The Elders are here," I whispered. A creeping sense of fear began to envelop me, getting under my skin and chilling my bones. I clung to Xavier tighter but he pulled away from me.

"Xavier?" I asked. I looked into his eyes and gasped. They'd gone a strange, translucent white.

He brushed loose strands of my hair with his fingers before giving me a wide, manic grin. "Hello. You're right, sweet innocent."

Right about what? Realization dawned on me. "No."

"Yes. We're here."

Chapter 27: Kiev

I watched as the young woman set the tray of food on top of the aluminum pushcart. Strawberries, pancakes, delicacies that I would never have the pleasure of tasting. *Ones Derek Novak is somehow now able to enjoy… wherever he is.* The man had been off our radar since the day he'd somehow escaped our capture.

That means only one thing. He's no longer in this realm.

"Everything's ready, my lord." Downcast eyes and clasped hands faced me.

"Let's go then."

Olga was the beautiful brunette tasked to bring Sofia her meals every day. She'd been held captive at The Blood Keep since she was a baby and she'd been serving as a kitchen girl from childhood to her teenage years. I knew I could trust her to do whatever I told her to do, so when the subject of who to send to cater to Sofia's needs had come up, Olga had come to mind.

Unlike the other servants, the teenager didn't tense at the very sight of me. She respected me more than she feared me and I liked that about her. She knew her place in my life and she served it well.

"How is she?" I asked her as we walked along the corridors of The Blood Keep, headed for Sofia's bedroom.

"I don't think she gets enough sleep. She seems anxious as of late."

"Did she try to talk to you again?"

"Yes. Always. She wanted me to help her. Begging. She was talking about escape."

Sofia, you little fool. "And what did you do?"

"Nothing. I ignored her. Like you told me to." Olga paused and caught her breath.

I'd practically raised the young servant. I could read her expressions very well. "You're keeping something from me. Spit it out, Olga."

"She hit me yesterday. She got really angry that I wouldn't respond to her pleas." Olga's round face paled.

She hit Olga? I couldn't picture Sofia doing something like that, especially to an innocent just like herself. *The darkness is getting to her.*

"She's not like she was when she first came. She's losing it, my lord. She's withering away." A deep sigh escaped Olga's red lips, her eyes glistening. "I feel for her."

You feel for her? The thought riled me up. I grabbed her arm and yanked her around to face me before gripping her jaw. "Know your loyalties, Olga."

She didn't cower like others did. Her hazel eyes met mine, unflinching. "I know where mine lie, my lord. On the other hand, I'm not sure where yours do."

I knew her so well, but for some reason, I was never quite able to wrap my mind around the idea that she knew me just as much as I did her. In fact, she knew me better than anyone else—apart from the Elder—did at that castle.

Olga knew that even though she was my lesser in terms of station at the castle, we were both just captives of the Elder. I was the Elder's so-called son, but I was not much different than every other slave and prisoner he kept at The Blood Keep. I didn't have a will of my own.

I slapped Olga across the face for her insolence. "I have no idea what you're talking about." I was lying, and I could see in her stoic face that she knew it. I let go of her and she turned away from me and once again began pushing the food cart forward. Her long brown hair sashayed over her waist, her hips swaying as she walked along the castle's dark corridors.

Still, as we neared Sofia's chambers, Olga's words haunted me. The idea of Sofia "losing it" bothered me. *Have I allowed her to get to me? That can't happen. Remember what happened to the last girl you took a genuine liking to, Kiev.*

Natalie had been the love of my life. The rogue vampire herself. We'd planned to elope, to find a place in the world where the Elder wouldn't be able to find us. We were such fools—Natalie and I.

I shuddered at the memory of the things the Elder had made me do to her. I'd ruined the girl I loved. Those nights tormenting Natalie were the worst nights of my life. It was the Elder's way of showing me that the darkness inside me was far greater than the light, because I couldn't say no. I did to Natalie what the Elder pleased. After we released Natalie, I knew she would never be able to forgive me.

I'd lost her.

Back at The Shade, when we'd found her inside the Sanctuary, I'd seen how she looked at me. Natalie was the vampires' ultimate diplomat for a reason. She was peace-loving and cordial. She never hated anybody. She was on no one's side. She was the middle ground, but at that moment, as our eyes met, I knew that she hated me. I couldn't bear it.

Her hatred had caused me more pain than I could imagine a heart could handle, so I did what any child of the Elder would do. I punished her.

Natalie Borgia, the woman I loved, had died in my hands, because I was a sick, sick bastard, who would forever be a prisoner to darkness.

Natalie's face was still etched on my mind when I entered Sofia's bedroom. Though her lovely countenance would forever haunt me, I felt nothing over her loss. Years under the Elder's power had done that to me. I was forever numb. Or at least I thought so.

All callousness dissolved when I saw Sofia's bloodstained bed. I couldn't even explain what I felt. The sense of deep, deep loss came over me like a flood and I had no idea how to handle it.

Did she miscarry? I walked toward the empty bed. *That's too much blood.* I scanned the room to look for the redhead and found no sign of her or the beast I'd assigned to guard her. *Stupid mutt.* Olga ran towards the bathroom to check if Sofia was there, and I followed suit.

Olga's gasp confirmed that Sofia was indeed there. I was already thinking the worst so I actually sighed with relief when I saw that Sofia was on her feet, pulling a dress over her shoulders, shocked by the unannounced intrusion. Sitting beside her, licking his own fur, was the beast.

My claws came out. "You good-for-nothing monster!" The beast yelped when my claws cut through its flesh the first time, but within minutes of the abuse, it was snarling and growling at me, poised to attack.

I grinned, ready to take on the beast's challenge. I had every intention of killing the dog.

"Kiev, please. The dog didn't do anything to me."

I creased my brows in surprise, wondering why on earth she would come to the defense of the beast. "What happened then?" I asked her.

She withdrew from any attempt to defend herself or the animal and just stared back at me, no word of explanation coming out of those lips. She'd clearly been crying, but it wasn't sorrow that I was seeing in her eyes. It was anger—not just that, it was hatred. I found it unbecoming for someone like her.

"Did the beast hurt you?"

She shook her head.

I had half a mind that she might have been trying to escape and the beast must've sensed it. I was losing my patience with my lovely captive. "Then why is there blood all over the bed, Sofia?"

Again, she didn't respond to me. At least not in words. Instead, she turned around and slightly pulled her unzipped dress down her shoulders, exposing her bare back to us. The stripes on her back were too familiar for me not to recognize.

"The Elder came to you."

Her voice was so raspy, so soft, I barely made out the words. "What is he?"

A monster. I swallowed hard. The fact that the Elder was able to do this to her meant that she'd allowed darkness in. The months of captivity had relentlessly chipped away at her resolve, covering up anything good about her.

"Leave us," I instructed Olga. The servant quickly complied. She knew better than to be around something like this. "Your children?"

"They're unharmed." Sofia pulled her dress over her shoulders once again and placed her hands over her belly. "At least I think so," she added, her voice coming out as a soft croak.

I marveled at her strength. Another woman would've crumpled in a corner and felt sorry for themselves. I retrieved a dagger tucked beneath my belt and cut a gash over my palm. I walked towards Sofia. "Drink."

She took one look at the blood and shook her head adamantly. "Never."

"You would rather remain in pain?"

"I can bear it."

"Don't be a fool, Sofia. You have your children to think of."

"Maybe it's better that they never become a part of this sick, sick world, Kiev."

"Suit yourself." I shrugged. I really couldn't care less what she did with her children. If she was looking for someone to talk her out of her insanity, then she was speaking to the wrong person. I stared at my bleeding palm. The gash was about to close. "I'm not going to cut myself again. Are you going to drink or not?"

I noticed then how pale she was. *She's lost a lot of blood. If she doesn't drink, we're going to lose the children for sure—even her perhaps.* I could see the wheels in her mind turning. She drew a short intake of breath before grabbing my wrist and drinking from my palm. She was only able to take a couple of sips since the gash was already closing. I wasn't sure if it was enough so I none too gently grabbed her and yanked her to one side so that I could see her back.

The lashes healed.

"I never thought I'd see the day when the Elder had enough power to get to you, Sofia."

"I need Derek."

"Well, he isn't here, is he?" I began running my fingers over her spine, enjoying the feel of her bare flesh under my skin.

"What will it take for you to help me, Kiev? There must be something you want from me. You've been kinder to me than you ought to be."

I chuckled. "Have I? Or has the Elder's attack just made you delusional? Tell me, what exactly did you do to get him to pay you such a violent visit?"

"How am I supposed to know what's going on inside your father's twisted mind?"

I didn't get a full grasp of the darkness that had already consumed our beautiful captive until she spun around and looked up at me with a heated gaze. I knew then that she was true to her word. She would do *anything* for me to help her. All the wicked possibilities ran through my mind. I was with Sofia Novak at her most vulnerable and every part of me was screaming to take advantage of that fact.

"So how about it, Kiev? What exactly do you want from me? What do I have to do…"

I wanted her in my bed. Every part of my being wanted to experience what Derek experienced with Sofia. I laid her on the bed and allowed my eyes to ravish her lovely form.

Then I saw her eyes. The tears, the fear… I didn't know why, of all the many times that I had taken advantage of other people, my conscience decided to make itself known at that particular moment. I stared down at Sofia and saw her trembling and I knew that if I went ahead and took what she was offering, not only would I completely destroy any hope of her ever going back to the light, I would also destroy any chance that I had to do the same.

You're going to regret this, Kiev, I chastised myself as I looked at the beauty beneath me. Sofia was far from willing, she was just desperate. I wanted to believe that I was still capable of light.

"Don't worry. I don't want to do *this* with you. Not like this. Not while I know that you belong to him." I knew I was going to pay for those words, that there was no way the Elder wouldn't find out that I'd had the chance to make Sofia Novak completely mine. I was going to get severely punished, but for reasons even I couldn't completely understand, I couldn't do it. I couldn't destroy Sofia.

I rose to my feet and tried to gather myself together.

Sofia was still shaking when she sat up on the bed. "Kiev?"

"I had no idea darkness has already consumed so much of you, Sofia. You're right. We need to get you out of here."

"Why? Why would you help me? I have trouble believing that it's simply out of the goodness of your heart that you want to suddenly assist me."

Despite the fact that she was shaking like a leaf, Sofia still had that fight in her. It seemed she always did. I doubted anything could kill the embers of this little spitfire.

"Why do you care what my reasons are, Sofia? I'll help you escape. That's all you need to know."

"You must want something in exchange, Kiev."

"Perhaps I do." I shrugged. "What I want, Sofia, you'll know in due time. Let's just say for now that you owe me one."

I could see the apprehension on her face, but considering what she'd been willing to do just moments before, I doubted she had it in her to object.

Why indeed am I helping Sofia Novak? Is it her? Is there something about Sofia that just makes people want to be good around her?

For the first time in a long time, I dug deep within me, scouring my memories for an answer. Then there it was. A memory I'd desperately longed to forget resurfaced. I found my answer, and every fiber of my being wished that I hadn't.

Gruesome memories of a past I'd buried deep into my subconscious came to the forefront of my thoughts and as much as I tried to keep it from happening, I actually shuddered. I had plenty of reasons to want to rescue Sofia from the Elder's grasp. Should those reasons be examined, it would be quite clear that none of them had anything to do with light.

Every reason I could think of for wanting to help the young woman was born out of selfishness. My identity had never become clearer than it did at that moment.

I was a child of the darkness and nothing I did could ever change that.

CHAPTER 28: VIVIENNE

"No… What have you done to Xavier? Where is he?" I could hardly breathe. I stood frozen trying to comprehend what had just happened.

"He's right here, my sweet. I can hear his screams and demands to get out. Annoying really, but it pleases me to use him as a vessel. I hear the taste of human blood is exquisite when enjoyed through the flesh of our mutations."

Mutations. We are mere mutations of the Elders.

"What do you want?"

"What's your name?"

"No." I shook my head. "I refuse to tell."

He laughed—a sound that didn't seem to have any true pleasure in it. "Well, I was only trying to heed your customs as humans. It doesn't matter if you don't tell me, princess. We all know who you are. You and your brother did us Elders proud for so long. That is until your brother decided to fall in love with that little redheaded worm. You betrayed us, child. It will be interesting to see what we can do to make you pay for what you did."

I stepped away from him. I was having trouble hearing those words through the voice of Xavier. He had been my rock for hundreds of years. To see him this way, with eyes empty... I trembled, more out of fear of losing him than fear of what they had in store for me.

The Elder noticed the way I shook. "You fear me. Good. It means you know your place. You may be princess to our mutations, but you are nothing but a slave to the Elders." He stepped forward and pressed his lips against mine, firm hands holding my waist and pulling me against him.

I squirmed away from him, knowing that it was someone else who was holding me, not Xavier. Of course, there was little I could do to keep him from having what he wanted.

When our lips parted, I looked at him for a sign of whether or not he even took any pleasure in what he'd just done. He seemed so empty of emotion. "Take me to the humans."

I tensed at the thought of what they wanted the humans for.

The Catacombs.

Out of breath, I didn't have time to think it through. My immediate thought was to get to the Catacombs before the Elders could use the vampires there to devour the humans we were trying to protect. I sped to the caves, hoping to leave the Elder behind.

It took but seconds before the visiting Elder gripped the back of my head painfully. "Where the hell do you think you're going?"

"Please, these humans... they're our friends."

"Friends?" White eyes turned red.

I doubted I'd ever been more terrified than I was at that moment.

I stared up at Xavier, his handsome face distorted by veins coming out of his skin, as if his body was straining to contain the unwanted invasion of the dark force inside him.

"You make friends of these worms? They're good for nothing but their blood." He grabbed my wrists and squeezed tight. "Has your nature taught you nothing?"

I yelped when he pulled me against him before raising my wrist up. Claws popped out of Xavier's fingers, cutting my wrist and letting blood flow.

Red eyes turned back to white. A smile crept into the corners of Xavier's lips.

I could practically sense the Elder's hunger. Since I'd become a vampire, I hadn't known what it was like to be a prey being hunted by a predator—to be the morsel being craved. Nothing prepared me for when the Elder bit into my wrist and drank deep.

By the time he was done, I felt weak and in need of blood myself. I wondered then if it was actually possible to bleed a vampire dry.

The Elder threw my wrist aside, blood dripping from the corners of his mouth as he straightened to his full height. "Not as sweet as a human, but it will have to do for now."

Screams began to fill the atmosphere. The sound was coming from the Catacombs. My heart dropped. The thought of suffering any more loss than we already had was tearing me apart.

"Please."

I wasn't given a moment to speak. Instead, I was yanked toward the sounds of death.

Chapter 29: Aiden

Claudia's face twisted in horror when Yuri's eyes turned a shade of blood before he began devouring the first girl he got a hold of.

"Get out of here! Now!" She pointed at Gavin, who, along with Zinnia, and Craig, one of the hunters, was already running toward a dark corridor inside the cave system. I didn't bother to look around me.

I was never the kind of person who ran away. I preferred to stay and fight. Had it been just the vampires or the strange giant dogs that came with them, I would've stayed, but invisible monsters that took over the bodies of friends... I had no idea how to battle against something like that. The only recourse was escape. That way, we could figure out what to do.

I took one last look at Yuri, a man whom—even though he was hundreds of years older than me—was almost like a son. My heart fell when he held a young woman who'd grown up at the Catacombs and bled her dry. Claudia tried to pull him away from the girl, but with one blow, the blonde vampire was thrown several feet away from him.

I stepped forward to help the beautiful blonde only to have Gavin hold me back. "Aiden, there's nothing we can do to help. All we can do right now is save ourselves."

Despite my inclination to stay behind, Gavin was telling the truth. I would've been a fool to remain, so I ended up following Gavin into a series of tunnels I'd never even known existed at the Catacombs.

"Where are we going? Where are you taking us?"

Since I met her, Zinnia had never been the picture of sanity, but as Ian led us through narrow tunnels that led out of the Catacombs with only a flashlight to shed light before us, she was insufferable in her delusion that she was still in control.

"Shut her up," Gavin seethed through gritted teeth.

"I demand to know where we're going!"

"Be silent, Zinnia," I reprimanded her. "If you want to come with us, then it's in your best interest to keep those lips sealed."

Gavin, who was ahead of the pack, stopped. He began moving the torch from one side to another, the light flickering with the motion.

Several unsavory curses flowed out of the lips of Craig. "What the hell is this? It's a dead end."

"Shut up," was the only explanation any of us got from Gavin, who began feeling along one side of the wall. "This passage will lead us to the Port. From there, you guys can do whatever you want. Right now, just shut up."

The screams behind us escalated right before several piercing howls echoed in the corridor behind us. Rabid monsters began barking, their growls getting louder and louder.

"They're coming!" I announced. "Gavin, what's going on?"

Gavin remained silent, feeling through the wall for a couple of seconds—more serene than any of us were.

I pulled my gun out. I looked at Zinnia and Craig, who began retrieving their own weapons. "We're better off putting up a fight."

Right when I said it, one of their mutant dogs appeared, bright yellow eyes betraying its hunger and ruthlessness. Zinnia shot at it with the gun, bullets tainted with ultraviolet rays, designed to kill vampires. It hit the dog in the leg. The animal whimpered in pain, but unlike the effect one of those bullets would've had on vampires, the dog quickly recovered and pounced right on me.

Before I knew it, I'd been tackled to the ground, with the dog's sharp fangs biting into my neck. Craig and Zinnia fired more shots. I heard more growls. My vision began to blur. With whatever strength I had left in me, I stabbed the dog on top of me with my dagger. I twisted the knife inside it and threw it away from me. I struggled to my feet. That was when I realized that there had been no other dogs on its tail. All shots had been fired at the animal that had tackled me.

What on earth? I was beginning to feel dizzy. I wondered what the dog bite would cost me.

Zinnia's eyes were wide with horror. "We kept firing at it. It wouldn't die."

"What is it?" Craig hissed.

"Are you all right?" Zinnia checked on the wound on my neck.

I nodded, pressing my palm over my neck. "I'm fine. How's it going over there, Gavin?"

"I got it!" Gavin pressed against what appeared to be a well-hidden panel. There was a rumble within the narrow tunnel and before we knew it, an opening appeared where there was once a dead end.

"How are you so sure that this leads to the Port?" I asked.

Gavin grimaced as he looked at my wound. "I grew up here, remember? We have our secrets. Anyway, can you even make it? We're going to have to crawl through this."

I nodded curtly at him. "Let's go."

This time, they made me go right after Gavin with Craig taking up the rear end of the group. It felt like hours before we were able to finally reach the end of the tunnel.

When Gavin finally crawled out of the tunnel we were crouched in, my heart dropped when he gasped. I thought for sure that we had crawled right to our deaths. Dread washed over me even as I battled to keep my consciousness, suffering from the blood loss caused by the attack from the Elders' pet.

When I finally dragged myself out of that tunnel, I drew a sigh of relief when I saw welcome comrades standing before me.

Derek and Corrine.

"Aiden?" Derek creased his brows. "What happened to you?"

"Where's Sofia?" was all I could think about to ask. "Where's my daughter?"

Sorrow came over my son-in-law's face. "You need some rest. Corrine, get him into one of the rooms."

The worst possible scenario swept over me. "No." I shook my head. "Sofia… Derek, where's Sofia?" I didn't know whether it was the blood loss or the fact that Derek was standing in front of me without my daughter, but I was losing control. I tried to lunge for Derek, but my knees gave way beneath me, and my consciousness gave way to a memory.

I sat comfortably at the back of the black limousine, a safe distance away from the playground where my little girl was soon going to be. It'd been a year since I last saw her. The longing was almost unbearable.

It felt like hours before the bell rang for their lunch period and she appeared amidst a flurry of children her age. She walked beside Lyle's son, Ben, a fine young man by my estimation.

The first thing I noticed was how lackluster her eyes were. That was unlike the Sofia I knew. My little girl had bright curious eyes. My eyes. She was always looking for adventure. She looked at the world like she believed that she could conquer it if only she could explore all its secrets. From the moment she could walk, it'd been difficult to keep her in one place.

This time, however, while Ben hung out with the other boys from their class, she sought a quiet corner and brought out the items from her lunch bag. She ate her sandwich quietly, not minding anyone around her. She had an air of disinterest, detachment. She seemed disconnected from reality and I couldn't really blame her.

"What have I done to her?" I found myself saying out loud.

"Sir?" the driver asked.

"Nothing. I was just speaking my thoughts."

Sofia was no longer where I last saw her. I scanned the playground and saw her running toward the far right side of the school building—toward the sandbox.

My heart skipped a beat when I saw her face. She was clearly agitated. Ben and two other boys surrounded a much smaller boy who was trembling and retrieving from his pocket an inhaler. One of the boys pushed him to the ground.

Sofia came just when Ben was about to reach down and get the kid's lunch box. She didn't say anything. Instead, she planted her hands on her waist and just stared at Ben. No words, not even a single action. Just her presence.

I couldn't help but think about how beautiful she was, standing up to those boys. She helped the little boy up and shook her head disapprovingly at her best friend, who seemed truly sorry for his actions.

Ben caught up with her, clearly trying to explain himself, while the other two boys followed them, heads hung low.

"Your daughter has leadership."

I drew a short intake of breath when I realized that Arron was leaning on the limo, right by the window. He had his arms crossed over his chest.

He looked my way and without a hint of any expression said, "I think she takes after you."

"Sir... What are you doing here?"

He tapped on the car door. "Let me in."

I gulped as I opened the door, embarrassed that I was caught watching Sofia.

He took a seat beside me and shut the door. "What do you think you're doing?"

"I had to see her again."

"I thought you made your choice. She is a thing of the past."

"She's my daughter."

"You only torment yourself and endanger her if you keep doing this. If you can't stand being away from her, then take her back and raise her up as a hunter."

"I can't do that. She deserves a better life than the one we're living."

"Then leave her in your past. It's for her own good."

I wanted to object, to spout out all the reasons I couldn't be away from Sofia, but there was truth in what Arron was telling me, so all I ended up saying was, "Don't worry. This won't happen again. I just wanted to see her one last time." The confession slipped out of my mouth. "I really just want to see her eyes brighten up again."

All I got was a scoff from my superior.

"Let's just drive, shall we? We have a lot of business to see to today."

As the limousine began to move forward, I took one last look at my beautiful daughter, proud of her. Still, Sofia's eyes were void of life and I *blamed myself for it.*

I didn't know then that it would be years and years later before I would see my daughter's green eyes brighten once again—not until the first time I saw her look at Derek Novak.

Chapter 30: Derek

"You have to keep your calm, Derek." Corrine reminded me of the same thing Ibrahim had been telling me over and over again during my stay at the witches' Sanctuary. "You don't want to blow the Port up."

Aiden had been brought to one of the cells at the Port. Corrine had taken care of his neck wound and left the two hunters, Zinnia and Craig, to look after their former boss. I had half a mind to feed him my blood only to be reminded that I was no longer a vampire. Reminded of how I'd healed back at the dungeon at The Blood Keep, I wondered if it were at all possible that I retained my healing abilities. Given my tempestuous struggle with fire, however, I decided that I wasn't about to experiment on my father-in-law.

Seated around a circular table, feeling helpless despite the power I contained within me, I felt the heat rising up to my palms as I tried to wrap my mind around everything that Gavin reported to me.

Fear took hold of me at the thought of the dangers my people were facing. *How on earth can we even attempt to rescue Sofia when we're in so much chaos ourselves?*

"And you weren't able to rescue anyone else?"

"It was chaos, Derek. There wasn't much we could do," Gavin explained. "Your sister had a plan to get all women and children to the Chilling chambers, to hide them from the Elders, but the Elders found out where they were and they..." The redhead's face drained of all color.

I didn't even want to ask about the details. I doubted I'd be able to control the fire burning within me. "Where's Vivienne?"

"I haven't seen her at all. I'm not sure where she is."

"What happened to Aiden?"

He visibly shuddered. "The Elders came with these dogs. I've never seen anything like them before. One followed us to the tunnels. We couldn't kill them even with the guns. It was only when Aiden stabbed the dog that it stopped, but the dog had already bitten into his neck."

My brows rose. Eli had mentioned not long after I woke up from my slumber that he'd done some work with The Underground. Something about turning stray dogs into vampires. It didn't quite work out the way they'd expected. The dogs had the same bloodlust and heightened senses that vampires had, but killing them was another thing. Ending them required silver. "They must've taken the beasts when they attacked The Underground. Eli would know how to control these things. Do you have any idea where he is?"

"They took him to The Blood Keep several months ago. No explanations. They just said that he was needed at the Elder's castle."

Somehow, it gave me relief to know that Sofia wasn't alone at The Blood Keep, that Eli was there with her.

Still, I feared for her. The dreams hadn't stopped, the dark premonitions of our possible future—a future I was determined not to allow to happen.

Lost in my own turmoil, I barely paid attention to the young man staring at me, awaiting my orders.

"Derek." Corrine spoke up. "What do you want us to do?"

I rose to my feet and began pacing, thinking everything through. My primary goal was to find a way to attack The Blood Keep and save Sofia. I had to believe that she was alive, that she was waiting for me. To do that, I needed my people—a people the Elders were destroying.

"We'll have to go back to the Catacombs. We have to save as many of them as we can."

"That's suicide." Gavin said.

I could sense his hesitation. I couldn't blame him. They knew that without Sofia, I was a volatile force that no one could control. We'd gone a long way in terms of building a trust and a friendship, but I was still Derek Novak, the ruthless leader who'd built The Shade, and considering how I was oozing tension at that moment, he was probably expecting my temper to erupt any time. I had to maintain control, or I would lose whatever trust these men still had in me.

The two hunters stepped out of the room. I eyed both of them—Zinnia and Craig. I recognized them from the time I had to spend at the hunters' headquarters. I was fond of neither of them.

"He's awake," Zinnia announced, not bothering to hide her disdain for me. "He asked to see you."

I made my way to the cell. The last time I saw Aiden, he'd been walking Sofia down the aisle. Guilt came over me. *He trusted me with his daughter, and now she's...*

"How are you doing?" I asked half-heartedly.

"You need to get my daughter out of The Blood Keep." Aiden's voice was low, cold, almost accusing.

"My thoughts exactly."

"No, you don't understand. You don't have much time. You need to get her out of there. Now."

"Not much time? What are you talking about?"

"She's going to give birth soon, and the Elder... he's after the child. You can't just..." He paused when he saw the shock in my eyes. "You didn't know?"

Suddenly, all of it made sense. The witches had kept on saying that I had time, that there was no rush. *They figured that the Elder wouldn't kill Sofia—not until she gave birth.* The news began to sink in and the fire began to build up. If I didn't get out of there, I would burst into flames and end up murdering Aiden and the rest of the men.

Not sure if I still had my speed, I leapt up and started running. Within a few seconds, I was in the wide open field that separated the Port from the thick dark forest of The Shade.

I didn't have the time to process how I got there so quickly, because within a few breaths, flames shot out of my palms as I screamed in agony over all the worry, all the pain that I felt over my Sofia's predicament. That she was carrying my child, that I could even have a child, was supposed to bring me the greatest joy. Instead, at that moment, all I felt was guilt that I wasn't there for her, that Sofia was going through her first pregnancy without me. Tears spilled from my eyes.

A forest fire was now well on its way. I had no idea how to quench it, so I was relieved when Corrine appeared, whispering words to conjure a mighty wind to battle the flames.

When the fire was gone, she approached me.

"Did you know about her pregnancy?"

"I…"

"Corrine, did you know?"

Corrine nodded.

"And you allowed her to go through it on her own? I thought you were her friend!"

"There was nothing I could do about it, Derek. The Ageless wouldn't allow me to intervene. Not in this case."

"The Ageless can appear at The Blood Keep and whisk my wife to safety anytime she pleases and yet she chooses to remain perched in your Sanctuary, looking down as the rest of us in the other realms suffer. She sits there high and lofty as *Sofia* suffers! How can that not matter to you, Corrine? What's the point of all that power if she doesn't use it?"

"We're only allowed to intervene to maintain the balance. The Ageless saw fit to keep you alive in order to do that. You would've been killed if she hadn't taken you to The Sanctuary. She has done her part."

"I can't believe you're defending her."

"We have our parts to play in the grand scheme of things, Derek. The Ageless cannot, under any circumstance, abuse the power she has been given to…"

"Stop. Just stop, Corrine. My wife is held captive by a sadistic monster who won't hesitate to bend and break her any way he can. She is more fragile than she ever was before, now that she's with child, and I come home to this! How am I going to help her, Corrine? I can't even get a grip on these powers that *your* ancestor bestowed upon me!"

That was it. I'd reached my breaking point. I was at the end of my rope. I had no idea what to do and I couldn't help but blame the witches for not helping.

"The way I see it, Derek, the battle has always been between the vampires and the Guardians. We exist to maintain the balance between the two. You humans... you're simply caught in the middle. Here at The Shade, the vampires are starting to get the upper hand. If you want an ally, you have to go to the Guardians."

"How on earth do I do that?"

"You go to the hunters."

What she was implying sank in slowly—a revelation. The war between our realm's vampires and the hunters was only a miniscule version of the greater war that was going on in realms that weren't our own.

I knew then what I had to do. I was about to return to the Port to let them know that we were headed for hunters' headquarters when Cameron staggered into the field, bleeding, barely able to breathe.

"Cameron," I gasped.

"You need to stop it, Derek. I was barely able to escape. They're turning all the humans into vampires. They're going to kill everyone who was loyal to you. I..." He broke into a sob. "Liana..."

Cameron, one of the strongest and toughest men I'd ever had the pleasure of meeting, crumbled right before me.

I looked back through all the years that I'd fought and bled with Cameron. I couldn't remember a time when the Scottish warrior had been as distraught. I wasn't even certain if I'd ever seen him cry before.

A million thoughts whirled through my mind—questions, fears, apprehensions, doubts. All I could do was stand there and clench my fists, desperately trying to rein in the heat building up inside of me. I had half a mind to just run into the forest and burn everything down. I fought to maintain control, focusing all my concentration on keeping all those emotions and questions locked in.

It's not like Cameron can answer them anyway. Before Sofia came into my life, I couldn't have cared less that my friend was in pain. I would've pried all the information I could get from him—with force if necessary. This time, I couldn't dishonor the legacy Sofia had left in my life, because if I did, I wouldn't be able to face her again.

Corrine wasn't as sympathetic. "What happened? What's going on at the Catacombs? How were you able to get away? What did they do to you?"

Cameron's already pale complexion grew several shades lighter. He was white as a sheet, and his eyes grew distant as tears continued to stream down his face. "We're nothing to them. Just toys they can play with. Creatures they can embody. Vessels."

Vessels. I had no idea what Cameron was implying, but the moment it came out of his lips, fear carved itself into my bones.

Corrine didn't seem as moved. She was more focused on Cameron's wounds, her brows furrowed as she examined him. "What do you mean by vessels? How were you able to escape?"

"I didn't escape. Liana did this to me."

My breath hitched. *How is that possible?*

"One of the Elders used her as a vessel. Then they forced me to fight her. I couldn't do it. No matter how Liana hit me, fought me, I didn't have the heart to strike her. I knew that it was the Elder, but…" Cameron broke down.

I understood. There was no way he was ever going to hurt the love of his life. Centuries of marriage had made Cameron and Liana one of the most loyal and loving couples I'd ever met. I'd stood witness to many of their fights and fallouts, but there was never a question that they were going to stick together.

"How then were you able to escape?"

"One more blow, and she would've ended me. She would've killed me. She raised her hands and when she did, I saw a tear run down her cheek. My Liana was still there, conscious even as that monster took over her body. She was about to deal the final blow, but they stopped her."

Corrine pushed at his rib and he groaned in pain. "They used some sort of spell on you to suppress your healing abilities."

I stared at Corrine, wondering if she was even the same person who'd once convinced me to treat Sofia as an equal and not as a slave. *Would she act this way if Sofia were here?*

"Why? Why wouldn't they just let her kill you?" The words had already slipped out of my mouth before I realized how insensitive they were.

Cameron seemed unfazed by it. His eyes were still distant—somewhere far, somewhere painful. "They let me go to find you. They know you're here, Derek."

"Then why aren't they coming for me?"

"They want you to surrender. They sent me as a messenger. They want you to willingly give yourself up to become one of their vessels."

"Why on earth would I ever agree to..." Blue-violet eyes flashed into my consciousness. My heart stopped. "Vivienne," I muttered. "They're going to use her against me, aren't they?"

"One of the Elders has made a vessel out of Xavier. If you don't surrender yourself, they're going to make Vivienne fight him to the death. Tonight."

The heat shot out of my palms before I could control it. To my relief, the flames didn't go toward Cameron, or it would've been the end of him. It felt like an eternity before I could reel the fire back in and gain back my self-control. By the time I was able to stop the fire, I had collapsed on the ground, while Corrine conjured a couple of spells in order to keep the fire from burning down The Shade.

I stared up at the witch who had kept The Shade protected with her spells and found myself both angered and curious at what exactly she was capable of. *Whose side is this woman on?* I'd once thought that she was on our side, especially seeing her fondness for Sofia and the way she'd gained the respect and loyalty of the Naturals, earning herself a prestigious position of honor at the Catacombs. This time, however, after having met her superiors, I wondered what game she was playing.

Before I could keep myself from doing it, I stood to my feet and grabbed her by the wrists. My palms still sweltering with heat, she screamed in pain as my touch seared her skin.

Defiant brown eyes looked at me and I could've sworn then that she was going to come up with a spell to destroy me. Instead, Corrine tried to tolerate the pain as she stared directly into my eyes. Through gritted teeth, she muttered, "What do you want?"

"How powerful are you, witch?"

Her lips were sealed tight, but a thought came to me—as if she had communicated with me telepathically. *More than you can ever imagine.*

"You're going to help us," I demanded.

"Why would I do that?"

"Because you are Cora's descendant, and no matter what the Ageless or the witches of The Sanctuary stand for, you are loyal to your ancestor. You can't deny that."

"An ancestor *you* killed."

"You know why it had to happen. Don't tell me you wouldn't have killed her yourself had you been given the chance. Emilia was just a shell. Cora would've wanted her dead. For all we know, Emilia might have also been just a vessel."

Moistened eyes stared back at me. Corrine tightened her jaw, as if she were trying to fight me.

"Don't pretend that you don't care about us or The Shade. You might have been brought here under circumstances you aren't entirely pleased with, but you can't look me in the eye and tell me that you hold no affection for this island. Don't tell me that Sofia— or the fact that she's bearing my child while in the grasp of a sadistic monster—doesn't mean anything to you."

"I care about Sofia and you know it." Even as the witch said those words, affection flashed in the otherwise stoic expression at the mention of my wife's name.

My heart warmed at that gesture. Sofia had a way of doing that to people, getting them to care. "Then why aren't you doing something to help us? Do you really think Sofia would still see you the way she did if you don't help us? Is she not this place's queen? You know she loves the people being tormented by these Elders."

Corrine's shoulders sagged in resignation. "What do you want me to do?"

"First, answer my question." I shrugged a shoulder. "*Exactly* how powerful are you?"

Chapter 31: Sofia

Walking was getting harder as my belly grew. I was beginning to have my doubts about our escape plan. As we walked along the gardens so I could get a breath of fresh air, I hooked my arm over Eli's and expressed my apprehensions.

"Is this going to work, Eli? Can Shadow even carry us?"

"He won't have to carry me. I'll still have my speed. Granted, it won't last long, but I think I can make it. The Elder's people won't be able to come after us, not in sunlight."

"Maybe it's too big a risk. We don't even know where we are, Eli. How are we supposed to know where to go? How on earth are we going to get to the hunters?"

"All we have to do is get to a phone or a computer, anything that will allow us to get in touch with the hunters. You still have contacts from the time you were there, don't you?"

I nodded. I had one. Julian was the man my father had assigned to train me in combat while I was in hunter headquarters. I never quite did catch on. I was ever the pacifist. Lately, I'd been wishing that I'd listened more to him when I had the chance. *Maybe then I wouldn't be in situations like this. I wouldn't need men to save me.*

I gave Eli an apologetic look, ashamed that I wasn't giving him any security or reassurance when he was risking his neck to help me.

Eli returned my gaze, concern traced over his features. "Do these doubts have something to do with the Elder attacking you?"

I drew a breath. The slightest mention of the unpleasant encounter still made me shiver. A couple days after the visit from the Elder, I was still so jumpy, afraid that he was around, that he was listening in on my conversations. The only assurance I had that he wasn't around was the recollection of his presence.

If the Elder is around, it's impossible not to know. Anybody could sense the wickedness, the fear, the incapacitating cold.

I had no idea how to tell Eli that since the attack, Kiev had been talking about escape. That meant that I wasn't sure if Eli could be there with us. I felt responsible for Eli's presence at The Blood Keep. *If it weren't for me, he'd still be back at The Shade. Safe.*

My conscience scolded me. It was one thing to consider leaving Olga behind—we didn't have a history together. But Eli... we might not have had a personal connection, but he was risking his life to help me escape The Blood Keep. Not only that, he was one of Derek's dearest and most loyal allies.

Eli must've considered my lack of a response as a *yes.* "Sofia, the Elder can't touch you unless you have a significant amount of darkness within you. That's why he was never able to get to Derek after you came to The Shade. Your light took over."

Eli's words were tearing me apart. I was trying not to cry as I listened to him remind me of a light I no longer had. I was torn. I hated to admit it to myself, but I was willing to consider escaping with Kiev. *I have to do this for my children.*

"Eli... I need to tell you something."

Eli remained silent, waiting for me to speak up.

"Kiev has been talking about helping me escape. He has been since the Elder's attack and..."

"You're considering it?" The tinge of apprehension was evident in Eli's voice.

"I'm going to give birth soon, Eli. I'm just afraid that..."

"I understand," he assured me. "If I had even the smallest amount of trust for this man, I would recommend that you go, but this is Kiev we're talking about. He was in love with Natalie Borgia and yet he tortured and killed her right in front of all of us. Are you sure that he's after your safety?"

"I'm not certain at all, but..."

The mention of Kiev being in love with Natalie took me aback. I'd had no idea. Kiev was a wildly unpredictable person and I'd never quite figured him out, but it had never dawned on me that he could ever be in love. *Why do I see that as a positive thing?* I tried to dwell on what Eli said—that Kiev had killed Natalie—but for some reason, I was holding on to the hope that Kiev could still be saved.

"I will respect whatever decision you make, Sofia. I know the risk of my plan for escape. I won't blame you if you choose to trust Kiev and you won't need to worry about me. I can take care of myself. I just want to be sure that you know what you're getting yourself into."

"Thanks, Eli. I need to think things through." I was relieved that I'd told him. "Right now, what do you know about Kiev and Natalie?"

As Eli told me what he knew—not that there was much of it—I

saw then what Derek saw in him. I'd always seen Eli as this intelligent person we all went to when we wanted to figure out how to do something at The Shade, but his rational nature also brought out a side of him that was good. He didn't take things personally. He understood why I was torn, why I felt I had to do what I had to do.

Genuinely grateful for Eli and his support, I knew I had several things to figure out and soon. *Can I really trust Kiev?*

The fact that he hadn't taken advantage of me was, to me, a sign that there still was a flicker of good inside of him, but I was uneasy. Eli was right. Something was wrong. Something about Kiev suddenly wanting to help me didn't sit right with me, but I couldn't afford not to take this into consideration. I had to at least see if Kiev meant it, if Kiev could possibly provide me a way out.

I owe my children that possibility. I can't deprive myself of that chance.

Deep inside, however, I knew that this wasn't me. I was being selfish, putting my own needs before the people around me, but as hard as it was for me to admit it, I no longer cared.

CHAPTER 32: VIVIENNE

I'd never thought that my heart could break for Claudia the way it did that night. As Yuri—or at least the monster within him—dealt her another punch, I couldn't help but cringe at the way she looked at him, the love in her eyes, pleading with him to overcome whatever it was that had taken over him.

Yuri's eyes, on the other hand, remained pure black, sometimes flashing a bright red when Claudia's blood splattered all over the floor. I couldn't even imagine the pain Yuri was going through. I whispered more prayers than I ever had in my entire life, hoping that he wasn't conscious, because as much as it pained Claudia to be beaten up by the man she loved, I knew Yuri enough to know that even if he had been possessed by this dark spirit, he would still blame himself.

I looked across the makeshift arena the Elders had had several of the humans put together. It was a large circle, lined with thick ropes, and was situated right smack at the middle of the Catacombs. Sam and I were chained together on one side. Ashley and Xavier stood on the other side. Ashley had her hands planted on her waist, eyes shifting from a pure yellow at one point to a powdery white at another. Xavier, on the other hand, had his arms crossed over his chest. His eyes were just a pure black. His brows furrowed. He didn't seem to be having any fun at all.

Based on body language, the Elder who had grabbed hold of Xavier seemed to be higher in position than the rest of them. I stared at him, my heart aching.

Is he still there? Does he see what's happening? What's going on inside his mind right now?

"Princess, look." Sam nudged me on the side.

Liana bit into the neck of one of the humans. I wondered why on earth Sam would want me to watch my best friend drain a human dry, but it quickly became evident that Liana wasn't killing the human. She was turning him.

"They turn the humans to vampires. Why is that necessary?"

"I think it's because they can only use vampires as vessels." I was barely able to squeak my theory out.

I looked away from Liana, wondering how she felt about almost killing Cameron moments ago. When they'd stopped her from ending Cameron's life, I'd been so relieved. It would destroy her to know that her beloved had died at her hands. When the Elders had revealed that they'd stopped her from ending Cameron's life only because they intended to make him give Derek a message—me in exchange for him—all the relief I'd felt quickly faded away. While the idea that Derek was on the island gave me a shred of hope, the recollection that he was human once again, devoid of the power he'd once wielded as a vampire, quickly made me wish that he hadn't shown up at all.

I would rather die than be the reason for my brother's death. I told myself that he was the only family I had, but remembered that this was no longer true. *I have Sofia, and now that she's with child, I'll have her children too.* I'd never thought I could ever think of a hunter as family—the notorious Aiden Claremont especially—but he had become family too.

Are they enough to replace losing my brother? I caught the thought, surprised that I could even think it. There was a time when I would've readily given my life for my brother's, but if I were to be honest with myself, at that moment, I wished that things would change. I knew that Derek would give his life for me, but I'd never wanted him to until that very moment.

I realized that I wanted what he had. *I want the chance that he got. I want to experience falling in love, getting married, going on my honeymoon, raising a family. I've only done one of those. I fell in love. With Xavier.* As I stared at the shell that he'd become when the Elder took over his body, I realized that I wanted to become human and I hoped that he wanted that too, that he wanted to be the father of my children, and that we could live finite, mortal lives together.

That was why I was hoping that Derek would indeed give himself up for me. For the first time in my life, I was actually dreaming of a future that I truly loved and desired.

"Enough!" Xavier screamed, clapping his hands as he gave Yuri an approving nod.

That jolted me to attention. My heart dropped. Claudia lay in the arena, unconscious, bruised black and blue, barely able to move. I immediately checked her chest, watching for it to heave and sigh, wondering if we had lost her. I was never too fond of Claudia—apart from Yuri, none of us were—but she had only begun to live out the second chance that Yuri's love had allowed her. I didn't want to see her meet this kind of end.

I held my breath when it seemed that she was no longer breathing.

Yuri was standing over her. His claws retracted. Blood dripped from his fists. A cold sneer was on his face, manic and disturbing, almost as if the grin had been pasted on his face. I searched for a sign that he actually found pleasure in what he'd just done and found none.

Are these creatures even capable of real pleasure? Or do they just do all of these things in order to make us all miserable?

"Is she dead?" Xavier asked one of the humans he'd sent to check on Claudia's body.

The trembling middle-aged woman who was stooped over Claudia's motionless form shook her head after she checked Claudia's pulse.

Xavier frowned. He set his eyes on Yuri. "Do you want to kill her off?"

Yuri flexed his muscles and cracked his knuckles. "I'd rather wait for her to heal and beat her up again. Pretty little Claudia was such a disappointment to all of us. She had such potential to be true evil, a perfect vessel for us, but no, she had to fall in love with that dismal sap."

"That dismal sap would be you, fool," Xavier responded without a tinge of amusement in his voice. Just contempt. I wondered if he was seeing his fellow Elder or just Yuri—another one of the vampires who'd 'betrayed' their kind by being loyal to my brother.

Yuri chuckled dryly before shrugging. "I forgot. I'm not used to such weak vessels."

"You can always end him once you're tired of him."

"Only after I make him kill the love of his life."

We were in the presence of pure evil and even though they'd only occupied several of us—Xavier, Yuri, Ashley and Liana, as far as I knew—I could sense that there were more of them lurking, waiting for a vessel to make their own. Invisible creatures surrounded me, just waiting to take over. I shuddered even as one of the humans dragged Claudia out of the arena.

Yuri walked out almost listlessly. The moment he stepped out of the arena, he grabbed hold of the nearest human and bit into the man's neck. After several seconds, he drew away from the man and screamed, "Blood! Invigorating blood!"

"They can't do this," Sam muttered next to me. His hand clutched mine—completely unlike the vampire guard, who had always acted in a friendly, albeit rather stiff, manner around me. I squeezed his hand as tight as I could.

Ashley walked toward the middle of the arena, crouched down on the ground and dabbed her finger into Claudia's blood still splattered all over the stone floor. She grinned as she took a whiff of the blood. Her eyes flashed a brilliant red.

It was as if she were gaining power from just the smell of the spilled blood. Unsettled, I looked for Xavier.

I found him grabbing Liana's arm and planting a kiss on her lips.

I swallowed hard, finding it difficult to see any other woman in his arms—the fact that it was my best friend made it worse. It seemed he sensed me looking because after kissing Liana, he sped toward me.

"Jealous, princess?" he asked me mockingly. "You should've given yourself to this man while you still had the chance. But don't worry. I can still let him—and you—have your kiss." He kissed me full on the mouth.

I'd never thought that I could find a kiss from Xavier disgusting. I had to keep reminding myself that this wasn't Xavier, but I couldn't help but feel betrayed.

Why isn't he strong enough to fight this? Why aren't any of us? I wondered what it would be like for Sofia and Derek. *Would they be able to fight this?* I recalled all the times that Derek had been able to fight the darkness just because of his love for Sofia. Just hearing her hum their song or even just seeing her... It turned him to light.

I found myself resenting them for their love. *Now, they're even immune to being turned into an Elder's vessel. They're both human.* Should I ever get out alive, I would turn human as soon as I could. I would go as far as force Sofia to let me drink her blood just so I could have an immune's blood in my system.

Xavier pulled his lips away from me. I looked at him and all I saw was the monster that he now was.

He backhanded me in the face. I was thrown on the ground several feet away. It was only then that I realized that I was already unchained and that Sam was already at the arena, being dealt his first blow from the Elder who possessed Ashley.

Xavier grabbed a fistful of my hair and made me focus on the fight. "Watch, Vivienne. Watch your friends bleed."

To my surprise, Sam fought back, pushing Ashley to the ground with one massive upper cut.

My heart sank. *What has become of us? They're turning us into* them. Only then did I realize that maybe that was their intention all along. They wanted us to become just like them. *That's why they spent hundreds of years turning humans into vampires. But why?*

Xavier gasped with seeming delight as Ashley rose to her feet.. "This just got interesting. I knew it all along. Your love is weak. None of you have the kind of love Derek and Sofia had for each other. But don't get me wrong, princess. If they were in your situation, they wouldn't be able to fight this either."

I recalled how Derek had been able to break Emilia's hold over him. Desperate to stop the madness, I rose to my feet, pressed my body against Xavier's and whispered into his ear, "Please. Drink my blood."

I hoped that as Sofia's blood running into his veins had jolted my brother out of Emilia's curse, my blood running into Xavier's might have the same effect. I wasn't human nor was I an immune like Sofia, but I had to try.

Just as Xavier's fangs were about to sink under my skin, my brother's voice boomed across the cavernous walls of the Catacombs.

"Stop this madness right now!"

Chapter 33: Sofia

"What's bothering you, Sofia?" Kiev tucked a loose strand of my hair beneath my ear.

We were in my bedroom. I was on the bed, sitting with my back against the headboard. He had taken the liberty of resting his head on my lap before, after hours of telling me one morbid story about his past after another, he knelt on the bed, facing me, and asked me that question.

"Nothing," I lied. "Why would you think that something's bothering me?"

"I don't know. You haven't spoken much for the past hour or so."

That's because you're doing all the talking. Frankly, I wish I could unhear the things you just told me. Hearing stories from a vampire who'd spent hundreds of years serving the evil that was the Elder didn't exactly make for a peaceful night's sleep.

I shrugged. "I just don't have much to say. That's all."

"I appreciate that you listened."

He was being kind. It was terrifying to be around this version of him. I was always on my toes, wondering when he was about to burst out in fury over the slightest mistake.

To worsen my already bundled-up nerves, he began rubbing my belly. "Are you excited to meet them? Have you decided on names?"

During our honeymoon Derek and I had playfully talked about the children we were going to have. We'd always fought over what to name our child should we have a girl, but we'd both agreed on what we would name our son. *Benjamin.*

There was no questioning that. Ben deserved that honor.

Not knowing what had become of Abby, and having been strictly ordered never to inquire about her again, I said the first thing that came to mind. "Ben and Abby, I guess." I was bothered by how curious Kiev seemed to be when it came to my children. Since his plan for escape, he'd been fawning over me almost as if he were the father of the children I was bearing.

Though it unnerved me, I had to run with it if I were to have any chance of compromise with my captor.

So, whenever he was in one of these moods, I plastered a smile on my face, pretending that I was flattered—even delighted—by his attention.

Kiev stared at me. "Ben and Abby? That's sweet, but just so you know, it would be an honor if you named your son after my father. Serghei."

I gave him a look, wondering if he was joking. "His name is Ben."

A flash of anger crossed his face, but he reeled it in.

What is going on? I wanted to believe that this was a sign of goodness in him, but I'd never felt more unsettled by him than I did at that moment.

"Kiev…" I spoke up tentatively. "Are you really going to help me escape?"

His eyes darkened to a bloody crimson. I could sense his suspicions rising. "Why do you ask?"

"I'm in my third trimester. I would really like to not have to bear my children here at The Blood Keep and you mentioned that you would…"

"Just be ready. I don't need to tell you about my plans. You just have to go along with what you are told to do and everything will be okay."

"Can you not give me a hint or something? Anything? I just really want to be able to hold on to some sort of assurance that…"

He grabbed my jaw and forced me to look into his eyes. "I'm your assurance. Drop this subject, Sofia. Or I will make you bleed."

I nodded. "Fine," was my curt reply.

He let go of my jaw, took a deep breath, stared into blank space for a few seconds then began caressing my hair gently. "You're going to be all right."

He's a madman. Eli is right. How can I ever trust him? His mood swings were so erratic, I couldn't keep up with them.

Silence took over the room. I asked myself what I would've done had I been with Derek. I remembered how I'd coped through everything at The Shade.

I did it through laughter. All those times I'd spent with Derek, cutting through the tension between us by making him watch movies or pulling him to the music room and charming him to play me some music.

I was intrigued by whether the approach I'd used on Derek would work on Kiev. I was sick of always feeling like I was at the edge of my nerves when around Kiev.

If there's any hope of Kiev ever coming to the light, of ever embracing goodness, then this has got to work.

Without thinking things through, I moved over the edge of the bed and got on my feet. Facing him, I took both his hands in mine and met his questioning gaze with as joyful an expression as I could conjure.

"Dance with me, Kiev."

"What?"

"Come on, don't you miss dancing?"

"Seeing as I've never danced in my entire life, no. I don't miss it."

"Seriously?" My eyes widened. "You're what, fifteen thousand years old?" I teased him. "And you don't know how to dance?"

"Why would I ever want to dance?"

I should've known that Kiev's sense of humor would leave much to be desired. I rolled my eyes. "Why are you so devoid of joy?" *He lives at The Blood Keep, Sofia. What's there to be joyful about?*

"How is dancing supposed to give joy? Only fools find pleasure in flailing their arms around, swaying to music and acting like complete fools."

"Were you always like this? I mean, even before you became the Elder's spawn?"

Kiev seemed bothered by the question. "I'm not going to dance. You shouldn't be dancing either. You're going to give birth anytime."

"Way to dampen the mood, vampire." I rolled my eyes. I walked away from him and toward the large grilled windows in my bedroom. I leaned against one of the windows and drew the curtains back. I found myself staring at the dark night sky. "I need sunlight. There's barely any light in this place." *There's barely any light in* you. *I'm not even sure if you have any!*

"We give you plenty of vitamins to make up for the lack of it."

"I need my husband." I bit my lip. I was gearing myself up for a rough hand gripping a fistful of my hair or perhaps even a slap in the face, but this time, Kiev didn't seem angry at all.

It was beyond me why he seemed fine with me mentioning my need for Derek when all the other times I talked about my husband, it drove him to a frenzy. He was perhaps in another one of those mood swings of his and that particular moment, he was more considerate than freakish. He almost looked sorry for me, as if he sympathized with my plight.

"I see it, you know."

"See what?"

"How you brought light into his life… how you were able to do the impossible and influence the notorious Derek Novak for good."

His kindness was more unnerving than his acts of terror and I tried to keep the tremble from my voice when I coyly asked, "Oh yeah? How?"

"You are light itself."

"Right," I scoffed. "I don't seem to be lighting you up, do I?"

"Maybe I'm too soaked in darkness to ever be consumed by light."

I shook my head. Truth be told, I doubted I had any light left in me. Nights still terrorized me. Considering all the dark thoughts I'd entertained lately, I was always fearful that the Elder would come to me.

Just talking about Derek felt like healing to my longing soul.

"Derek had the light inside of him all along. I never told him before, but he brought light into my life just as much as he says I brought light to his. He just needed convincing that he still had good in him. You are who you choose to be. No matter how much light is shed upon you, if you still choose to remain in darkness, that's your doing, not anyone else's."

I felt like a hypocrite saying the words. I needed to follow my own advice, but I justified my situation. *Who can blame me? No light has been shed upon me at all since I was last with Derek.* I missed him so much, the pain was almost unbearable. *I don't deserve this.*

Kiev rose to his feet and stood behind me. His hand brushed through my hair. His touch gave me goose bumps, sending shivers down my spine. He wrapped his arms around me and began stroking my belly, I could feel him press his face against the back of my neck, breathing my scent in.

I hated when he touched me. He didn't have the right to. *It should be Derek with me right now, holding me.*

"I hate that I ever got to know you, Sofia."

The feeling's mutual.

"I hate that you gave me something I never should've had."

That he would think that I'd freely given him anything sickened me. "And what's that, Kiev? What did I give you exactly?"

"Hope."

That was when I realized for certain how embittered I was by the months I'd spent at The Blood Keep. I felt nothing for Kiev. Instead, I hated him. I hated him for taking me away from Derek. The Blood Keep had changed me and inside, there existed a darkness I'd never known I could possess.

"You are light, Sofia, and I rue the day when that will be ruined. I'm sorry for what you're about to go through."

My heart stopped. He was a man of riddles. When he was speaking good, it still felt like the words were laced with an underlying wickedness. I never quite knew what to expect with him and that was both thrilling and fearsome to me. "What are you talking about, Kiev?"

He shook his head as he clung to me tightly, pushing my back against his chest. "I can't tell you, Sofia, but when it happens, know that there's nothing I could do to stop it."

A mixture of indignation, desperation and anger came over me as I broke away from his grasp, shaking my head. "No. Hell, no." I stepped away from him and spun around so he could see how enraged I was. "Nonsense. You have a choice. There is *always* a choice. If what's about to happen to me is so awful, you can help stop it. Don't tell me that you can't. You want to know how Derek turned to light? He stopped playing the part of a victim and began taking responsibility for his own actions! That's how. He owned up to his choices instead of cowering away from them."

Kiev stared back at me coolly. He seemed to be unmoved by my outburst. In fact, he seemed amused. "Interesting," he noted. "We're going to escape, Sofia. Soon. Just be ready." His stare went from my face to my belly and I could swear I saw hunger spark in his eyes.

I shuddered, wondering what on earth he had in mind. I couldn't figure him out. I felt like a toy whenever I was around him, and it seemed he never tired of playing games with me. Now, however, seeing the way he was staring at my stomach, as if he could see my unborn children, I knew that I would be a fool to trust him.

"Is all this just a game to you?" I hissed.

He shrugged. "What if it is?"

I remembered the first night I'd spent at The Shade when Vivienne had told me that I was just a pawn. That memory was quickly followed by another one with Vivienne telling me that I wasn't a pawn after all. I was the queen.

Neither matters. Pawn or queen, they're just pieces to be yanked around by whoever is playing the game.

I was tired of feeling so powerless. Aside from Eli, there were only two people I encountered on a daily basis at The Blood Keep: Kiev and the servant girl. I'd taken note after note of their every move. I didn't understand either of them fully, but the little I knew, I had to use to my advantage.

It might seem like Kiev was the one in control, but he was just a piece in the game like me.

There is always a choice, I'd screamed at Kiev only moments ago. It was time I lived up to my own ideology.

In an upsurge of bravado, I determined to myself that I was no longer going to be played. By anyone. I made a decision to take control.

Kiev was right. *What if life is just a game?*

I gave Kiev my sweetest smile, and answered his question with a wink. "I'm wondering if you could teach me how to play."

He was intrigued. I saw it in his face, but at the same time, he stayed true to his character. He was taking on the role of a player. I'd just made my move. Now, he was about to make his.

He didn't leave that room until he was certain that he had me under his control and cooperation. I played the part of a student, eager to learn from the master.

Of course, the moment Kiev left and I met up with Eli for a walk in the garden, I was delighted to find how Shadow responded to him with seeming eagerness and loyalty.

"So?" Eli asked. "Have you made your decision?"

I nodded. "Yes. Let's get out of here."

I thought I was playing Kiev. I was a fool to think that I could win against him. I had no idea just how good a player he was. I didn't know it then, but I had already lost before the game even started.

Chapter 34: Derek

Xavier, a man I'd trusted with my life more times than I could count, strutted toward me. He was barely recognizable, his veins sticking out of his neck as if he was about to burst, his eyes sallow and a haunting white. He had Vivienne's back pressed against him, gripping her hair while the other arm coiled around her waist. The tension inside the room was electrifying. Currents of fire were beginning to build within my veins. I felt like I could explode any time.

However, there was a strength in Vivienne's eyes that I'd never seen before. I was expecting her to tremble, to shake and cower at the danger surrounding her, but no, something had changed with my twin and I was left wondering whether it was a change for the good. She glanced at me and quickly looked away. A sick feeling formed in my gut. Something was wrong with her and I knew it.

Noticing that my attention was no longer on him, Xavier—or whoever had taken over his body—grabbed her by the hair and made her yelp. Considering that Ashley and Sam were still in this makeshift arena pounding on each other, it was difficult for me to focus on Xavier, but it seemed he was one to fight for all the attention he could get.

Who knew Elders could be such attention whores?

"Well, if it isn't the king of The Shade, honoring us with his presence." Xavier's eyes lifted toward mine, narrowed and intimidating. He began groping my sister, never losing eye contact with me in order to taunt me with my own helplessness.

"What do you want?" I clenched my fists, praying that I wouldn't end up exploding and burning everyone there.

"That's not a very diplomatic way to welcome your guests, is it now, oh powerful king? I think we ought to start with the pleasantries as is human custom, don't you?" The sneer on Xavier's face reminded me of every psychopathic villain I'd ever seen in those movies Sofia got me to watch during the first few months of her stay with me at The Shade. I had no question in my mind that whoever had possessed Xavier was one cold-blooded murderer.

Xavier fidgeted in a seeming attempt to recall "human custom". "So how does this actually go…" he muttered as his hand continued to violate my sister, his lips sickeningly close to her ear. "Oh yes…" He looked my way with an air of triumph. "Hello there, your highness. It is truly a pleasure to finally meet you."

I swore at him in response. I couldn't hide the spite that I felt toward him.

My disgust only amused him. He cocked his head to the side and hissed like the snake that he was. "I guess you're not very diplomatic, are you? It's always been this lovely creature in my arms who's been the picture of The Shade's diplomacy." He ran his tongue over Vivienne's cheek.

I wanted to snap his neck in two.

However, his taunts were not yet over. "Deciding not to kill Cameron paid off after all. How could it not when the message he gave was so powerful? When this beauty is within our grasp?"

Cold winds began to rush all around me. *Are they trying to quench the fire?* If so, they were failing at it. However, even with the power I possessed, I had no idea how to use it. It wasn't like I could just burn Xavier. The Elder would leave Xavier's body and find a new vessel.

"Let her go," was all I could manage to say.

"You're not in a position to be giving out commands here, king. I'm the ruler of this island now."

In retaliation over my audacity, he spun Vivienne around and kissed her. I could only imagine what all this was doing to both Xavier and Vivienne. My friend's affections toward my sister weren't lost on me, but Vivienne had seemed to be quite oblivious after all the centuries that Xavier had stood by her side.

What does Vivienne think of him now?

There was no way for me to find out, because as my stomach turned, my mind warring over the idea of ending Xavier's life, Xavier snapped his fingers and two firm pairs of hands gripped me. I would've fought back, but I was too stunned by what happened next.

Ashley pierced through Sam's flesh and pulled his heart out.

The shout that ricocheted across the cave walls was a chilling sound that seemed to come straight from hell.

Xavier pulled his lips away from my sister. His eyes began to burn a bright red-orange—almost as if flames had taken over his pupils. "Now, look what you've done. You made me miss out on all the fun."

I felt the blood drain from my face as Sam's body fell to the ground. I watched Ashley for a flicker of emotion—any indication that she was still in there, that she was torn over what she had just done. Nothing. She stood over Sam's dead body, gripping his heart in her hand, blood dripping from her fingers. Her eyes were pitch black, an indication of the darkness that had taken over her. As if that weren't blood-chilling enough, she grinned. Maniacally.

Vivienne crumbled in Xavier's arms. I knew she had just reached her breaking point. When Ashley sneered, I couldn't take it anymore.

Gathering up all the strength I could muster, I hit both men holding me with my elbows, grabbed their necks and the fire just went out of control. With one loud scream, my palms burst into flames, evaporating my own tears as the two men who were holding me got incinerated into ashes.

Xavier's eyes widened, taking on the shade of red before turning into a midnight blue. I wondered what each shade meant. His shoulders were trembling.

"How did you do that?" The hoarseness of his voice betrayed his terror. "There's no way you could've... You can't kill an Elder."

Realization washed over me like a flood as I watched the piles of ashes that accumulated on either side of me. *The Elders are dead.* I swallowed hard, realizing that I didn't even know which of my men they had possessed.

I turned toward Vivienne. When her eyes moistened with tears, my knees almost buckled beneath me.

What have I done?

If Xavier was encouraged at all by my momentary weakness, it didn't show. He was still staring at me, white as a sheet. "It can't be. Our kind is immortal. How is it..." His eyes slowly turned into pitch-black night.

Winds started to move all around me.

Chills ran down my spine as all the vampires possessed by Elders set their sights on me.

Before I said the word that would signal Corrine to use her powers to retrieve as many of our comrades as she could, Xavier screamed, "He has to turn back into a vampire! Turn him now!"

He threw my sister to the ground. That was when I said it. One word. "Now!"

The moment the word came out of my lips, chaos followed.

My vision blurred as the strong winds carried all the Elders right toward me in one quick swoop. It was a full-on massive attack and I had no idea how to get out of it. All I knew was that I couldn't allow them to turn me back into one of them, because the moment they possessed me, whatever power I had would immediately belong to an Elder.

When I pictured my young wife's face, an overpowering desire to live came over me, but should it come to it, I had no choice other than to die.

CHAPTER 35: VIVIENNE

The sight that unfolded before me was one of the most awful, breathtaking sights I'd ever seen.

Derek Novak had always been powerful. He was my brother and I knew him better than anyone else in the world, but at that moment, he was almost unrecognizable. His face took on a determination I'd never seen before.

I watched in horror as one of the vampires possessed by an Elder—Landis, Xavier's brother—bit into Derek's neck. When Derek pressed his hand against the man's chest, I was sure that I was about to see one of us die—just like those two guards' lives had ended just a couple of minutes ago.

However, as the mysterious fire once again flowed from my brother's palms, touching Landis just as he was about to turn Derek into a vampire once again, the man simply collapsed to the ground.

Derek's fire formed a flaming tornado. Screams of invisible—and supposedly immortal—Elders filled the air. As the lives of one Elder after another ended, Xavier, Liana, Yuri and Ashley moved away from the pack. Xavier took one look at the other three before they all disappeared. My heart sank. The Elders had taken them away from us. Hostages—people they would use against us.

I was so focused on Derek that I hadn't noticed Corrine standing in the middle of the bloody arena, mumbling words that made no sense to me. Her eyes were as lightning, her long brown hair being blown away by invisible winds.

By the time I looked back at my brother, a dozen of the recently possessed vampires lay all around him. The flames—along with the Elders' shrieks—subsided.

I had no idea what had just happened, but Derek, now covered in soot, looked completely exhausted. My heart dropped when he collapsed to the ground.

I rushed past the several levels of the Catacombs that separated him from me. I knelt on the ground beside him, raising his head and laying it on my lap. He was barely conscious.

"What was that?" I whispered. "How... What did you just do? You were able to kill Elders, Derek. How were you able to do that? What happened to you?"

I probably should've been more concerned for his wellbeing, because he didn't appear to be doing well at all.

Derek's lips opened to say something, but instead tears began rushing down his face and he sobbed. "I killed them all. I killed…"

I looked around at our people lying on the ground around us. They were all moving. Claudia looked through the mass of bodies. A disheartened expression was on her pretty face, her shoulders sagging in defeat, even though most of the people there were alive. "Claudia?" I whispered, unable to wrap my mind around everything that was happening.

"I don't understand," she whispered.

I could practically see Yuri's countenance reflected in her eyes. My heart went out to her. *Is Xavier's face reflected in mine?* I could still feel his hand on my body and I couldn't suppress a shudder. Once he was free from the Elder's grasp, would I be able to let him touch me without thinking of that moment? Of that moment when he wasn't Xavier, but instead a complete monster. The regret, guilt and depression swept over me as I recalled my missed chance to let him know how much I loved him. *Why didn't I just say the words?*

I realized that the most difficult times of my life had been when I had been taken captive by Borys Maslen and that time when I had been taken by the hunters—both times were made even more difficult because Xavier wasn't with me.

Now wrapped in my own pain, I knew I had to snap out of it or it would eat me alive, so I did what I had to do. I switched the emotions off, even if I knew that it was an entryway to the darkness. I wondered to myself what darkness Xavier had in him so as to have an opening for an Elder to take over him.

Snap out of this, Vivienne. I once again caught sight of Claudia, looking lost as she stared blankly at the people surrounding her. I couldn't be like her. I couldn't be a lost, whimpering little girl, pining for Xavier. I had to be the leader Xavier had challenged me to be if I was to have any chance of getting him back.

Landis was the first to sit up. He looked me straight in the eye, this time no longer possessed, his irises clearly showing.

"Are you all right?" I asked him.

He nodded, but he also frowned. "I think I have a fever."

"Vampires don't have fevers." Claudia wrinkled her nose. I thought she had half a mind to break Landis' neck.

His jaw tightened. "Exactly. It feels... strange." He groaned as he tried to get up. "Ugh!" he exclaimed. "My head feels like it weighs a million tons."

"Derek, you didn't kill them. They're all right." I turned toward my brother, but he lay unconscious in my arms.

"They're human," Corrine explained.

I almost jumped out of my skin. I hadn't even felt her approach behind me. "How is that possible?"

"Derek's powers mixed with mine. It burned the Elders' magic away from them—including the original curse that turned them into a vampire."

"His powers? How on earth does he have powers?"

"We don't have time to..." Corrine stopped her sentence short. Her eyes widened with shock. My eyes followed her gaze and found a woman with stunning silver hair standing right before us.

"What have you done, Corrine?" the woman asked. "Do you know what your intervention just cost us? Do you have any idea at all..." The woman's voice broke.

Corrine stood to her full height before bowing her head slightly. "I am sorry. I know I have done our kind wrong, but my loyalty is to this clan as my ancestor's was."

"Cora's loyalty was to the vampires!" The strange silver-haired woman attempted to keep her calm. "Do you honestly realize what you have just done? You have exposed Derek Novak to the Elders. You have made them weak and aware that they can be killed. The Elders are now out to kill him and the Guardians. Who knows what they will do once they know?"

"I had to help. They're family."

"I'm sorry this has to happen, Corrine. I should've done this to Cora when I had the chance." The woman breathed in some air and began to mutter inaudibly.

I saw horror in Corrine's eyes. "No. Please. Please…"

I was expecting something to happen. Wind. Fire. Anything to match or even exceed the display of power shown by my brother only moments ago. Nothing.

"I'll send Ibrahim to watch over you. When he deems that you can be trusted, then you'll have what I say you have the right to have. If you want to be a witch again, you have to earn it, Corrine."

Corrine swallowed hard, tears running down her face as she steeled herself against what the strange woman was saying. Just like that, the woman disappeared, replaced by a handsome-looking man with a black goatee.

"I'm sorry it had to be this way, Corrine," he said.

"What is going on?" I spat out. "Who was that, Corrine? What did she do to you? And who is *this?*"

"That was the Ageless, leader of the witches. This is Ibrahim." Corrine trembled as she revealed to me the price she'd had to pay in order to help us. "The Ageless just took away my powers."

"And she's going to have to spend her whole life atoning for her choice. I hope it was worth it, Corrine."

Corrine stared at Derek's unconscious form. She grinned. My heart leapt when she said with conviction, "Trust me, Ibrahim, if this helps save Sofia, if it helps save the Novaks, then yes… it was worth it."

Chapter 36: Aiden

When I woke up to find Derek Novak lying on the cot across from mine, barely breathing, I almost lost it. I wasn't a stranger to loss and grief, having been surrounded by violence and warfare all my life, but something about seeing my son-in-law, proud and powerful, looking as weak as he did just rubbed me the wrong way.

I sat up over the edge of my bed and scoped the room. No one was there aside from us. *What happened?*

We were no longer at The Shade. That was for certain. We were in a closed, windowless room. I had a feeling we were on some sort of vehicle. *The submarines. We're moving.*

The door swung open and Vivienne appeared. She seemed surprised to see me awake.

"What happened?" I asked. "Are we in one of the subs?"

She nodded slowly, eyeing her brother with concern. She motioned for me to follow her. I obliged, overcome by curiosity, not only at what had occurred during my sleep but also at what their submarines looked like. The last time I'd been in one, I was unconscious.

Vivienne led me to a small living area where Claudia sat on one of the lounge chairs, her eyes fixed on vacant space. Zinnia and Craig were also there, along with Gavin. All had loss written all over their faces.

Vivienne sat on a wooden chair and motioned for me to take the seat across from hers. She began to recount what had just happened, from the Elders' attack at The Shade up to Derek's arrival and eventually what had happened to Corrine, and how we now had another witch amongst us—one we weren't certain we could trust.

I found it difficult to swallow everything that she was telling me. "So where is this Ibrahim person now?"

"He's with Corrine." Vivienne's eyes were unfocussed, her brain likely recalling the eventful afternoon. "You should've been there. Derek… these powers he has… I think he's even more powerful now than he ever was as a vampire."

"That's good, is it not? That means we have a better chance of rescuing my daughter."

"I'm not sure, Aiden. All of these… I don't understand. I just have a bad feeling about all this. Especially Sofia. We've just discovered that Derek *can* kill Elders. That makes him the largest threat to their kind. Do you really think they're not going to use Sofia against him?"

A sick feeling settled at the pit of my stomach. Derek Novak had just became the hunters' most valuable weapon. I wondered whether Arron even knew about this. *Where is he anyway?* I was sickened to think that I had given so much of my life serving the cause of this coward, someone I used to fear and respect. *All the years I lost running after the hunters' cause... years I could've spent with my daughter.*

"We need to save my daughter and her child, Vivienne. We just have to."

Vivienne's face twitched. I could tell there was something she wasn't telling me.

"What is it?"

"That's the thing. Right now, we're headed toward hunters' headquarters. Derek doesn't know. Soon after what he did at the Catacombs, he lost consciousness. With him out, we thought of bringing him to Sofia's quarters at the caves, but the Elders returned. We were barely able to escape. They have The Shade now and everyone we left behind."

"Who's with us now?"

"We have Cameron, Claudia, Gavin, Zinnia, Craig and Landis."

"That's it?"

"The humans who were left behind were either bled dry or turned into vampires. The vampires, on the other hand, I think they're all vessels now. Xavier, Ashley, Yuri and Liana... they're all vessels now." Her voice broke, pain etched in her eyes.

I recoiled at the recollection of what the Elders had made Ashley do to the man she loved. "We're dealing with monsters, Vivienne, but if we're headed for hunters' headquarters, I'm not sure we're going to deal with creatures who are any better."

I was expecting a question from the princess, but all she did was nod. "I know, but do we really have any other choice? Derek is set on attacking The Blood Keep to find Sofia. We can't do that without the help of the hunters."

"They won't help us without anything in exchange. You realize that they may demand Derek's loyalty."

"You know my brother, Aiden. He's never bowed to anyone

before—not even the Elder. He's ruler of The Shade for a reason. He won't just pledge loyalty to the hunters."

"Even for Sofia?"

Vivienne hesitated. "What else are we going to do?"

She was clearly fighting back the tears. I saw the exhaustion behind her distant blue-violet gaze. Vivienne Novak was one of the most resilient women I'd ever met, but it was clear that she was nearing her breaking point.

"Have a rest, Vivienne. It looks like you need it."

"I'm going to check on my brother." She gave me a curt nod and made her way out of the living area.

Zinnia and Craig were quick to approach me the moment she left. My eyes zoned in on the blue star on Craig's temple. Something about it seemed innocent and playful—attributes that had become increasingly lost in our world.

"I never thought I would see the day when vampires would run to our headquarters for help," Craig said quietly.

"Do you think Arron would even allow them to set foot in headquarters?" Zinnia mused.

"The only vampires here are Vivienne, Claudia, and Cameron— all three desperate to fight against the Elders in order to have their loved ones restored to their arms. They're hardly our enemies. Arron would be a fool not to work with them."

"Especially Derek Novak."

I didn't miss the hint of admiration in how Craig said the king of The Shade's name. "Are you actually beginning to side with the Novaks, Craig?"

His eyes widened. "Of course not." His denial came too quick. "Never. Still, being at The Shade, seeing how crazy things are for the vampires…"

"You're not flaking on us, are you?" That was typical Zinnia, defensive of the hunters and whatever cause they were still fighting for, but even when she said it, there was a loss of edge to her loyalty and determination.

I could see it in the once ruthless hunters' eyes. They were realizing that in the world we were moving in, nothing was black or white. The lines were getting blurry and it was difficult to tell which side we ought to stand on.

I, however, didn't share their uncertainty. I had one goal in mind, and that was to get my daughter back.

Saving her was not going to be easy. I didn't care. I would willingly give my life to secure my daughter's future. If I had to sell my soul to the hunters to make that happen, I would do it.

When we arrived at hunters' headquarters, I watched without saying a word as they cuffed the vampires with more force than was necessary, considering how none of the three were putting up a fight. I remained calm as one of my most trusted hunters, Julian, who was now apparently leading the hawks since my absence, faced me.

"I never thought I'd see you back here again, Reuben."

"The name is Aiden. Aiden Claremont."

"So I heard. I see you've brought us vampires. Influential ones at that." His eyes focused on Vivienne and Claudia, his gaze lingering on the blonde more than the brunette. "Two of whom were once guests here already. What are they exactly, Aiden? Peace offerings?"

"No. They're my friends and they will be treated as such, so I would appreciate it if you would unhand them at once."

"And why on earth would we do that, Aiden? You're no longer one of us. As far as we're all concerned, you should be in cuffs too." He eyed Zinnia and Craig who were both standing behind me. "Have you two betrayed the hunters too?"

I was expecting both hunters to adamantly deny the accusation. Instead, they just stood by me.

"None of us mean any harm toward the hunters—especially these two. They are hunters by heart and will *always* be hunters."

"And you, Aiden? Are you no longer a hunter?"

"I'm a father whose daughter is about to give birth inside a sadistic evil creature's castle. I want her out of there and you're going to help us do it."

"Help you? For what reason?"

"For one, how about the fact that apart from me, Zinnia and Craig, every hunter you sent to The Shade was either killed or turned into vampires by these Elders? Isn't the lifeblood of this organization the desire for revenge? Why not redirect that revenge toward the original vampires—these Elders—and not just their mutations, the vampires we've always known and hunted?"

From the way Julian tensed, I could tell that we were getting to him.

"The Elders have taken over The Shade and that is something that none of us want. So, we're here to offer up an agreement with Arron."

"Arron? There's no way we can get in touch with Arron."

"Don't play me for a fool, Julian." I chuckled. "I know this organization far better than you ever will. I know how important the Novaks are to him. I know that he would want to be a part of this. Release Vivienne, Cameron and Claudia. Give us accommodations as guests of the hunters. Two witches—Corrine and Ibrahim—are also present, along with Derek Novak. I'm sure if you tell Arron all these things, he would be more than willing to discuss terms with us. Consider this a diplomatic visit."

"A diplomatic visit from whom, Aiden? The vampires? There is no diplomacy between hunters and vampires."

"No. This is a diplomatic visit from The Shade, from people who are loyal to loved ones, and no one else. We are rogues and if you play your cards well, you just might get us on your side. Don't tell me that Arron or the seniors of this organization don't want that."

Much to the chagrin and audible objections of the hunters present there, Julian snapped his fingers and motioned for the release of the captured vampires.

By the end of the day, Vivienne, Derek and I had a meeting with Arron, set the next day.

Before the meeting, I geared myself up for what would be asked of me. I was willing to pay any price to get my daughter back. I just had to trust that Derek and Vivienne—our family—were willing to do the same.

Chapter 37: Derek

When Vivienne stepped into the bedroom provided for me at hunters headquarters, I was in the middle of a workout, having already done more push-ups than I cared to count. Sweaty and not having yet taken a shower, I was the farthest thing from presentable, but as I stood to face my sister, she stared at me like I was the most magnificent thing she'd ever laid eyes on.

"What?" I asked when her stares were beginning to make me uncomfortable.

Her mouth opened but all she did was inhale. Tears began to brim her eyes.

"Vivienne, what is it?" Despite the fact that I was sweaty, I approached her and pulled her into my arms. "What's going on?"

"You're human," came her hoarse whisper. "Derek, you're human."

"Um yes. We found a cure, remember? I was already human when

I left The Shade with Sofia." Even as I said my wife's name, pain gripped my heart. I couldn't bear the idea that she wasn't with me. It had been months since I was taken from The Shade. *Does she think that I abandoned her? She wouldn't think that, would she? She knows me better than that.*

Vivienne had a knack of reading my mind, so I wasn't too surprised when she said, "I'm sure she understands, Derek. Sofia knows you more than any of us do. She saw goodness in you when the rest of us saw only darkness."

I remembered Sofia's kisses while we were in the darkness of that dungeon. "Vivienne, she's pregnant. Sofia's pregnant."

"I know." Vivienne nodded as she pulled away from me. She squeezed my arm. "We're going to get her back, Derek. Her and your child. Everything's going to be all right."

From the moment I'd woken up, I'd been consumed by the desperation to have my wife back in my arms. I was married to the love of my life. I was supposed to wake up in the morning and find her in my arms, beautiful and radiant like she always was, but lately the only memory I had of her was the dream I always had—blood dripping from her mouth, poised to kill. The image haunted me. I found myself spilling out the words to my sister, grateful for a confidante.

Vivienne said the same reassurances I kept telling myself, but still, it didn't seem enough.

"You've made it through so much already, Derek. Both of you can still make it through this."

"How? We don't even know where The Blood Keep is."

"I think Corrine knows. Wasn't it the witches who got you out of The Blood Keep to begin with?"

Hope surged within me. Still, an unshakable dread had settled over me. "What if she's already given birth? What are they going to do to our child? What are they going to do to her? Vivienne, what if…"

"Stop tormenting yourself, Derek. You're having a child! There was a time in your life when you never even imagined that you could ever fall in love, much less sire a child, and now you have that. Sofia is resilient and strong. You know that. Forget the dreams."

"How can you say that? You're the Seer of The Shade. You live by the dreams and visions that you see."

"And I've also seen many die by them. Maybe my visions have been accurate because I allowed them to be. All the war and bloodshed at The Shade, it all happened. I saw it beforehand, all that darkness. What I didn't see was all the light. I didn't see how Sofia would influence you to light. I didn't see the cure. I didn't see myself falling in love with Xavier. I am a seer, yes, but I am also so blind to many things."

I had to interrupt. "You and Xavier? Finally?"

A strange mixture of delight and sadness crossed her lovely countenance. "You knew?"

"Of course I did."

"And now he's a vessel, used by the Elders for whatever purposes they wish." Her voice broke and she began sobbing.

I had no idea what to do. I wasn't used to seeing Vivienne break down, so I just ran my hand across her back, like I did to Sofia whenever she seemed down. Vivienne sobbed into my chest for a couple of minutes before getting a hold of herself.

"We're going to get Xavier back," I promised her. "We're going to find a way." For centuries, my twin had been fighting for me to fulfill my destiny. She'd never asked for anything in return. Now, she was about to lose the love of her life. I wasn't about to let that happen.

"You're going to help me, aren't you?" she asked, almost as if she wasn't certain if I would bother.

I cupped her face between my palms. "Of course I will. You know I will. We're going to find a way to save all of them—Sofia, Xavier, Liana, Yuri and Ashley. They're our family. We are family."

There were so few of us left surviving. Never had I said words regarding the men and women loyal to me with as much conviction as I did then.

That was all it took for Vivienne to calm down. A promise from me that everything was going to be all right.

Once she gathered herself together, she gave me a curt nod, and looked me straight in the eye, "That's it then, Derek. Forget those ugly nightmares you have of Sofia."

My heart sank. "How can I? My dreams have a way of coming true."

"Whatever we see in dreams or visions, those images are merely part of a story—and they are rarely the end of the story. Should your nightmare of Sofia come true, you can trust that it's only a snippet of what is to come. If there's anything I've learned watching you and Sofia blossom into the couple that you have become, it's that we hold our fate in our hands. We always have a choice. Don't settle for less than the future that you dream of with her."

I couldn't help but smile inwardly at the words my sister expressed. "Thank you." I walked away from her and toward the phone installed on my bedside table. I dialed a number that had been etched in my head since Sofia and I had visited those homes in California. "Monica Andrews, please?"

A couple of minutes of conversation and I had just agreed to buy my first house. Not because I wanted to abandon The Shade, but because the house, to me, had become a symbol of the family I wanted with Sofia. That house—and seeing my wife and children live and grow up inside of it—was a future that I had always dreamed of.

That afternoon, it became the future that I was going to fight for no matter what came our way.

CHAPTER 38: KIEV

The night sky was starless, the moon absent. The evening was as dark as night could be, yet nothing could keep Sofia from her regular evening stroll with the genius of The Shade. I watched from a distance, the beast not far away from them, lurking, paying attention to my captive's every move.

Olga sat on my lap as she fed me blood from her wrist. I drank deep even as my eyes centered on the redhead who had captured my attention from the very moment I first heard of her.

Are you foolish enough to actually want to escape with this man, Sofia? I sensed jealousy over their closeness. I hated that Sofia had found a confidante in anyone other than me, but having him around had been good for her pregnancy. I stared at her belly, swallowing a large gulp of Olga's blood at the thought of the wonderful creatures it contained—morsels for the taking.

Eyes set on the wiry man who towered over her, I flinched when

Eli ran his hand over her back several times as if to comfort her.

I pulled my lips away from Olga's wrist, quickly wiping blood away from the corners of my lips. "I hate that he's touching her."

Olga glanced at her wrist before pulling out a bandage. She began to tend to her wound, oblivious to my outburst.

"She's mine."

I sensed the amusement in my servant's countenance. "What is it about her that has got all you vampires so wrapped up in her dainty little fingers? The legendary Derek Novak, you... who else has been cast under her spell?"

I pushed her away from me, annoyed. "Do you think she's planning to escape with him?"

"I'm sure of it." Olga said.

"Well, I'm already offering to help her escape."

"And you think she'd just trust you? After that last encounter she had with you?"

My stomach knotted at the recollection of her smile, of her sweet laughter as she tried to convince me to dance with her.

I hated her. I hated that moment. I hated that it could make me feel so hopeless, knowing that the light I saw in her could never be mine.

Or maybe it still could.

The voice came unbidden, like a whisper of a conscience I'd long ago shut out.

I pushed the thought away, shaking my head.

Olga knelt at my feet, absent-mindedly running her fingers over my kneecaps. She was comfortable around me in a way that only she was capable of. "Why do you want to help her anyway?"

"Help who?"

I tensed at the familiar, grating voice behind me. *Clara.*

I dared not turn around. I didn't want to see her face. If there was one person I hated more than anybody in the world, it was Clara. Of all the vampires the Elder had sired, she was decidedly the worst. She was his favorite. She was the one who actually enjoyed his torture. She was the one who was most like the Elder. I shuddered to think of the consequences should she find out that I was planning to escape The Blood Keep with Sofia.

I did my best to keep my voice calm and cool. "Sofia," I responded, even as Clara's hand brushed over my hair.

We had once had a competition—a sick game the Elder had played at our expense. Clara had won. As a reward, I was given to her. A pet for her to toy with. She was allowed to do with me whatever she pleased and I was not to retaliate in any way. Clara had placed me in more degrading positions than I could think of just because of this loss. I was hers for a hundred years. We'd barely even gotten to twenty.

Clara pushed Olga away and perched herself on my lap. "I missed you, brother," she whispered.

Disgust came over me at the mention of me being her brother. I wanted to push her away but knew that I couldn't. I knew what torment under the Elder's hands meant. I did not want to go through that again.

Clara's lips found mine. I tensed. It seemed to me that she loved it when she saw my disgust over her advances.

"I've always wanted you," she whispered to my ear.

The amusement was unmistakable.

"It's too bad Father doesn't allow you to come with me on the missions he sends me on. You should've been at The Shade when the Elders arrived, Kiev. It was quite a sight to see how Vivienne Novak trembled when she stood before the vampire one of the Elders possessed. Her beloved himself, Xavier Vaughn. I didn't want to leave, especially when they made the vampires fight some of the vessels. There was an arena and everything, but of course, Father had to drag me back here."

"Oh? Why's that?" Of all my brothers and sisters, Clara was the only one who seemed to find pleasure in calling the Elder her father. *Sick conniving bitch.*

"He's worried about you. He says you spend too much of your time mooning over our lovely captive. Are you actually falling for her? Have you fallen under her spell? What, did you lie with her? Did you finally give in to your longing to have what Derek Novak had? I know you want to."

I stared at her, unwilling to address her taunts, hating every bit of her, revolted by her touch.

"What are you helping the queen of The Shade with, Kiev?"

"Her pregnancy. Isn't that my task?"

"Don't play me for a fool, Kiev," Clara purred.

I fought the urge to gag. She always did that, almost like she thought it was cute.

"Look. I don't know what you're up to, brother, but I must say that I'm not pleased to see you mooning over an immune—especially one as tainted as she."

"Tainted?"

She wrinkled her nose as she spun her head to catch a glimpse of Sofia. "She has an ex-vampire's spawns growing inside of her. She is and will always be tainted with light. That makes her the enemy, Kiev. Always."

I can't wait for the day I see you die, Clara.

"Well, anyway, whatever you're thinking of helping her with, I'm here now. Father told me to keep my eye on you, and I'm going to do just that, Kiev." She pressed her palms on either side of my cheeks. "I'm going to love every minute of it. Aren't you glad I'm back?" She was so close, her lips were pressing against mine as she spoke.

All I could respond with was, "You're disgusting."

She slapped me across the face with the back of her hand. She chuckled. "Good. I'd like to know how revolted you are by me once I come to your bed tonight. Be ready."

I glared at her. I was about to speak against her but her lips crashed against mine. Crushing. Demeaning. Wicked in every way.

By the time she left me, I had one thought ruling in my mind. *I need to escape from this hell hole. It's the only way I can get away from Clara. It's the only way I can kill her.*

Escape was easy. Being safe from the Elder's rule once I was gone was a whole different thing. My eyes once again wandered back to Sofia.

She really is my only way out.

Chapter 39: Derek

Not long after the conversation I had with Vivienne, I took a quick shower and we were off to breakfast with Arron in a dimly lit room with no windows, as a way of protecting my sister from the sunlight.

Breakfast consisted of pancakes, butter and maple syrup. I was starving, so the moment food was served, I had no inhibitions in wolfing my breakfast down.

Aiden, who seemed to be satisfied with his cup of coffee, stared at me like I had somehow gone mad. Vivienne watched curiously while Arron had his typically deadpan expression on his face as he stirred a cup of tea for himself.

"I see the king's being human has made him appreciate *our* delicacies more than the delicacies enjoyed by vampires such as yourself, princess," Arron said.

Vivienne just shrugged a shoulder. "I can't deny that I envy him. It's been centuries since I last enjoyed a meal."

"Ah, yes… you're one of the rare few who never killed a human for his blood. I admire that about you, Miss Novak."

Vivienne seemed ill at ease.

I couldn't have cared less. I hadn't eaten since I left The Sanctuary and I knew that if I didn't enjoy the spread we were given now, there was a big possibility I wouldn't be able to wolf down a meal anytime soon. Unlike when I was a vampire, I could only last so long without food as a human. I bit into my last slice of pancake and took a gulp from my orange juice.

I swallowed then laid my palms on the table in front of me. "Let's get to business, shall we?"

"About time."

"I'm not going to play around with you, Arron. I know who you work for and I know why this organization is so hell bent on ending vampires. But we both know that it's not this earth's vampires that you really want to end. You just want to win this war you have with the Elders. We humans are just caught in between."

"I see the witches have been talking about us while you were in their realm."

"They have. Now, what must we do to secure your help in rescuing my wife and all the other citizens of The Shade whom the Elders held captive?"

"First of all, you're going to speak to me with respect, boy. I don't care how old you are. I am an immortal and you will address me as such."

I noticed the spark of interest in both Vivienne and Aiden's faces.

"An immortal? You?" I challenged. "See, I don't even know what you are. Why on earth should I speak to you with respect?"

"Because it's my help that you need."

"Really? So the fact that I was able to kill at least a dozen Elders doesn't matter to you?"

Arron's eyes grew wide. "What are you talking about?"

"Back at The Shade," Vivienne spoke up, "when he arrived to find the Elders making us fight one another to the death in an arena, Derek was able to kill the Elders who'd possessed some of the vampires there, using them as vessels. At first, he also killed the vessel the Elder inhabited, but with Corrine's magic protecting the vessels, Derek was able to end the lives of the Elders with his fire."

"Corrine? The now powerless witch?"

We all nodded.

"The Ageless took away her power for helping us."

"Typical," Arron mumbled beneath his breath. He then turned toward Aiden. "Is this true?"

Aiden nodded. "I wasn't there when it happened. I was unconscious after one of their beasts attacked me, bit me right in the neck." He showed Arron the wound.

Arron seemed disconcerted by the sight. "Beasts? Their vampire mutts? What happened to them?"

"I hadn't noticed." Vivienne shook her head. "Everything was happening too quickly. I'm assuming they're still at the Catacombs."

"Hm. Anyway that doesn't matter. What matters is that you are right. For once, we want the same thing. We want to stop the Elders. It's bad enough that their kind have entered this realm, but they're turning so many humans into vampires for a reason."

"What's that?"

"They're building an army against us."

I drummed my fingers on the dining table. "Sounds to me like you need us more than we need you."

"Don't be a fool, young king. We both know how desperate you are to have your wife back in your arms."

I waited for him to talk about Sofia being with child. *Doesn't he know?* I wondered what they would think once they knew. *Would they want my child too?* I chose to keep it a secret, and considering that neither Aiden nor Vivienne spoke about it, I imagined they also thought it best that the Guardians not know.

"Fine. We all have something at stake. So? Can we now agree to work together?"

"Not until we've discussed several conditions. Do you have any?"

"We are not pledging any loyalty to the hunters. We are loyal to our loved ones. We are loyal to our own conscience, to what we believe is right."

"This means what exactly?"

"It means we can leave this place when we please," Aiden verified. "Once the task is done, our commitment to one another is over."

"I'm afraid that won't work out. You see, we can fight against the Elders without you. The only thing you have to offer that we don't have is the location of The Blood Keep. I'm not even sure you know that."

"You don't have Derek," Vivienne added. "Remember what he can do?"

"I must admit that I've never seen an Elder die while in this world's atmosphere. There's something about your world that makes them immortal, so I can't deny my curiosity about this power you are boasting of, but I don't see why it would be of utmost importance to us. We can just blow up The Blood Keep. All we have to do is kill the Elders' possible vessels."

"That doesn't make sense," Aiden hissed. "They would just turn more people into vampires!"

"You've been a hunter all your life, Aiden. We both know how cutthroat this operation can get. That was never hidden from you.

244

We're willing to sacrifice necessary human lives in order to further our cause."

"I thought the cause was to further the good of the human race." Aiden spoke up.

Arron chuckled. "We had to make you think that, but I think you've seen enough of our worlds and our kind to know that isn't true. It is the Guardians' cause that the hunters are furthering."

"What are Guardians?" Vivienne asked the question that was most likely running through all our minds.

"You'll know soon enough, princess. For now, we need to discuss terms. I think we've both established who needs who. So again, let's discuss conditions."

"The Shade and everything that belongs to us is safe. We will have an autonomous rule, away from the control of your kind," I asserted. "My family especially—that includes Vivienne, Aiden and all the people of The Shade I brought with me here, their loved ones included. None of us are to be harmed."

"Fair enough."

"I want Anna, Ian and Kyle back. They are my subjects. The hunters have no right to take them."

"That's more complicated than it looks, but fine. I can give you that."

"What do you mean it's more complicated?"

"They're not here at headquarters. They're in our realm—the realm of the Guardians—The Aviary."

"What! Why? What have you done to them?"

"Don't worry, king. They were treated as welcome guests. They will return to you perfectly unharmed—just like they were when we took them from you. Is there anything else you want?"

I wasn't thrilled about stopping the discussion about Anna, Ian and Kyle, but it was clear that Arron was no longer going to speak about any of it, so I said the one thing that came to mind when it came to our list of conditions: "I refuse to be under your control. I refuse to be a hunter."

"You've served us more than you know, Derek. I wouldn't imagine pushing our vendetta on you. Besides, you're too volatile a power to play with. Is that all?"

I gulped, realizing that we hadn't exactly come here prepared. Going to the hunters' headquarters had been an act of desperation to break away from the chaos at The Shade.

"I think that's all." Vivienne nodded after looking to both Aiden and me for confirmation. My father-in-law was pale as a sheet.

What is going on with him? "Aiden?" I asked. "You all right? You have anything to add?"

"All my properties and wealth, accumulated over the years and also inherited from my father, are to be given to my daughter and her husband, Derek. None of it will go to the cause of the hunters."

Arron raised a brow at this. "You're talking as if you're about to die, Aiden. I can't say I'm pleased with this seemingly last will and testament of yours, considering how your family's wealth is largely due to the backing of the hunters, but sure. We don't need your money or your properties, but why *are* you talking as if you are a dying man?"

"I know you, Arron. I just want to make sure that whatever you ask of us, of me in particular, my daughter and her family will be secure."

For the first time, Arron took on an expression that was anything other than stoic. It was pure delight. "We weren't wrong in choosing you to be one of our prime hunters, Aiden. You always were one of the best."

"What is he talking about?" I couldn't bear the anxiety any longer.

"I have two conditions. One is that all three vampires now within our custody be turned into humans the moment we rescue their loved ones. I wouldn't want them to turn human before facing off with the Elders, because the Elders are already a threat to them as vampires—how much more as humans? Do we agree on this?"

"Claudia's not going to like this," Vivienne muttered under her breath. We exchanged glances but all I could really do was shrug. She nodded at me.

"Fine." I nodded. *Sacrifices have to be made. Besides, this is what I've always wanted for my subjects at The Shade. Freedom from this curse. They may not like it, but it is what it is.* "What else do you want?"

"I want Aiden to agree to be turned into a Guardian. Not just a vessel for our kind, like the body that I have now taken hold of, but actually one of us. A true Guardian. That would mean that he would agree to be transported to our realm."

Aiden trembled, and though I didn't know the extent of what Arron was asking of him, I could tell that the sacrifice Aiden was about to make was beyond what I could imagine.

"Only after my daughter has been saved." Aiden spoke before I could object. "Only after I'm able to hold her in my arms and say goodbye."

"Goodbye?" I burst out. "What? Aiden, you don't have to do this." *What exactly does it take to become a Guardian?*

Vivienne grabbed his arm and squeezed. "We're family."

The words made Arron grimace, almost as if it was the most disgusting thing he could think of to be called our family.

"I have to do this." Aiden nodded. "It's because we're family that I need to agree to this. I know Arron and he won't stop until he gets what he wants. Isn't that right, Arron? You'll never stop trying to destroy my family until you have me at your side."

Arron remained expressionless, except for a slight twitch of his lip.

I wondered what kind of history the two had with each other.

"This is me putting my family first," Aiden assured both of us.

"It's a deal then?" Arron asked.

I looked at Vivienne, whose eyes were fixed on Aiden with concern.

It was Aiden who sealed the whole deal. "Fine." He nodded. "It's done."

"You agree to this, king of The Shade?" Arron raised a brow at me.

I felt trapped even though my instincts were speaking against this. "Aiden... Are you sure? I don't think Sofia would..."

"If there was any other way, Derek, I wouldn't agree to this, but you and I both know we need them."

Trapped in a corner, all I could do was nod. "But not until you show us what you can do."

A smile formed on Arron's face. "Very well then." He stood to his feet and stepped a distance away from us. "First things first..." He drew a deep breath and when he exhaled, massive, magnificent wings sprouted out of his back—wings that resembled that of a hawk.

If I hadn't known any better, I would've thought him an angel, but he was the furthest thing from such honorable creatures. Whenever I looked at Arron, all I saw was a devil in disguise.

Chapter 40: Sofia

Tonight was the night. I woke up in my bed, shaking, breaking out into a cold sweat. The night had been restless. My sleep was plagued with nightmare upon nightmare. My heart was pounding and my breaths came in pants.

I turned to my side and saw Shadow nearby, intimidating as he always was. "Is this really the right thing to do, Shadow?"

He sat to attention almost as if he understood what I asked him—like he tensed at the suggestion of what we were about to do. Our plan was insanity, and that was why I thought it would work.

They'd never see us pulling something so simplistic. The element of surprise is on our side.

I kept telling myself that by the end of the day, we would be out of that place and headed toward hunters' headquarters where we could seek sanctuary, where I could give birth.

Still, there was a nagging feeling of foreboding inside. I felt a kick inside my belly and I held my breath. *Please, please, don't come now. Give Mommy more time.* I was heavy with child and was due to give birth soon. That was why it was necessary to escape then, because if Eli and I waited any longer, I would have to give birth at The Blood Keep and that thought alone was the most terrifying thing I could think of happening.

I was certain that should I give birth at the Elder's castle, I would never see my children again. I shuddered at the recollection of the Elder's visit to my chambers and swore to myself that my children would live as far away as possible from evil like that.

This plan has to work. It just has to, I told myself for about the millionth time. I struggled to get out of the bed and up to my feet. I groaned. *Who am I kidding? I can barely walk.* Carrying twins was more difficult than I'd ever imagined it would be. *I should be on bed rest or something, not planning an escape from a madman's lair.* I glanced at the dark creature that lay on the bed nearby. All our plans—all our hopes—hung squarely on one beast's shoulders. A beast that still terrified me with just one of his yellow-eyed glares.

A knock on the door almost made me jump out of my skin.

Like clockwork.

I didn't need to acknowledge the knock. The door swung open and Olga stepped in a few seconds later. The beautiful redhead smiled at me. I immediately noticed the bruise on her face.

"What happened?" I asked her. "Did I do something to displease Kiev? Why did he hit you?"

"It wasn't your fault, miss," Olga responded. "Mistress Clara paid him a visit last night."

My stomach turned in knots. Clara was creepier than Kiev ever was—and Kiev already brought me more creeps than I could keep track of. "I'm so sorry."

"I'm used to it. It will heal. I'm sure Master Kiev will allow me a drink of his blood. Now, shall we prepare your bath, miss? Sir Eli will be waiting at the gardens for your daily walk."

"Please." I nodded.

Olga assisted me toward the bathroom and helped me into the tub. She allowed me some privacy before returning to assist me in dressing. It was while I was dressing that Kiev entered the room. He sat on one of the couches, oblivious to my state of undress. In fact, the cad seemed to delight in watching me struggle to get dressed, needing Olga to support me.

Just think of it as him being relaxed, thinking that I couldn't possibly escape given my current state. It was the only piece of comfort I could give myself given the awkward predicament I was in.

"You can barely move without help, Sofia," he noted. "Perhaps a stroll around the gardens with your friend isn't good for you. Maybe you should just be resting."

My heart skipped a beat. *Does he know?* "I need the fresh air, Kiev. I enjoy the strolls. I think it's good for the babies."

Kiev didn't seem pleased with my request. "I think you spend too much time with Eli."

"The only times I spend with him are the times you allow me to, Kiev." *What is going on with him?*

"Tell him this is the last time you'll be spending time with him."

Olga helped me pull a sweater over the light pink dress I was wearing. "Why? Have we done anything to displease you?"

"No." Kiev shook his head, his bright red eyes sparkling with something akin to excitement. "We're going tonight."

"Going? You mean…"

"Yes. Tonight's the night, Sofia." He stood to his feet, seemingly pleased with himself. "Get ready."

"What do you want me to do?"

"Just be prepared to do whatever I tell you to."

"Okay." I nodded, paranoid over the coincidence that Kiev would schedule his escape on the same day Eli and I did. "Thank you, Kiev."

He walked up to me and ran his hand over my belly. I tried to suppress a shudder at how he looked at my stomach. "You're shaking."

"I'm cold," was the only excuse I could come up with. I wanted to get as far away from him as possible.

"Maybe this will warm you up." He pulled me into a tight embrace. I could sense him breathing in my scent.

I forced myself to stop trembling. I was revolted by his touch. I couldn't understand what he wanted with me. If he was so interested in me, then why hadn't he just taken me to his bed when I'd willingly offered myself up to him out of desperation?

Kiev was a great unknown and what I didn't know left me on edge. I was relieved when he finally let go of me.

"I'll take you to the gardens." He offered his arm and I linked mine with his, despite the fact that all I wanted was to be far from him.

Shadow followed behind us—at a distance, seemingly wary of Kiev ever since Kiev had clawed at the beast's skin.

When I saw Eli waiting at the gardens, I was both relieved and mortified. I knew what we were about to do and the consequences should we fail.

"Eli." I tried to smile.

"Pleasant evening to you, your highness," he greeted. "Have you eaten yet?"

"Breakfast always comes after our stroll. You know that." I

couldn't help but note the edge in Eli's tone of voice. His asset had always been his brains and not his brawn. Should we be caught, there was no way he could defend me or even himself. Eli Lazaroff simply wasn't a man of battle.

Kiev eyed the man from head to foot. "Don't tire her. She needs rest. She'll be giving birth soon."

"Of course, sire." Eli nodded. "I'll see to it that she doesn't overly exert herself."

Kiev kissed me on the cheek before leaving me with Eli, who watched as the Elder's spawn faded into the distance.

"What was that all about?" Eli asked when Kiev was finally out of earshot.

I shrugged. "He's been touchy-feely all morning. I think it has something to do with Clara's visit to him last night."

Eli didn't ask more questions, to my relief. After all, we had more urgent matters at hand. "Okay then. Are you ready?"

I nodded. "As ready as a mother can ever be, I guess."

As we talked, we walked steadily toward the boundaries. With Shadow tailing us, none of the vampires or the caretakers or the beasts who saw us suspected what we were up to. They were all expecting Shadow to pounce on me like he had the last time I tried to step over the boundaries of where I should and shouldn't be.

Once we were right at the very edge of the boundary, we stopped. I slipped out the vial I tucked into my sleeve and handed it over to Eli. It contained my blood. He drank every drop of it.

We didn't have to discuss the plan. We knew it by heart. We'd whispered about its pros and cons for weeks.

"You remember the hut?" Eli asked, careful with his words, in case someone was listening in on our conversation.

I nodded.

"Okay then?"

There were no further cues required. I took a sharp intake of breath. Eli whistled and snapped his fingers. Shadow lunged forward. As he did, I climbed onto his back and within less than two minutes, all three of us were outside the boundaries of The Blood Keep and right into broad daylight.

We were headed for a hut that Eli had heard one of the servants speak of. It was several miles away and they used it to store grain. That was our meeting place.

It turned out that Shadow was a lot faster than Eli. I could only hope that no one noticed our departure, because if they noticed, they were going to send the beasts after us. They might not catch Shadow and me, but Eli was in danger.

It felt like we'd been running for hours and I wondered if Shadow was getting tired of carrying me as he continued to sprint forward. The sun was beginning to burn the beast's skin and I could tell that he was in pain, but I was amazed at his resilience. He just kept going and I was grateful for it. I tried to look back to see how Eli was doing, but I could barely move, as I was focusing all my attention on holding on to Shadow for dear life. All I could do was wish that Eli was unharmed. That he was safe. Should this escape succeed, I owed my life to him... him and Shadow.

I was relieved when we reached the hut. Shadow's skin was beginning to burn off and given my current situation, I was fighting my urge to vomit all along the way. My back was screaming in pain and I was afraid of what the ride had done to the children I was carrying.

I staggered toward the hut, dying to take a seat. Shadow retreated to a dark corner in order to recover from the pain the sun had caused him. *Seems like vampire dogs have far more endurance than their human counterparts.* I couldn't deny my amazement over the creatures created by Eli and The Underground. *It's too bad most of them are under the Elder's control now.*

I had to wait for Eli there. I'd barely reached the door when liquid ran down my thighs. *No. This can't be happening. Not now... It can't be. Not now.*

Sure enough, I saw a puddle of water beneath me. *My waters just broke.*

Tired and afraid, I stepped inside the hut. I tried to get comfortable. It felt like hours before Eli arrived. By then, I was screaming from the waves of labour pains washing over me.

When Eli arrived, he barely had any skin left on his body. The sun had burnt away his flesh. "I think I have to stay in the sun for the whole process to finish, Sofia," he managed to tell me from outside the door. "I can't help you. We have to get away from here. They'll be on our tails soon."

I tried to get up on my feet, but another wave of spasms sent me back to the ground, reeling in pain. Shadow whimpered from outside the cabin, as if he too could feel my pain.

I shook my head in desperation as I stared at Eli. "I'm so sorry. I can't. I just can't..." Tears were streaming down my face when I realized that I was going to have to give birth there. With no one to help me.

That was when Eli retrieved an item from his pocket—something so precious given the situation we were in. It was a phone. "I stole it from one of the servants. I don't know if it works, Sofia, but it's worth a try." He threw the item at me. He then shut the door and ran to the woods where the sunlight still burned out the vampire's curse, my blood still coursing through his veins.

I grabbed the phone and opened it. I was relieved to see the LED screen light up. There was the tiniest signal on there. I dialled the one number I knew—hunters headquarters. The line was so crackly, I could barely make out what the hunter was saying, but from what I could hear, a group of hunters was already at The Blood Keep. I had to keep myself on the line until she could figure out my location, using the phone's signal to track me down. Waves of reassurance came over me when the hunter said, "Okay. Just hang on, Sofia. I'll try to get in touch with one of the hunters stationed outside the Keep. Hopefully someone will be there shortly."

The wait was excruciating. The labour was painful. When I heard shouting outside, I thought that it was the end of everything. *They know we're gone. They sent the beasts to get us.* I was expecting to be found anytime even as I drifted in and out of consciousness from the pain.

When the door swung open and I saw the handsome face of my beloved husband, Corrine standing alongside him, I thought I was hallucinating.

"Sofia." His voice broke as he ran to my side. I felt his firm grip on my arm and his lips on mine, but I wasn't sure it was for real. I just knew that I was thankful that he was there. My Derek was there.

Everything seemed so surreal. Corrine had taken over. The pain was making everything so fuzzy. I just kept staring into Derek's face, unable to believe that he was really beside me.

"You can do this, Sofia. You're doing fine," he encouraged as I pushed at Corrine's command. I clung to Derek for dear life, wondering if I was hurting him.

"You're doing fine, Sofia."

I heard a small cry. Then I saw tears in Derek's eyes.

"We have a boy. Sofia, we have a son," he announced. He reached for the child. I tried to lift my head to catch a glimpse, but then another spasm of pain came. I screamed.

"There's another one!" Corrine announced.

I saw the delight in Derek's eyes. He wanted this. I wanted this. I had been at The Blood Keep alone with this pregnancy for so long I had forgotten that we'd dreamed of this. Derek and I wanted to have a family.

I stared at him. *Is he really here?*

"Push, Sofia! Push!"

Out of instinct, I responded to Corrine's screams. The pain had reached a peak so that I could barely feel it. I wasn't certain if the whole thing was even real, but I did as I was told.

When I heard a second cry, I looked up at Derek again. I saw pure joy on his face.

"It's a girl," Corrine announced, relief in her voice.

Derek held both children in his arms, and looked at me with such delight. "Everything's going to be all right, Sofia," he told me, then worry immediately replaced his joy. "Sofia?" Panic came with the way he said my name. "Corrine, take the babies."

The witch quickly obliged and within seconds, I was in Derek's arms.

"Derek, where were you?" I began to sob into his chest as my head spun from everything that had just occurred.

This is too good to be true.

"Sofia, darling, I'm so sorry. I tried to get here as soon as I could and I just... I'm sorry." I felt his kisses. I felt the strength of his embrace. I felt the heave and sigh of his chest and the beating of his heart. I felt the warmth of his breath on my skin as he showered me with apologies.

I was exactly where I had longed to be, but just as I was beginning to accept what was happening, the door swung open and the man with red eyes stepped in.

Night had fallen. The darkness had come. Perhaps it was mercy that stole me away from that moment and allowed me to fade from consciousness, because I probably wouldn't have been able to survive what was to happen next.

Chapter 41: Derek

The state Sofia was in was tearing me apart. She needed immediate medical attention.

"She needs to go to a hospital."

Kiev looked at her. "Yes. She does."

"But if you think you can take her away from me…"

"Save your threats. It's not her I want." He paused and stared at Sofia.

I noticed the way he gulped as he eyed her blood.

He smirked. "Well, maybe I do want her, but not more than I want something else that you have."

Before I could respond, he rushed out of the hut. Corrine screamed outside. I wanted to get up, but Sofia was cradled in my arms and I was afraid that if I let go, I'd never be able to hold her again.

Within seconds, Corrine burst into the door, holding one baby instead of two.

My eyes widened in horror. "No!"

"He took your son. I'm sorry. I couldn't do anything to…"

"No!" I screamed. I looked at my unconscious wife, cradled in my arms. *How am I ever going to tell you?* "Where's Arron? Where are the others? What are they doing?"

I knew the answer. The Guardians were back at The Blood Keep wreaking their havoc there. Aiden and Vivienne, along with the rest of our crew, were probably lost in the heat of battle.

As if we weren't already surrounded by enough chaos, another unwelcome guest arrived in a flash of light. The silver-haired vixen herself. The Ageless.

"What do you want?" I hissed at her.

"Forgive me for what I am about to do, Derek, but our intervention at The Shade came with a price. Corrine knows that every time a witch intervenes in the manner that she did, there are always consequences. The Elders are demanding justice for their loss."

"Justice? After all the injustices they put us through?" I hated the witch more than I'd ever thought I could. "Do you see my wife right now?"

"Sofia is strong. She always has been. Her spirit is perhaps even stronger than yours. I have no doubt in my mind that both of you will survive what is to come."

"What are you talking about?"

"I'm sorry," she repeated, "but the payment they demand for what you did is your wife."

I clung to Sofia for dear life, afraid that I would crush her, but unwilling to let go. I pressed my lips against her even as I turned desperate eyes toward a creature more powerful than any of us.

"Please. Don't."

Sadness showed in the Ageless' eyes. "This must be done. I'm sorry." The Ageless turned toward Corrine. "I know you risked everything for her, but you and I both know that this is the price that must be paid. Cruor demands her. Cruor will get her. It's the only way to keep the balance."

"This is unfair. And you know it," Corrine pleaded even as she clutched my daughter in her hands. "Sofia had nothing to do with what happened."

"And yet she is the price they demand, the price we are going to give." The Ageless turned her eyes toward me. "I trust that she will someday be back in your arms."

"No. Please," I pleaded even as I sensed my body heating up. I began to fear that I would burn my own wife to ashes, but there would be no time for that. The witch was about to rip my heart away from me.

It took less than the blink of an eye—just a snap of her fingers. And both the witch and Sofia were gone.

"No!" I screamed out. As if she knew what had just happened, our daughter cried right along with me.

The fire was building up inside me and I knew there was nothing I would be able to do to control it. I was in more pain than I ever was before. I turned desperate eyes toward Corrine. "Get away. Get as far away as you possibly can." I looked at the child she was holding. "I'm not about to lose her too."

Corrine ran as far away from the cabin as possible. I held the fire back as long as I could, but what was to happen was inevitable. The ground shook when a loud explosion burst from inside the small hut, incinerating everything within half a mile.

To have held Sofia in my arms only to have her ripped away from me was the farthest thing from justice. As the fire came out of me, all I could think about were the few words Sofia was able to utter to me.

Derek, where were you?

Epilogue: Sofia

When I woke up, my head was pounding and my heart was thumping so hard it felt like it was about to burst out of my chest. Every tooth ached terribly. I felt cold—colder than I'd ever felt before.

I shuffled out of the bed and stood to my feet. My knees almost buckled beneath me. I held on to one of the posts of the bed for support. I looked around me. My surroundings were unfamiliar. Everything was white. The floor, the walls, the ceilings, everything.

"I've gone mad." I tried to recall what had happened to me and my mind came up with a huge blank. Instead, I felt a shower of kisses on my temple, strong arms wrapping around my frame. The strange sensations came with a sense of comfort that left me unnerved even as a flash of bright blue eyes came through my thoughts.

I jumped from where I was standing when a baritone voice assured me, "Everything's going to be all right, Sofia."

The words came like an embrace. A promise I had to hold on to.

Sofia. That's my name. I was certain of it. I looked around me in search of some assurance of who I was. I couldn't remember. I had no idea who I was. All I knew was that the name was mine. Those kisses were mine. Those eyes were mine.

Right about then, a loud whoosh caught my attention. I turned toward the sound and a door opened where I'd thought there was only a wide white wall.

A young woman dressed in white from head to foot entered the room. She held a tray on her hands. In the middle of the tray was a glass of blood. The bright red colour was a stark contrast to the bare white surroundings.

My eyes immediately focused on the glass and the strangest sensation came over me. *Hunger... hunger unlike anything I've ever felt before.* It took over my senses. *Is this what Derek used to feel whenever he looked at me?*

I wondered at the strange thought. *Who's Derek? Is he the man with the blue eyes? The man from whom those kisses came, whose arms wrapped around me and whose voice reassured me?* A wave of affection swept over me for this stranger whom I was sure I loved with every fiber of my being.

"What's going through your mind, Sofia?"

I was right. Sofia. That's my name. "A man," I admitted, even if I had no idea who the woman standing before me was. Brown hair. Beautiful. Darkness evident in her eyes.

"A man? Who?"

"I don't remember," I lied for reasons I couldn't fathom. *Why can't I just tell her I'm thinking about Derek, whoever he is?* I stared at the blood.

"Do you remember me?" She seemed annoyed that I wasn't even

looking at her. "Stop staring at the blood, Sofia. Look at me. Do you remember who I am?"

I shook my head. "No. I don't."

"I'm Clara. Now do you remember?"

I tried to recall, but I remembered nothing. I found myself drawn to the blood. I swallowed hard at the sight of it. I wanted it. I craved it. I had to have it. I took a step forward and reached for it.

Clara stepped away and pulled the tray away from me. "Not yet, Sofia. Not until you answer my questions."

"Do you remember who I am?"

I shook my head. "No. Can I have a drink now? Please?"

She appeared pleased this time. "Sure. Have a sip. But just one sip."

She handed the glass over to me and I took a sip. My eyes lit up at how invigorating the blood was coursing through my veins. I gasped when Clara pulled the glass away from my lips.

"Now let's talk about that man you remember. What does he look like?"

"I don't know. I don't remember."

"What's his name?"

"I don't remember."

"Don't lie to me, Sofia. I'll never give you any more blood if you lie to me."

I swallowed hard. I wanted that blood.

"That man is keeping you from all the blood you want, Sofia. All you have to do is give me his name and the blood is yours."

Something raged within me, and I was so desperate for the blood that I almost said the name out loud. *Derek.* But I couldn't. I simply couldn't.

But I still wanted that blood and there was only one person

keeping me away from what I wanted. It wasn't Derek. It was Clara.

I glared at her and before I could even make sense of what was happening, I was holding her heart in my hands and staring at her motionless body on the ground. The glass of blood was secure in my other hand. I smiled, not feeling an ounce of remorse over what I'd just done.

Then I drank the glass of blood—every drop of it. The blood caused memories to come over me like a flood. Memories I couldn't make sense of, random images of a life that I wasn't sure was mine.

When I swallowed the last of the blood, a wave of shame and guilt washed over me. *What is happening to me?* I staggered toward a full-length mirror placed on one side of the room. I looked at my countenance. I was white as a sheet, almost as if I had no blood inside me. I was cold. I looked at my aching teeth and gasped when I saw fangs.

Something inside told me that this wasn't supposed to be, that this simply *couldn't* be. But when claws suddenly appeared from my fingers, I knew the reality of it all. I could no longer deny it.

I knew it was impossible, but there it was.

I had turned into a vampire.

WANT TO FIND OUT WHAT HAPPENS NEXT?

Visit www.bellaforrest.net for information on Book 7!

Note from the Author

Dear Shaddict,

If you want to stay informed about my latest book releases, visit this website to subscribe to my new releases email list: www.forrestbooks.com

Also, if you subscribe, you'll be automatically entered to win a signed copy of A Shade Of Vampire!

You can also check out my other novels by visiting my website: www.bellaforrest.net

And don't forget to come say hello on Facebook.
I'd love to meet you personally, and sometimes Derek Novak takes over as manager of the page:
www.facebook.com/AShadeOfVampire

Thank you for reading!

Love,
Bella

Made in the USA
San Bernardino, CA
05 April 2016